IN ANOTHER COUNTRY, AND BESIDES

IN ANOTHER COUNTRY, AND BESIDES

—— A Novel ——

MAXWELL JACOBS

NEW YORK

NASHVILLE • MELBOURNE • VANCOUVER

IN ANOTHER COUNTRY, AND BESIDES
A Novel

Published in New York, New York, by Morgan James Publishing. Morgan James is a trademark of Morgan James, LLC. www.MorganJamesPublishing.com

The Morgan James Speakers Group can bring authors to your live event. For more information or to book an event visit The Morgan James Speakers Group at www.TheMorganJamesSpeakersGroup.com.

ISBN 978-1-68350-531-0 paperback
ISBN 978-1-68350-532-7 eBook
Library of Congress Control Number: 2017905327

Cover Design by:
Rachel Lopez
www.r2cdesign.com

In an effort to support local communities, raise awareness and funds, Morgan James Publishing donates a percentage of all book sales for the life of each book to Habitat for Humanity Peninsula and Greater Williamsburg.

Get involved today! Visit
www.MorganJamesBuilds.com

THIS BOOK IS FOR
SUE AND JON

"Thou hast committed—Fornication: but that was in another country, and besides, the wench is dead."

—Christopher Marlowe (*The Jew of Malta*)

IN ANOTHER COUNTRY, AND BESIDES

BOOK I

CHAPTER I

IT WAS DARK NOW as it always became dark quickly after sunset. The wind was in from the east, and a smell of sewage came across the canal. I turned back to the north so the odor wasn't as strong. I knew I was alone. I could see prisms in the dark canal water stretching ahead with calmness. The clouds were building up in the sky and gave a blurred reflection onto the water. It always feels lonely on the streets of Venice, and I thought how some men feared being alone.

Looking up past the low fog, I could see white cumulus clouds building up in piles of thickness against a dark sky. In that moment I had no thoughts and no feelings of any kind.

It was cold now. I rubbed my hands against my trousers. An aeroplane passed overhead on its way to somewhere warm. I watched its blurred reflection in the canal, thinking it must be very strange in an aeroplane. I wonder what Venice would look like from that height.

The moon was rising. I had no way of judging the time. I wasn't clear enough in the head. I'm as clear as this cloudy night, I thought. "I must sleep," I said out loud. I should sleep when the sun sleeps. Even the ocean sleeps on certain days when there's no current and it's flat and calm. I must remember to sleep. I could go without sleeping, but that would be too dangerous. Maybe I'm half asleep now. And bed, I thought. Bed is my friend. Just bed. Bed would be wonderful.

I stopped and took out a cigarette. I blew the smoke out into the distance, and it disappeared and mixed with the fog. I sat down next to three wrapped-up canal boats with my legs over the side, almost touching the water. Wet green weed hung from the lines of the rope that held the boats in place. I dipped one foot in and it made a swirl, and I watched the ripples flow off to the far side. If I had no sense, I would splash this dirty water on my face and wake up. I looked up to the sky. There will be bad weather in the next days.

The next thing I registered was the hotel bed. My face pressed down on the soft white sheets. I raised myself up, lit the gas lamp beside the bed, and looked at my blood-soaked hands. Best not to think about it. Oh, that's swell advice. Try and take it. Try and take it.

A knock at the door broke through my thoughts. I jumped up and ran to the bathroom and turned on the shower, which gave a large hissing sound.

"In the shower, please come back later," I shouted with strange terror and waited for a moment before walking slowly over to the peephole. It was the maid. "Si, signore," she said, and as she left I quietly attached the chain.

In the shower I scrubbed myself until my skin was raw. I never used to realize it. I try and play along. I try to not make trouble for people. Probably I never would have any trouble if I hadn't, well… People are that way. To hell with people. I got out, naked and dripping, and went straight to the mini bar. I opened two small bottles of Irish whiskey and, pouring them both into a glass, gulped them down and collapsed onto the bed. I wish it had really been a dream, I thought. It might have turned out well.

By the time an hour had passed the room was a misty fog of smoke. I kept wondering if anyone had found the body and if I had been careless on my way back. I went to get another drink, but my hands were shaking now and I dropped everything on the floor.

I sat down on the bed with remorse and looked around the room. It was large, wide and high ceilinged on the side of the Grand Canal. I opened the windows and the east wind came into the room. The canal was becoming as gray as painters had once painted it on one of its grayest days.

I washed down the sheets and lay them to dry. Cleaned the knife, checked the room and pulled the door, got into the elevator, and looked in the mirror. There was a painted, frightened expression on my face, and I knew as soon as the elevator hit the lobby floor I would fly out the door and run—and keep running.

I took a deep breath and fixed my tie and waited for the halt with the slight hydraulic inaccuracy of the elevator, and when the brass doors slid open, I moved through the hotel lobby slowly and calmly, looking around for people's reaction and checking anything that I may have touched on the way up to the room. But nothing seemed strange or out of place, and nothing particularly unusual transpired.

CHAPTER II

IT WAS BRIGHT THAT NIGHT and the atmosphere of the city had changed as the evening went on, as if something had left Venice and the city was now putting on a show just for me. It was a colossal show of water taxis and costumes, the hurrying of people on the streets and the voices with no real purpose, and me, walking with the moving crowd through Piazza San Marco and down toward Harry's Bar. The canal seemed as gray as steel now with its quick, failing winter light.

Inside, against the bar and tables, was a small crowd. It was hot. I took off my coat and placed it on a hanger on the wall next to the entrance. I went over to the bar and sat down on a tall stool that left my feet dangling. I couldn't help but think that I'd dreamed up the whole rotten business. I kept my stare until the thoughts had passed, and in the mirror behind the bar, between the bottles, I saw myself.

The sound of the bar came sudden to me, and I looked around the room then back down at my whiskey.

Isn't the literary life a funny one. This night had truly been a frightfully hellish experience. But shouldn't we all make more sacrifices for literature? I know it's awfully hard. But in the end, isn't it all for literature?

I was a little drunk. Not drunk in any positive sense but just enough to be careless. I sat there against the zinc bar and did not talk. I was pretty well through with the subject. I had probably considered it from most of its various angles.

I watched a good-looking girl. She looked up and I caught her eye.

Now there's a girl you could write about. No, girls are not the problem. It's the conversations. That's the tricky part. A good writer needs to be able to remember conversations, not girls, and I'm terrible at remembering conversations. Therefore I must be a lousy writer.

A crowd of young American men came in, some in jerseys and some in shirtsleeves. I could see their faces and hair newly washed. The bartender looked at me and smiled. I looked on at the girl and she looked at them and they looked at her and I felt pretty rotten.

One of them stood by the bar and looked at the girl again and said, "I do declare. There is an actual harlot," and they all laughed. He looked a great deal like a compatriot who must have looked like that when he saw the promised land. I wanted to swing at one and shatter that superiority. Instead I took notice of her movements, her eyes, and the way she talked. She wasn't doing anything in particular—just smiling and laughing, but for a moment she started to hold my world together.

Her hair was dark, with a light touch of mahogany that flowed down in thick waves, which curled up at the tips and flicked at her face. She was wearing a carnival mask, and it was the type that looks like a cat's face so her mouth and chin were exposed and the eyeholes were wide enough to see bright brown eyes and long dark lashes. I couldn't see her nose, just her full red lips.

She smiled at one of the men and I looked away and took on a sudden look of reflection. To hell with women. I took out a ten lira note from my pocket and placed it on the bar.

"You go now? So early?" the bartender asked.

"Yes," I said and started for the door.

I walked for some minutes, passing Piazza San Marco and the big protruding bell tower with its fluted orange and square brick shaft. I walked by the water on the walkway until the walkway finished. Looking around and seeing nobody, I took out the knife and threw it far into the Grand Canal. My head started to work again. I smiled and walked with thoughts of the girl, and suddenly I felt good and warm and safe.

I do not know what time I got to bed. I remember undressing, putting on the bathrobe, standing out on the balcony. I knew I was quite drunk, and when I came in I put on the gas light next to the bed and started to read. I was reading Faulkner. I read the same page over several times. The pressure in my head seemed to loosen. I was very drunk and did not want to shut my eyes. If I kept on reading perhaps the feeling would pass. I thought I had paid for everything.

I could now feel the two ladies whispering and looking on. I leaned back on my stool and opened the note. It read:

SATURDAY NIGHT. HARRYS BAR. NINE O'CLOCK. DON'T BE LATE. CLEO.

I placed the note in my pocket, paid, and walked out of the bar and onto the side street facing the canal. I took out a cigarette, lit up, and inhaled. What a lovely name Cleo is, I thought.

CHAPTER III

IN THE MORNING it was bright and cold, and they were sprinkling the streets down as I had breakfast. Venice is a very clean town. I went out onto the street and walked up to a cathedral but started to get an uneasy feeling. There was a long line of boats in one of the slow canals that carried water from the Brenta where the great villas are, with their lawns and gardens and plane trees. I'd like to be buried out there, I thought. I know the place very well, although perhaps it's not possible. I could ask Cleo; she might think it was a bit morbid, though.

I walked up to the newsstand and bought a local paper, then up toward a pizzeria I had seen the night before in a very narrow street. Strings of beads were hanging from the doorway and a decanter of wine stood on every table. There were six tables in total, and I knew it was the kind of place you could sit for hours and not be disturbed. I sat there until three o'clock reading the paper and trying to understand in my best Italian what the authorities had said.

The article had taken up one whole page, and my Italian failed me. But with the help of a dictionary I learned that his name was Massimo. He was thirty-seven years old, a wealthy Venetian, married with two kids. The article said that he had been stabbed and they had yet to find the murder weapon. The police suspected it was close by in the canal. It also said they had a lead from a witness who described a blond-haired man without costume, wearing round black spectacles. The witness said he certainly didn't look Italian. I took off my glasses and slipped them into my pocket.

A breeze blew, and you could feel it and that the air came from the sea. There were pigeons out in the street, and I did not want to leave the café.

I asked for the bill, and while I was waiting I saw a rat perched on the stone wall next to the canal and it must have been seven inches long. I pointed him out to the waiter, who briskly ran over and shooed it away.

I got up and walked off and headed straight back to the hotel. As I walked, I took off my jacket and placed it into my backpack.

Back in the hotel room I took a whiskey from the mini bar and sat on the bed and considered my options. I could leave now, I thought. Perhaps I could even go to the police and confess. But reasoning deterred me.

Desperately I tried to turn my thoughts back to Cleo. The idea of seeing her tonight excited me but also made me anxious. What the hell does one talk about these days? What does anyone talk about? I figured in the last few years I hadn't really been in the company of another woman. Would I be a bore? Would she see through me and ask to leave after one drink? Oh, to hell with women anyway. Who needs them? Women make such swell friends, but that's about it.

When I got to Harry's Bar later that night it was busy and I had to wait outside for a place at the bar. When the waitress came out and called me in, I finished my cigarette and went inside, looking around to see if there was anyone from the night before. I ordered a whiskey sour and settled in.

In the bar, standing, there was what looked like a post-war rich from Venice, tall, dark, fat, and hard as only the Venetian can be with his dark suit and expensive-looking face and an extremely desirable mistress. He had thick black spectacles and a heavy mustache. They were drinking negronis and mopping up oil and vinegar with pieces of thick bread. Negronis are a mixture of two sweet vermouths and seltzer water, and I wondered how much in taxes the man had escaped to buy that sleek girl in her long mink coat. They both stared at me for a moment. Had I seen him here the night before? She was damned beautiful. I wondered what it would have been like if I had ever had the money to buy me that kind and put them into a mink.

Outside I could hear the music of a procession going by. The carnival was still going strong.

"Due Bellini, grazie," the tall dark man said across the bar to the barman.

"Si, signore," said the barman, who was dressed in black plants, white shirt, and black tie with a heavily tailored white double-breasted dinner jacket. He took out the pre-made purée from the fridge and served it and looked at him with his wise Italian eyes, not merry now.

The tall dark-haired man raised his glass toward me and smiled meaninglessly before taking a sip. I raised my glass and nodded courteously.

One of the ladies across from me eyed the tall dark-haired man from another table close to the entrance. I could see her newly washed hair in the light from the door. He noticed her and grinned. She turned red and looked away.

His was a tough face, a worn-out face, and it seemed out of place. He wasn't talking to the girl he was with, or anyone else for that matter, but I could feel him. I could feel his looks. Did he follow me here? Was he a policeman of sorts? A detective perhaps?

Staring at the door, I figured they couldn't give me more than two years in prison for messing with the scene of a crime. Maybe three, with good behavior. I suffered a moment of desperate regret.

Was he the kind of man they send on a job like this? It would start by him looking over from across the bar, and then bang! One hand on the shoulder and the other hand holding a policeman's badge. Harry Hoffman, you're under arrest! I kept a watch on the door.

Perhaps he's really just a local having a drink with his girlfriend and the reason they're not talking is because they had a fight on the way over here. Perhaps I should talk to him, I told myself. Perhaps.

I was drinking red wine now and felt uncomfortable. I looked around the room.

Just then he smiled at me with his big glazed eyes, just standing and smiling with the woman with bare shoulders next to him. He did not even nod.

"Did I see you here last night?" I asked over the bar.

"Yes, you are right," he answered in a serious tone. His voice sounded croaky, like he was a heavy smoker.

"My name is Harry, Harry Hoffman," I said, before asking myself why I had just given him my full name.

"So that's why you like Harry's Bar." He smiled under his mustache.

"Ah, yes."

"You are American?" he asked.

"No, I'm British."

"You look American."

I turned the first available corner and waited there in the dark. There were a few lighted bars and late open shops on each side of the street. I looked back and stayed there for a moment just to be sure, and as I continued up the long narrow street I kept turning around but there was nothing. If there was any sensation I hated the most, it was being followed.

Walking back to the hotel, I reminded myself that I was probably just being paranoid and placed my mind firmly back on Cleo and the disappointment of the evening. I walked through the hotel reception and through the bar and out to the terrace, where I ordered a whiskey sour and took out a cigarette. For a moment I took stock of the situation and looked onto the magnificent view of the Basilica di Santa Maria Della Salute. Its huge gray dome filled the sky. What if he took the note from Flavio? I sat up.

When I got to my room I slowly took off my jacket and untied the tie, watching every move I made in the mirror as if it were somebody else's movements, and it was clear to see how differently I stood and the non-identical look on my face. I have no understanding of it, I thought, and I'm not sure I believe it. Perhaps it was a sin to kill. I suppose it was even though it had kept me alive. But then isn't everything a sin?

"Do not think, Harry," I said out loud. It's much too late for that. Let others think about it. I smiled to myself in the mirror and turned off the light.

CHAPTER IV

WHEN I WOKE in the morning I went to the window and looked out. It had cleared and there were no clouds. Outside under the window were some street carts and pigeons on the piazza.

Someone tried to enter the room and I jumped back. "Somebody in here," I called out. I realized I was naked and firmly gripped the door handle. "Scusa, signore," a woman's voice answered. I waited a moment and then put on a dressing gown and unbolted the door to fetch in my morning paper. The hall was empty and nobody was stirring.

I got back into bed, feeling the cold air rush in from the open window, and read the paper, then ate a fine breakfast of eggs Benedict with spinach and hollandaise sauce and a large coffee with warm milk, both served in a silver pot.

I dressed, put on my shoes, and went downstairs, making a pass at my hair in the mirror. As I was passing reception I heard my name being called out.

"Signore Hoffman, I say, Signore Hoffman, if you please." I turned around to see one of the receptionists beckoning me over.

"We have a message for you, Signore Hoffman," she said and handed me a note scribbled onto what seemed like the back of a torn-off receipt. It read:

HARRY. MEET ME IN THE MIDDLE OF THE RIALTO BRIDGE AT NOON. I'M WEARING A WHITE COAT. CLEO.

Pleasure emanated from me into the air. We are inhabitants of a splendid world. The receptionist smiled, sensing the pleasure on my face, so I smiled back and walked out through the revolving doors. My head felt like it had swollen up like a balloon.

I stepped out of the hotel and there was sunlight on the opposite side of the square, but the gondoliers were sheltered from the cold wind by lounging in the sunlight.

One of the cafés was just opening and the waiters were arranging the outside terraces. They were sweeping the streets and sprinkling them with a hose.

I turned back and stopped for a moment and looked at the church of Santa Maria del Giglio and thought what a fine building it was. I turned right and walked along the square to the paved street which turned off on the right and looked in the windows of the various shops I passed, the charcuterie with the Parmesan cheeses and the hams from San Daniele, and the sausages alla cacciatore and the bottles of good Scotch whiskey and real Gordon's gin, the cutlery store, the antique dealer's with good pieces and old maps and prints, a second-rate restaurant disguised expensively as one of the first class, and then the first bridge crossing the feeder canal with steps to be climbed. I don't feel so bad today. There is only the buzzing.

At a newspaper kiosk I bought a copy of the *New York Herald* and sat in a café with comfortable wicker chairs to read it. The waiter was in no hurry to come. I drank a cold beer to cool my nerves. It felt strange to think I was finally going to meet Cleo. The waiter came over.

"How does one sit outside in this cold weather?" the waiter asked.

"Well. Very well. One sits very well outside. After all this is Venice."

The waiter seemed a little offended, so I over-tipped him. That seemed to make him happy. It felt so comfortable to be in a country where it is so simple to make people feel happy.

I walked down and took an espresso at a standup bar and a check in the toilet mirror to fix my tie, and at eleven-fifty-five I headed out toward the bridge, and as I climbed I felt the twinges, and coming down the other side there were two lovely looking girls. They were beautiful and hatless and poorly dressed, and they were talking fast to each other, and the wind was blowing their hair as they climbed down with their long easy striding Venetian legs. I better quit gazing now, I thought to myself.

When I arrived, there was a policeman standing in the center of the bridge. He looked over at me and smiled. It made me feel uneasy. Then a large crowd of young men walked past the policeman and he disappeared into the crowd. There's a lot of oxygen in this air, I thought as I faced the wind and breathed in deeply.

I looked around for Cleo, and through the crowd I saw the back of a dark-haired girl in a long white coat.

I approached.

"Cleo," I said. She turned and grabbed hold and embraced me. She was trembling. I didn't say a word, and neither did she until she pulled away. She wore no makeup, and perfume cut through the crowd. She was shining in her youth and tall with the carelessness of the wind in her hair.

"I'm so sorry for not showing up the other night," she said, and to my relief she seemed sincere. I looked at her and couldn't believe how beautiful she was. She had such a romantic-looking face and a sugary voice. Her light olive-colored skin gave a profile that could break your heart, and her dark hair hung down over her shoulders.

"It's no problem, Cleo." I turned and saw the policeman again. "Let's get off this crowded bridge and go somewhere we can talk," I said, taking her by the hand. I kept in front and pulled her along.

"What's the matter, Harry? Why are we rushing?"

"I'm sorry, I just can't stand crowds."

We got off the bridge and she let go of my hand.

"Harry, before we go on, I feel I should explain why I didn't show the other night."

"It's fine, really," I said, looking back at the bridge now waiting for the policeman to come running toward us.

"No, it's not fine, please listen to me. I feel just terrible about it," she continued. "A friend of mine was murdered on Saturday night not far from here. Perhaps you heard about it? Anyway, I was in such shock that I completely forgot about our meeting. I'm sorry, Harry."

I stopped in my tracks and focused on her.

"My God," I said. I could feel my breath quicken. Thankfully she looked down with a sigh and could not see my face. Still I did not know what to say but knew I had to say something. "Come with me."

We walked off the canal and into the bar of a hotel for a cocktail. We sat on high stools at the bar while the barman shook martinis in his large nickeled shaker. I excused myself for a moment to visit the restroom.

I walked calmly down the hall and into the toilet with a door that didn't lock, and though it was grimy and looked as if a thousand people had left behind their own kind of filth and the owners had never lifted a hand to clean it, I closed the door and rested my head on the back and almost screamed. I turned to the large mirror on the wall. I was flushed and covered in sweat. I took a moment to calm down and set myself aright, putting my hands to the sides and lifting my head, trying to become a self-respecting man again. I wiped the sweat off and turned away from the mirror and went back outside.

"Are you okay?" she asked.

"I'm fine. Sorry I was a bit jumpy before. I just hate crowds. Can't handle them. Get claustrophobic."

"Oh, you poor thing."

She was wearing her hair down in the style of an old movie actress, with curly waves running through it. Her voice was low and delicate and she spoke English with caution. Sitting there, in the sun, she looked lovely.

"No matter how nice the hotels are, the bars are always vulgar in Venice," she said. "Do you mind if we go someplace else?" she asked before the barman came over to fix our drinks.

"Of course not, do you know somewhere?" I asked.

"Yes, there's a great café five minutes' walk from here," she said. "Do you mind walking for a little?"

"Not at all," I said.

"So, are you American?" she asked as we started to walk.

"No, I'm from England. Why does everyone assume I'm American here?"

"I guess it's because we get a lot of Americans in Venice."

"Have you ever been to England?" I asked.

"No, never, but I would love to go of course, especially to London."

"Then you should." I smiled. "Flavio mentioned that you are from Rome?"

"Oh, he did, did he?" she laughed. "My family lives there. I came to Venice for my husband's work, but he left a year ago and I stayed. I love it here. It's very peaceful when it's not carnival."

"And what do you do here?" I asked, curious to hear there was a husband.

"I paint," she said. "Not for galleries or anything like that. I don't make any money; I just do it for myself. I also play the piano."

We walked quietly for a while.

"And you, Harry? Flavio also told me something," she said with a grin. "That you are a famous writer."

"I wouldn't go that far. I wrote one book years ago and it sold well and fortunately still sells well."

"What's the name?"

"*Bitter Tulips.*"

We were now at the café and it looked nice and subsequently expensive. We took a table together; it felt like a long time since I had sat across from a beautiful girl.

"It isn't bad in here. It's a little chic, but the food is good," she said and ordered a bottle of white wine and made a joke, showing her lovely smile. We touched glasses. They were coldly beaded. Cleo was one of those girls who reminded me of how wonderful life is, not just because she was so beautiful; there was something else. We continued to sit at the table, and some people went out and others came in.

Someone called out from the other side of the room.

"Cleo, I say, Cleo Tremonte!"

"It's a friend calling me," she explained and stood up. She went over to a big table with about six people. After some minutes, one of the girls from the table came over with Cleo and introduced herself as Lucia.

"I was just saying to Cleo, you both should come dancing with us tonight," she said in English. Lucia was small and had a nice smile.

"What dance?" I asked.

"Oh, you must come, it will be wonderful," Lucia said, looking at us both.

"Do you have a carnival costume, Harry?" Cleo asked.

"Not yet, but I could go out this afternoon and get one. I'm sure it shouldn't be a problem."

"Well, it starts at ten-thirty but we could meet here before, say around ten o'clock?" Lucia said, and before I could say anything Cleo said, "Thanks, we'll be there." Lucia smiled, said something to Cleo in Italian, and returned to her party.

"Who are your friends? Lucia seems nice."

"Sons and daughters of Venetian aristocracy," she said. "But don't worry, Harry, they are nice people. Not at all snobs."

She poured out more of the wine.

"So what's the next book?" she asked.

"That's a good question," I said, grinning. "I've been having a tough time lately putting anything decent down on paper."

"Perhaps you just need to be inspired?"

"Perhaps. I would love to write a murder mystery of sorts," I said, and in doing so found myself saying something I had never actually thought before.

"Well, there's no better place than carnival and Venice to find inspiration," she said before adding, with a curious smile, "Maybe I can also help with that."

"With what?" I asked.

"Inspiration." She smiled and then seemed embarrassed.

We finished our wine.

"Come on," she said. "We're going to have a coffee with the others."

Cleo opened her bag and made a few passes at her face. As she looked in the little mirror she redefined her lips and played with her hair.

"Good," she said, smiling at herself in the mirror.

We walked over and everybody at the table stood up.

"Can I present to you Harry Hoffman?" Cleo said. I smiled and shook hands and gave kisses before we sat down and ordered two espressos.

"Are you related to Hans Hofmann, the artist?" one of the girls asked. "I was just at a gallery in New York, and I saw a wonderful selection of paintings by a man called Hans Hofmann. They were wonderfully exuberant." She was an upper-class local and had all their social graces.

"I don't know him," I answered.

"But you have the same name," she insisted cordially.

"No, I'm sorry." I smiled at her and then at the group. "How do you spell his last name?" I asked.

"Well, I suppose it would be H o f m a n n," she said, spelling out the individual letters.

"See, mine is spelled H o f f m a n."

"That would be why then," she replied and sat back in her chair.

"Have you been in Venice long? Do you like it here? You love Venice, do you not?" another girl with dark hair asked and smiled and showed all her bad teeth.

"Yes, it's wonderful here. You're very lucky to live in such a city," I replied.

"We can't stay long, as Harry needs to go find a costume for tonight," Cleo said.

I asked Cleo if she would like to come with me. "I forget you're a tourist," she said, and we said our goodbyes and left the café, then walked for some minutes without saying a word.

"Tell me, Cleo, why did you leave me that note at Harry's Bar?" I asked, too curious to stay silent.

"Are you happy I did?"

"Very much so."

"I left it because of your eyes. Did anyone tell you that you have very nice blue eyes? And there's something else about you that I can't explain."

I smiled to myself, then she leaned against me and I put my arm next to hers. She turned to look up at me and touched me slightly with one hand. It was a cold evening, and it was starting to get dark and the electric signs came on above the cafés and restaurants, and people sat out on the terraces in the squares watching people go by. We walked around the city for the next hour and passed the doors of the shops, with their windows lit, showing displays of carnival costumes and masks, and then on into the Cannaregio district with its narrow alleys and wide squares and stopped in different shops. I talked about my days in Paris and my life in Switzerland, and Cleo told me about her daughter Liv and how she missed her and would love for her to come to Venice and live with her.

"Why can't she?" I asked.

"It's a long story. I just can't handle being a mother right now," she said, and explained how she needed to focus on herself.

She spoke of being tired of this Venetian bubble and how she longed to travel and live somewhere new with her daughter. "I would like to start over again," she said, misty-eyed. She changed the subject by explaining to me that there are two separate Venices. One has quiet campielli squares and barges that deliver fruits and vegetables, and it's that Venice that belongs to her. The other Venice, which she dislikes, is filled with the booming voices of tour guides and loud microphones.

It was nice to be walking around and discovering Venice through the eyes of a local.

I did try on several occasions to bring up the husband and the murder, but at the same time I stopped myself. I didn't want to ruin the time we were having or to mix up the two things in my head. The truth was, I was having a wonderful time with Cleo Tremonte.

CHAPTER V

WE FOUND A COSTUME and I invited Cleo for one last apéritif. We watched the early evening crowd and stepped into the nearest quaint café and discovered it was quite empty, except for a policeman sitting close to the door and the wife of the proprietor, who sat by a window. The large proprietor himself was behind the bar. There were long benches and long tables that ran across the room, but no customers. At the far end of the bar seemed to be a dancing floor, but before I could look further, the proprietor's wife came over asking what we would like to drink. We ordered two martinis.

"Are you happy with your costume?" Cleo asked; I kept one eye on the policeman.

"Well, if you don't mind me walking around in knee-high socks, then I'm happy," I said. She laughed hard and put her hand on mine.

"I don't mind at all as long as you don't mind being with my friends."

"Not at all, they seem like a fun bunch. And what better way to get to know the city than to experience it with some young aristocrats?" She sat across from me with the window and street to her back. She began to talk about her paintings, but by this time I had stopped listening and focused more on her movements, her eyes, and the way she half-bit her lip after each sentence when she wasn't sure about her English. All her wallows and sorrows remained inferior, and this felt like her greatest asset. The way she talked about her passion inspired me and made me feel like I could do something good again with my life. For the first time, I started to open myself. If it had been any other person, I wouldn't have taken the risk. Humans are tricky, and Cleo Tremonte in that moment was the only exception. Without thinking, I reached over and put my hand on top of hers, looking her squarely in the eyes. Her voice faltered, and she stopped what she was saying.

"May I kiss you, Cleo?" I asked in a soft voice. She didn't respond at first, simply giving me that wonderful smile. She took a deep breath; her eyes became big and looked seriously into mine. I raised myself up from the chair and leaned over the table while keeping my hand softly on hers. I came 90 percent of the way, stopping just before her lips and made a slight smile, allowing her to come the last percent if she wished. We kissed and the kiss was soft, small, and warm. It felt wonderful against my skin. She brought the tip of her tongue out and it touched the top of my lip, and with each passing kiss I could feel the blood flow to her cheeks. They became red and warm, and as the kiss grew stronger I took my free hand and placed it to the back of her neck, pulling her slightly closer. For that moment I was hers and she was mine.

"Have a drink with me tonight before we meet your friends, just the two of us," I said, and was happy to see her smile and nod. We arranged to meet at a bar she knew at nine o'clock. She wrote down the address on the back of a napkin and we stood up and left.

She turned to me in the street and I saw her face in the lights from the open shops. I saw her face clearly. Her cheeks were still red from the kiss. The street was dark now and I kissed her again. We kissed for a long time, standing straight and kissing true in the cold, and our lips held tight together, and then she turned away and pressed against the corner of my face, as far away as she could get. Her head was down, and I felt a sudden sadness within her.

The corridor of the hotel was now not only beautiful, it was exciting, and putting the key into the lock was not a simple process. I relaxed with the windows open and drank in my room when the telephone rang.

"Signore, there is a person here to see you at the front desk," the receptionist said.

"Certainly, I'll be right down."

I instantly knew it would be the police even before I hung up the phone. I'd been thinking about how it all must look now that I was with Cleo, and if I was followed and they saw us both kissing, they would assume I had some sort of motive.

I stepped out of the elevator and saw the familiar figure dressed in a black suit and another younger man in a full police uniform at the reception. He looked much more serious and professional than when I saw him last. They looked over at me and extended a hand.

"Signore Hoffman, may we speak with you for a moment?" The tall dark-haired man flashed his police credentials, and the receptionist behind the front desk gave me a long hard look of disapproval. We entered a long hallway that led to the big stairs and to the elevator, leading on the right to the entrance of the bar and the doorway onto the Grand Canal.

We sat down with the window overlooking the canal, and the waiter came over. The two men ordered espressos and I ordered nothing. I looked out and saw a couple walking arm-in-arm, and as they went up the first bridge the wind lashed at them heavily.

"Signore, I apologize for not introducing myself the other night, my name is Inspector Marino from the Venezia Polizia and this is Sergeant Esposito. We are investigating the murder of a local businessman here in Venice."

"And how may I be of assistance?" I asked, trying to keep my voice neutral.

Inspector Marino quickly shot out the first question in a stern tone.

"How well do you know Cleo Tremonte?"

"We only met a few days ago," I said, pausing for a second to take a breath. "I was supposed to see her the night when we spoke outside Harry's Bar, but she cancelled at the last minute."

"And do you know why, signore?" Marino asked, his dark eyes fixed on me.

"She said she had some personal issues."

The younger sergeant was now taking down my answers in his notebook.

"And your relationship with Signora Tremonte?" said the inspector. "How would you describe that?"

"Just a new friend," I responded. "I will see her tonight actually. Am I in some sort of trouble, inspector?"

"Can you tell me where you were on the night of the second of February?"

"Why?"

"Please just answer the question, signore."

I pretended not to quite grasp what he had asked and so he asked for a second time, choosing different words.

"Can you tell me your exact whereabouts at eleven-thirty on the night of the second of February?" he asked, not taking his eyes from mine.

"Am I a suspect, inspector?" I asked, giving a carnival expression.

"Well, signore, that all depends on your whereabouts."

"I believe I was back in my room by eleven-thirty," I said, gesturing with open hands though I hoped the inspector would not confront any of the hotel staff.

"Do you know a man named Massimo Russo?" the inspector asked, showing a picture.

"I'm sorry, I don't."

"May I see your passport, Signore Hoffman?" the inspector asked.

"Of course, it's in my room."

"And what room would that be?"

"212."

"I'm going to need to see that passport, signore."

"Now?"

"Si."

"Of course." I stood up and left. The young sergeant followed me. I took the passport from the room safe and he strolled around the room with his hands behind his back and a relaxed air about him, as though he were strolling around a museum. He said nothing and we came downstairs. The inspector took my passport and gave it a long hard look.

"It is me," I said.

"I will need to hold on to this while we continue with our investigation," he said sternly. "I would ask you to stay in Venice for the time being. How did you arrive here?"

"By train, I came here from Zurich."

"Va bene. You mustn't leave without contacting me. Here's my card." He slipped it across the table and they both stood up.

"We will be in touch, Signore Hoffman," said the inspector.

"No problem, happy to be of further assistance," I said, raising my hands in a sign of service. He said nothing, just nodded and started to leave then turned around.

"Signore Hoffman, were you aware that Signora Tremonte was in a relationship with the deceased?"

"I wasn't, no."

"Very well." He turned and left.

I sat down and reflected on my behavior. I was calm, I thought, and composed and certainly not overstressed or anything of the sort. They hadn't really challenged me in any way yet, though the questions were very preliminary. I had a terrible alibi and the witness, whom they didn't mention, had my details. I kicked myself for coming down in my glasses, and what was all that business about Cleo and Massimo?

Standing up I walked outside and felt the cold air. There was a strong wind and mist all along the Grand Canal. I couldn't really see the other side. I took out a cigarette from my father's cigarette case. Happy for the distraction, I studied it. It was a silver case that all soldiers who fought in the trenches received, and it had his name inscribed in the back: R. Hoffman, 1914.

The waiter came outside and I ordered a whiskey and smoked three cigarettes while contemplating if it was possible to get back to Switzerland without showing a passport. I could always say I lost it.

Around eight-thirty that evening the barman came out to the terrace again stating that there was a call for me at reception. I walked inside. It was Cleo.

"Harry, I'm running late." She sounded upset.

"Cleo, is everything okay?" I asked.

"I've had the polizia here asking questions about you and about us and if you knew Massimo," she said, her voice shaking slightly.

"It's okay, Cleo. Everything is fine," I said, whispering and turning so the receptionist couldn't hear. "They came to my hotel too, asking the same questions."

"Did you know Massimo?" she asked.

"Of course not. I think they just made the connection because we met today. Really, there's nothing to worry about, Cleo."

"Do you think we should still meet tonight?" she asked.

"Yes, I do."

"Okay, let's meet at nine-thirty now as I'm running late."

"Sure, no problem. See you there."

"Ciao." Cleo hung up the phone.

CHAPTER VI

As I LOOKED out of the window onto the waters of the Grand Canal, I could see the big black hitching post for the gondolas and the evening winter light on the windswept water. Across the canal was the old palace and a wood barge, black and broad and was coming up, her bluff bows pushing up a wave even though she had the wind behind her.

As I walked outside I was again reminded that it was in fact carnival. People had been coming in all day from all over and were now outside drinking. They would not start in paying café prices. Instead they got their money's worth in the wine shops. Later it would not matter what they paid or where they bought it. As I walked down the open streets I could hear signing and dancing through open doors in shops, restaurants and cafés. All the nice wicker chairs had been replaced in most of the cafés to more solid and sturdy steel ones that sat next to small cast iron tables. People were coming in squares from all sides. In the crowd you only saw heads and shoulders and dancers going up and down. The carnival had really started.

I moved off the main square and walked up a narrow street and on to a smaller less busy square and looked around for the bar that Cleo had mentioned. I couldn't find it, so decided to stay on the square next to the fountain, hoping she would pass by.

In front of me on a clear part of the square a group of men were dancing to the sound of music playing from an adjacent café. It's inside light and neon sign lit up the cold dark square.

Their steps were very intricate and their faces were intent and concentrated. They all looked down while they danced. Their shoes tapped on the cobbled floor. The toes touched. The heels touched. The balls of the feet touched. Then the music broke wildly and when step was finished, they began dancing on up the street and around the fountain. Taking out a cigarette I watched on.

By the time Cleo walked by the fog had cleared and the small square was now lined on both sides with men and women dancing. It was starting to drizzle with rain.

She was wearing the same outfit she had worn when I first laid eyes on her. She spotted me, and as she came over some of the men formed a circle around her and started to dance. Cleo laughed and danced too. She looked over toward me, waving and gesturing. One of the men saw this, came over, and grabbed me by the arm, pulling me in. We all started to dance, and I moved close to Cleo and placed my hands gently on her hips.

"Buonasera."

"Buonasera," she replied.

"This is a nice way to start the evening," I said.

"You look very handsome, Harry, and very Venetian."

I took her hand and spun her slowly around until she was back in front of me. We had blurred out the others and stopped for a moment and kissed. Suddenly a roar erupted around us as the men started to cheer.

"Let's get a drink," she said, seeming embarrassed. We walked down the side street and away from the crowd and the lights of the square. We walked along the smooth narrow street with buildings on both sides. Most of the houses were old, with crusty red brick that jutted out toward us, and some houses were cut back. Everything was uneven. The wind was high and took the clouds quickly across the moon.

We came onto Calle Fava and followed it down to the end where music was coming from. A crowd was packed on the street and many of the shops were now shuttered. Further down, there was a small terrace with just a few tables and people sat drinking in costumes. A man left his seat, opened the door and entered the bar. Music rushed out to the street and as we approached and I could see through the window that it was very busy inside, with people lined up along a zinc bar. We moved in brushing past the crowds.

We stood at the counter. It was dark and dimly lit, with old Venetian paintings depicting the Grand Canal and small tables surrounding the bar with smoldering candles and empty bottles of wine. The place was full of costumes, except one man sat alone. He was holding a camera. Through the corner of my eye I could catch people looking at Cleo.

Back of the counter they drew the wine from wooden casks. One man from a crowd at the bar came over dancing and placed a wreath of garlic around Cleo's neck. "The whole city feels alive," I said. She leaned over and took my hand. "We are going to have fun tonight," we smiled at each other, but her smile faltered slightly, as if dark thoughts had just crossed her mind.

"You know Harry; these last days have been hard, especially having to deal with losing someone close. But it's also been wonderful to spend time with you today," she took a breath and continued, "I think you are wonderful and I'm happy to be sharing tonight with you."

"Well, here's a toast, to new friends and new memories." We picked up and touched glasses and I drew closer to her. I took off my mask, and kissed her very firmly and then pulled away and looked at her. Her face was half-lit by the soft light, which came from above the bar, and the light showed her beauty clearly and it worked down from her hair to the long line of her neck and when I kissed her again our lips were tight together. I pressed her against the counter and we both locked in as one.

I knew it didn't matter that we barely knew each other, nor did it matter that we lived in different cities. Such minor details seemed irrelevant.

There was a great noise going on now inside. Some Americans in sport clothes entered the bar and scattered and stood around one of the tables. One of the women stared at me. They were speaking loud and above the crowd.

"Excuse me, signore," I felt a tap at my shoulder. "Your table is ready."

We both half turned and smiled at the waitress and following her. We sat down at a table halfway along the room. Empty wine glasses and three empty coffee cups were still on the table. A waiter came with a cloth and picked up the glasses and mopped off the table. We ordered a bottle and some olives.

"Cleo, forgive me for bringing this up but I wanted to ask you about the murder. If you don't want to talk about it, I would understand, it's just that the inspector was asking all these questions and I really believe he thinks I had something to do with it. And…" I faltered, wondering how to proceed. "He even seemed to suggest that you were involved with this Massimo," remembering his name from the inspector.

"Oh Harry," she said as her eyes became glossy.

"Listen," I said. "I'm kind of caught up in all this now and I'd like to know exactly what is going on."

"How do you think the inspector knows?" she asked.

"So it's true? Were you having an affair with Massimo?" I asked.

She said nothing.

"Perhaps his wife knew or went through his things after he died," she said, almost to herself. "Maybe she found a letter or something."

"So it is true?"

"Yes. Oh, those poor kids, losing their father like that. Who would do such a thing?"

"I know," I said darkly, remembering the night. My mind snapped back.

"How long was it going on?"

"What?" she asked.

"The affair."

"Oh, I don't know," she said vaguely. "Some months, maybe longer."

I tried to keep my expression neutral though her vagueness disturbed me.

"I know what you're thinking, Harry, but please don't judge," she said. "Massimo was a friend, and sometimes we slept together. It was only recently that he started to ask for more. He started saying he would leave his family. I couldn't have that. For me it was nothing more than some fun on lonely nights. You understand that, right?"

"I don't judge, Cleo," was all I could say. I cleared my throat.

"I don't want you to get the wrong idea about me," she said, sensing my unease. "I'm just lost with it all."

"What do you mean?"

"My life is a bit of a mess," she looked away. "The situation with my husband and family is very complicated. Then there's Alexander who I have such a wonderful time with. He gives me nothing but peace and love and all of his attention."

She had been looking into my eyes all this time now. Her eyes held different depths now, and sometimes they seemed perfectly flat. Now you could see all the way into them.

"Who's Alexander?"

"Alexander von Horn. He's a guy I met in Rome just after my separation," Cleo said. "He's Danish and lives in Paris."

"Is it serious?"

"It wasn't for me, but over the last months Alex had become very demanding, even obsessive, so I broke it off only a few weeks back."

"And are you still married?"

She shifted uncomfortably in her seat and then sat up straight. She looked different to my eyes with a way she had of looking that made you wonder whether she really saw out of her own eyes at all. They looked on and on after everyone else's eyes would have stopped looking. She looked as though there were nothing on earth she would not look at like that, and she seemed afraid of so many things.

"Yes, but we don't speak anymore. Please ,Harry, enough with the questions."

"Sorry."

I was pretty well through with the subject. At one time or another I would have probably considered running from such a complicated situation, but she intrigued me and I couldn't start to question my feelings toward her. She broke the long silence.

"Do I scare you, Harry?" she asked in a small voice.

"You seem like trouble, Cleo," I said with a smile.

"Relax," she said with a small smile on her lips. "It's not like we're going to run off and get married. We are just having fun, right?"

"Right."

"Do you really think the inspector believes you had something to do with Massimo?" she asked.

"Well, from what I could piece together from the papers and the inspector, it seems that there was a witness who heard English being spoken at the scene of the murder," I said. "And it seems the attacker was blonde and wore spectacles. And of course now we have been seen kissing they think perhaps I'm some crazed jealous lover," it sounded horrible when I said it out loud.

"Do you think they are following us?" she asked.

"It's possible."

Cleo looked away and around the room, but I was not finished. "They took my passport and asked me to not leave Venice," I continued. "But I'm only booked up until Monday at the hotel and my train is scheduled to leave for Milan that afternoon. Perhaps you could go see the inspector and tell him we only met after the murder?"

"I already told him that."

We both sat in silence for a moment before she let out a deep sigh.

"I'm sorry you are mixed up in all this."

"Well, don't worry, everything will be fine," I said, with more confidence than I felt. "I'm sure they will catch whoever did this in the coming days."

My words seemed to work as Cleo's face brightened up.

"Would you mind very much if I asked you to do something?"

"Don't be silly. What is it?"

"Would you kiss me?"

"Of course I'll kiss you," I moved my chair closer and put my arm around her and she leaned back against me, and we kissed and became quite calm. She was looking into my eyes so I kissed her again. She opened her eyes and looked over at the wall, "Oh, look at the time, we should go," she said, pulling back and raising herself up. We quickly paid and left.

It felt good now to be outside even in the cold, and away from the noise and the crowd.

I took her hand in mine and we dashed across the street, past the parties and street parades. The cobblestoned street was wet from the evening rain and as we ran Cleo slipped and fell. She skinned her knee and as I went down to help her, I saw a little tear of blood running down her leg. To my surprise, she started to laugh. She was smiling and laughing, and in that moment, not knowing why, it seemed to me like she was the sweetest thing I'd ever seen.

CHAPTER VII

THE CONTARINA BALL was located in an old Venetian palace on the other side of the Grand Canal. It was built in a sestiere. Its façade showed a style from the early renaissance. It was well preserved. The night was clearing and the moon was out.

We arrived at a seven-arched iron gate and a tall man stood in front. He was holding a notebook with people's names written on the inside. Behind the gate I could see an outside staircase attached to the main building. It had three arches below and each one got bigger as the staircase rose up. Its middle arch had all been bricked up.

After some discussion in Italian that I couldn't understand we were allowed to enter and as we walked up the staircase we entered a large candlelit courtyard. Hundreds of little flames lined the walkway on each side of a deep red carpet, which cut through the center and entered a ground floor hall. Inside the hall and to the right a magnificent looking staircase rose up. We took a glass from one of the servers who lined the red carpet and stood straight in costume with a silver plate filled with glasses of Prosecco. We walked into the great hall and climbed the staircase, admiring the great dark paintings on the wall and then into the heart of the palace. It was a majestic ballroom and I had no reason to feel disappointed.

The ballroom overlooked the courtyard and had a grand terrace. There were table's spread around the room with red linen and in the center of each table were candles of all different heights and sizes. Flowers and Prosecco were set around the tables, which circled a large and creaky wooden floor.

There were dark oil paintings on each wall, accompanied by a description in Latin, and tired mirrors clung to the walls between the paintings that reflected their age with a smoky appearance and the occasional distortion that gave an unclear sense of the world seen through them. Two had been scratched with initials: 'M-A.H' and 'A.H' 1842. I took off my mask and looked carefully and painfully through the dirty glass.

The roof had long white candle chandlers draping down. Each table had a place setting with name cards and silver cutlery.

Stood around the big table of our group were Cleo, Lucia, Antonio, Lorenzo, Alfredo, Sofia, Arianna and several other people I did not know.

Antonio looked over and said. "Harry, it seems you don't have a place with us, perhaps they put you on another table?"

Cleo jumped in, "It must be a mistake. I'll look into it." And she left to find the manager along with Lucia.

Lorenzo came over and put his hand on my shoulder, gently steering me away from the group and out on to the terrace. He took off his mask. Lorenzo seemed painfully self-confidant and his face seemed like an honest face. A face any woman would be safe with.

"Ignore him," he said, his black hair flopping down onto his face, as he pushed it back. "Antonio has had a thing for Cleo for as long as I can remember."

"I figured as much, just by the way he looks at her."

"Just ignore him. It's nice to see Cleo in such good spirits and she seems quite taken with you."

"I like her too."

"Well, my only advice is don't go losing your head over her."

"How do you mean?"

"Cleo is, how can I say..." Lorenzo paused for a moment, clearly trying to find his English. "Cleo is very special and she's very beautiful. She attracts many men as you can imagine for a woman of such beauty."

"What are you trying to say, Lorenzo?"

"I'm trying to say this. Cleo has had a string of men who have been left heart broken."

"And why tell me this?" I asked.

"Because, I see the way you look at her, it is a look that I know well and Cleo is a nice girl to have fun with, but not to go falling in love with. If it was me in your place I would want to know these things." His English was now spoken with a heavy Italian accent.

"Well thanks for the information, Lorenzo, but I think I know what I'm doing."

"Okay my friend, now enough of this, let us go for a drink," he grabbed my arm.

We went toward the door and I looked back through the thicknesses of glass and saw Cleo at the table with the rest of the group and was talking to a man I presumed to be a waiter trying to sort out the table arrangements. He walked away, flustered. We came over.

"All fixed," she said.

"What was the problem?" I asked.

"Antonio, who organized this, forgot to tell the manager to add one more person to the table."

"But he added you," I said.

"I know, it's strange. He's strange," I grinned, happy to hear she felt that way.

"Perhaps he thought you wouldn't come in the end," she said.

"Perhaps."

"Come on, take your drink and let's go for a walk," she looked to me with that terribly bright smile. We took in the atmosphere, the building, the lights, the music and walked out to the terrace to take in the city by night. It was quiet on the Grand Canal except one or two passing motorboats. When we looked down to the courtyard we saw masked guests still arriving.

"It's wonderful here Cleo, thank you for inviting me."

"Don't thank me, thank Lucia." She carefully took off her black cat mask with its gold ornate features. She turned to the wind and let the freshness of the air cool down her face. It's a face that ought to be thrown on every single screen in the country, I thought. Every woman should be given a copy of this face. Mothers should tell their daughters about this face.

"You know I'm leaving on Monday, right?" I said.

"I do know that yes," I looked down and tapped the railing with my foot.

"Well, I was wondering if I could see you again."

"Don't go falling in love with me, Harry," she smiled.

"It's nothing like that, I'd just like to see you again, that's all. Is that wrong of me?"

"Of course not."

"Maybe you could even come to Zurich one time?"

"We could go up into the mountains and ski. It's really wonderful and not that far."

"Let's see, Harry," she said, saying no more than that, but looking at me brightly. At that moment, Lucia came outside and offered some cigarettes. She was a very small girl and heavy and walked with a great deal of movement. She waved and smiled. I took my mask off and felt the fresh evening air hit my hot face. We stood for a moment and had a smoke.

"We should go inside soon, I think they will start the dinner service," Lucia said.

We left the terrace and got to the table and I took off my coat and hung it over the back of the chair. Cleo was stood talking to Lorenzo.

There were twelve of us in total. I sat next to Cleo with Lorenzo to my right and Lucia to Cleo's left.

The waiter came over and described the evening's menu. I took the big jug from the table and filled Cleo's cup with water and then passed it to Lorenzo. Cleo looked at me and I took her hand under the table.

We were sitting apart but jolted close together. I leaned over and tried to kiss her. She leaned back. "Not here Harry," she gave me a smile and took a sip of her drink.

Watching her face, I knew she was wondering if I was offended. I sat back and said to myself, it was okay. I was just happy to be here with her and if she felt uncomfortable, showing intimacy then I can understand, given all she has been through.

"Everything's fine Cleo," I replied and she seemed relieved.

Masks were off now as the dinner service commenced. I looked at the clock. It was half-past eleven. During the course of the dinner, we all talked about one thing or another, but nothing in particular. Antonio did not talk or look over to me but I could tell that my presence infuriated him. His face was sweaty and taut and sallow. I looked at him carefully and saw his unshaved face with its blank pockmarks and flattened nose. If he were in a crowd nothing about him would stand out. My head started to work again and I could see he was becoming quite drunk.

As the dinner service wrapped up and we finished our digestives, the music suddenly became much louder and the sound of Prosecco bottles started to pop, and then the party suddenly exploded. There was no other way to describe it. Everyone was either stood up or dancing but even when dancing, everyone was drinking.

"Salute for alcohol! Hurray for carnival!" Alfredo had stood up from the table and shouted. He had a bold head with a thick dark beard and black-framed glasses.

"Hurray for the English!" Antonio shouted in a sarcastic manner, looking over at Cleo, and then at me then slamming his glass down and spilling his drink all across the table. She turned to him and smiled. He was not smiling now.

"Oh lighten up, Antonio," Lucia said, before turning to me. "Just ignore him, he's had a crush on Cleo since they met and hates to see her with other men."

"He does not have a crush on me," Cleo said and put her hand on my leg under the table and squeezed my thigh tightly.

"Oh darling, don't be so naive," Lucia said.

"Anyway, I've had enough of Italian men," Cleo said, before turning back to the group. "Now, let's make a toast before we all break up for the night. Where's Sofia?" Cleo asked.

"I'll go get her, I think she's by the bar talking," Lucia said.

We asked for another bottle of Prosecco and toasted to good health, carnival and anything else we could think of. Everyone was making an effort to speak English and it was something I really appreciated. They really tried hard to include me in the conversation, everyone except Antonio of course, who responded to everything in Italian.

After we finished we all stood up next to the table. I could feel Antonio wanted to start up again, but Lorenzo held him off. His hard-eyes watched me. It was not pleasant.

As the night progressed the dancing kept up, the drinking kept up and the music went on. It seemed as though nothing could have any consequence that night and people all around were losing themselves in the dance and the drink. I only had to look at around to know that this was a party that could set one free.

The whole nightlong you had a sense that, even when it seemed less quiet that you had to shout everything to make sure you were heard.

I went to the restroom and took off my mask. What a box to sweat in. The sweat in the light of my complicated face had fell from the crowd and changed and chased, sputtered and cracked, between the people. It was a changed face tonight, I thought. Perhaps this is why we can see faces in clouds, trees, or even from two dots on a line of paper. I wiped down and walked out. Cleo had disappeared, but I saw Lorenzo on the dance floor talking to some girls.

"Harry!" Alfredo shouted over from the side of the dance floor, pushing through the crowds. He put his hand on my arm and seemed a little drunk.

"Come here, my friend, I want you to meet some people. Come with me."

"I'm waiting for Cleo."

"Oh come on, she's fine, Lorenzo can go look for her," he was pulled me along.

"But have you seen Cleo?" I asked.

"She was with Lucia by the bar some minutes ago. Look, come outside and then we will go find her together. Come on, Harry," he was insistent.

"Okay," I said, seeing no point in resisting.

We walked onto the terrace. Half of the crowd was now outside smoking and drinking. I could feel the history of the country in the air and as we walked out above the singing and dancing, I could hear the sound of the city lost in its own festivities.

We walked up to a group of girls Alfredo knew. One of the girls had a bottle in her hand and offered us a shot of something or another, which I refused at first but she insisted, so I took a drink. It tasted of liquorice and warmed me all the way through.

Alfredo introduced them all around, and they started to talk in Italian, but there was not enough room where we stood, so we all moved over to the sidewall. A waiter came by and Alfredo ordered a bottle of Prosecco and glasses for everybody. There was a lot of talking outside. It was loud.

"Tell them you're a writer," Alfredo said loudly. "Go on, tell them."

"I'm ashamed of being a writer," I replied and could feel everyone listening.

"Go on. Tell them!" Alfredo said, looking up smiling.

"This gentleman," he said. "Is a writer."

"You're a writer," one of the girls replied.

"No, no. You must be confusing me with someone else," I replied.

Another one of the girls stepped forward, introducing herself as Viola. "Really a writer, what have you written?" she asked and smiled and showed all her bad teeth.

"Nothing of worth."

"What are you doing here?" she asked. "I've never seen a foreigner at this party before," eyeing me curiously. "It's really only a local affair and tickets are only sold to local families. How did you swing it?"

"Actually, I met a girl called Cleo Tremonte and she introduced me to Alfredo and his friends and they just invited me to come along. Do you know Cleo Tremonte?" I asked.

"Sorry, I don't."

"Well, anyhow, I really didn't know what to expect and didn't know it was such an event."

"Lucky for you."

There was shouting now down from the street and I looked out and over past the courtyard to see a group of teenagers setting off fireworks in the square next to a large fountain.

"Well, I really should go find my friend," I said.

"Of course, it was nice to meet you."

"What's your name?"

"It's Harry. Harry Hoffman."

I turned and looked at my watch. It was eleven minutes past one and I hadn't seen Cleo for over an hour. I noticed a dot of dried blood on my watchstrap. I licked my figure and rubbed it off.

I looked around and saw someone I thought to be Lucia sat down talking to people I didn't know, so I made my way through and walked over.

"Having fun?" I asked.

"Oh hello, Harry," Lucia said, turning to see me. "How are you?"

"I'm fine, just looking for Cleo. Have you seen her?"

"I was with her some minutes ago, I think she's down in the courtyard talking with one of our friends."

"Which friend?" I asked.

"Ricardo, he's a friend."

Lucia started fingering her glass and seemed distracted. One of her friends filled her glass and mine. Just then Lorenzo walked by. He started to smile at me, and then he saw Lucia with a big glass of Prosecco in her hand. He was with a woman with bare shoulders.

"You chaps have some Prosecco for me and my new friend?" he asked proudly in English.

"Sure." Lucia took the bottle from the table and stood up and filled both their glasses.

"I will go outside for a smoke. This table is full of drunks," Lucia said to the three of us.

"Okay, I'm going to find Cleo," I said, turning to leave. Lucia grabbed my arm.

"Just wait a second."

"What's the matter?" I asked.

"Look, Harry, they seemed to be getting quite, how do you say, cozy."

"Who?"

"Cleo and Ricardo."

"What does that mean?"

"Just that, if you do go see her… Please don't go starting any trouble."

"Was she kissing him?"

She paused. "I'm sorry, Harry."

I breathed through my teeth and I saw Lucia looking sympathetically at me.

Lorenzo was now on tiptoes proposing a toast. "Let's all drink to" he began and then looked at me. "Cleo," I said subdued.

Lucia looked at me very seriously, and we all touched glasses and drank it down, I rushed it a little.

"Well, thanks I appreciate your honesty I guess," I said to Lucia.

"Harry, stay here and let's get another drink," Lorenzo said.

"I need to find Cleo," Lucia looked at Lorenzo like Lorenzo already knew, so I gave them both a grin and left.

"Harry," I heard them shout as I walked off.

I walked around the ballroom checking people's faces and then turned out to the terrace. I felt anger running throughout my body. I couldn't see them anywhere. Antonio and Alfredo were outside.

"Have you seen Cleo?" I asked walking over. Antonio was holding onto the terrace railings, swaying slightly. Lorenzo and the girl came out behind me and joined us. I started to ask Lorenzo what he knew and Antonio kept interrupting me.

"Why do you keep interrupt me?" I asked.

"You don't know?" he said with a slight grin on his drunken face.

"It would seem our friend here is not feeling so well," Lorenzo said.

"I see, are you okay, Antonio?" I asked, hoping he felt horrible.

"What do you care, English," he spat down at the floor.

"Calm down, and for God's sake don't be so noisy," Alfredo, said clearly annoyed.

"Yeah, cut it out, Antonio," Lorenzo said.

"Where's Cleo, you ask? Well she's with another asshole. He's actually even a bigger asshole than you, Harry Horrffman. What is that, Jewish? Please don't get all superior and Jewish on us Harry," he continued. "Do you even think you belong here among us? People who are out to have a good time?"

"That's enough, Antonio." Lorenzo shouted, before turning to me. "Don't listen to him, he's drunk."

"But he's not wrong about Cleo and this guy right?"

"I'm sorry, Harry," Lorenzo replied.

"Yeah, I'm sorry too," said Alfredo. "I really thought she liked you and it's not so nice to invite you and then go off with someone else."

"Anyway, what do you mean don't listen to me?" Antonio slurred, only just realizing what was being said. "Anyway am I wrong about that bitch?"

"Cut it out Antonio. Don't talk about her like that," I could feel my blood starting to rise. "Especially if she's not here to defend herself."

"Why, what are you going to do about it English?" he said, starting to laugh.

"Don't be a fool, Antonio. I don't want to fight you."

"Why don't you see when you're not wanted? Go away. Go away, for God's sake," Antonio shout over.

Lorenzo put his arm around Antonio and shook him slightly. "Come on my drunken friend. Let's get out of here and go for a walk. Time to cool off."

"Speak in Italian. I'm sick of this pig language," Antonio said slurring his words.

"Come on Harry." Lorenzo shouted.

We walked down the stairs and into the courtyard; it was becoming clear to me that Cleo had left without any word to me or anyone else. We left the party and walked to one of the cafés just off the square with the fountain. It was now past two in the morning, but the party was still very much going in the city streets. We had just sat down and ordered a bottle of Prosecco and water for Antonio, when he stood up.

"Where is Cleo?" he demanded, looking at me.

"I don't know."

"She was with you."

"I don't know, Antonio," I repeated. "She's probably with Ricardo."

"Oh yeah, Ricardo," he was bitter now and his face sallow under the light. He was still standing.

"Tell me where the hell she is," he demanded once more.

"Sit down," I said. "I don't know where she is."

"The hell you don't."

"Antonio calm down," Lorenzo demanded. "You will get us thrown out of this place if you don't calm down."

"Tell me where she is you English bastard."

"Even if I did know, I wouldn't tell you. You're a mess."

"Oh go to hell. All of you."

At this, Lorenzo started shouting at Antonio in Italian. Lorenzo stood up and tried to get Antonio to sit back down.

"She's on her honeymoon with Ricardo," Alfredo said as a joke to lighten the mood and then realized what he had said and looked at me.

"Sorry, Harry."

"You shut up Alfredo and don't apologies to that pig." By now we were making quite the scene. People had stopped dancing and were looking over.

"Is that where she is?" Antonio asked.

"Of course she's not on her honeymoon, stupid," said Alfredo. "But she's probably with Ricardo."

Antonio now pushed the table over and all the glasses and the bottle of Prosecco hit the floor making a great crashing sound. He stood proudly and firmly waiting for an assault and ready to do battle.

"Calm down for Christ sake," Lorenzo cried out.

"Oh go to hell," Antonio screamed back. "I'll make you tell me you English pig!"

Antonio then launched himself at me and swung his fist to my face. I quickly stood up and saw it coming and ducked. I saw his face move sideways in the light and then he hit me with such a great wallop to the right side of my face that I fell down.

I sat down on the pavement, and as I started to get to my feet he hit me twice more and I went down backwards, crashing into the table. I tried to get up but felt like I did not have the legs.

I sat there and spat to the ground. I couldn't believe this damn drunkard had put me to the floor. I had to get to my feet and hit him back. Lorenzo came over and helped me up and Alfredo was now holding Antonio back. I stood up, took one look at him and then collapsed on the floor.

I could still hear Antonio shouting in Italian, but it all faded into the background and got softer and softer until it was gone.

When I regained consciousness, it felt like blood was pouring down my face. I looked up and it was Lorenzo pouring water over my head. He saw my eyes open and then he slapped my face hard.

"Harry! Are you okay?"

"What? I was?" I said, feeling dazed. I sent a probe out to gather information on my body and senses. I was terribly dizzy and had a strong headache. I turned slowly to my left and saw Viola holding my hand.

"What are you doing here?" I barely slurred out the words.

"She saw the whole thing happening from the terrace as did everyone else and got here when you were out cold," Lorenzo said.

"Where is that son-of-a-bitch…" I said, slurring out the words again.

"Your friend Alfredo took him home," Viola said.

I stood up with their help and sat down on a chair.

"I really have to apologize for Antonio, he shouldn't have hit you like he did," said Lorenzo, shaking his head.

"He moved like a boxer?"

"He is. Three times a week," Lorenzo replied.

"Lorenzo, you could have mentioned that when you warned me earlier," I muttered, nursing my aching body.

"Relax and drink some water," Viola said. I turned to her.

"How does it look? Do I still have a face?"

"It's pretty banged up," she said, frowning.

"Look we better get out of here, I'm pretty sure the owner called the polizia," Lorenzo insisted.

They lifted me up from both sides. I felt a little more in control now. My legs were not as shaky anymore.

"I'll take you back to the hotel," said Viola.

"Me too," Lorenzo said.

"It's okay, guys, I appreciate it but I can make it back on my own, I'm feeling better now."

"Don't be silly, Harry."

We started off. I looked back as Lorenzo stumbled up the stairs and table then saw him finish off one of the glass that didn't smash and he quickly necked it down. Viola was holding me up and looking straight ahead at nothing.

Outside on the square it had started to rain, and the moon was trying to get through the clouds. There was a strong wind blowing that swept through the square and was hard and old under my feet. The band and music were playing again, and the crowd was massed on the far side of the square where the fireworks had been set off.

As we walked we fell into the crowd. Then suddenly the magnesium fireworks exploded again and made me jump.

"Take it easy Harry." Viola said.

That was the end of it. We went on, and my feet seemed to be a long way off, as everything seemed to come a long way off, and I could hear my feet walking a great distance away.

We got back to the hotel and Lorenzo said his goodbyes at the entrance, saying he would call on me tomorrow. Viola asked for the key at reception and the man at the front desk asked if I needed the house doctor. Viola helped me to the elevator and into the room where she put me on the bed.

"You don't have to do this, Viola, it's really very sweet of you, but I'm okay, honestly."

"Just lie down and relax."

She went to the bathroom and came back with a wet cloth and placed it on my head. Before I knew it, I fell into a deep sleep.

CHAPTER VIII

ONLY ONCE IN THE NIGHT I woke and heard the sound of the wind blowing and felt the pain. When morning came, I opened my eyes with a headache and the noise of the café from the street below. Raising myself up off the pillows, I looked around the room and saw Viola curled up on a chair in the corner. She had a thin blanket and the thick pillow from the bed was on the floor.

I slowly got to my feet, stretched and rubbed my eyes and walked over to the window. The wind was still blowing hard. The light was coming through the clouds from the east across the Grand Canal, but my eyes could not see how rough the water was. Be a hell of a tide today. Probably flood the square. That's always fun, I though, except for the pigeons.

I could see one of the waiters from the café below sweeping out the floor and mopping down the tables. I turned and went to the bathroom, switched on the light and turned on the taps and the water ran cold. I sat on the edge of the bathtub. Hell of a night, I thought shaking my head then walking to the mirror to examine the damage. My right eye had been cut below the eyebrow and was puffed out and was partially closed and discolored and the left side of my forehead was swollen. "To hell with you," I said out loud and to the mirror.

I closed the door and got into the shower. I looked up at the faucet at first but the water hitting my face was too painful. I turned around with my head down and felt the water hit the top of my neck. As the water trickled down my face the pain subsided. I watched the water move in lines down my legs and flow off into the black hole and wondered why Cleo would do such a thing. She seemed like such a genuine girl. Well, what the hell do I know?

It was Sunday morning and I had planned to leave tomorrow. Now I had an unnerving feeling that I should perhaps leave sooner.

Surely the inspector would visit me today if he knew I was leaving tomorrow. I really didn't want him to see me looking like this. I wonder how much trouble I could really get into by leaving suddenly and not informing the inspector. What could they do exactly? Could they extradite a British national out of Switzerland?

I stepped out of the shower and felt less groggy. I rubbed down and wiped the mirror, I took another look at myself. I guess it's all downhill from here, and the thought of returning to Zurich turned my stomach. I walked back into the bedroom and the room was in disorder. I saw that Viola was still fast asleep in the chair. The young sleep late, I thought and the beautiful sleep half again as late.

After getting dressed, I started to pack my things into the suitcase, and by nine-thirty I was finished. I phoned down for breakfast to be brought to the room, asking them to knock and leave the breakfast cart outside. I took a smoke by the window and when the knock came I decided to wake Viola and sat for a moment by her side. I watched her slowly open her eyes, watching her breathing and wondered what she was dreaming.

"Viola, Viola," I said softly. She moved a little.

"Hey Harry."

"How are you?" I asked in the same soft tone.

"Me? What about you?"

"I'm fine, but I have a horrendous headache."

"You don't look so good, Harry,"

"I'll be okay."

"Viola, I want to thank you for looking after me last night, it was really kind of you to take me home and stay the night like you did."

"When I saw that jerk hurt you, I could not in all good conscience just leave you."

"Well, it's really very sweet of you and I appreciate it," I said. "Here, I've ordered you some coffee and breakfast. I didn't know what you liked so I just ordered a little bit of everything."

We talked over breakfast about what had happened and how I had been invited to the party and all about Cleo and the incident with Antonio. Viola was very understanding. She did not eat much and drank her coffee slowly. She told me she was a student of Environmental science at the Università Ca'

Foscar, which is a wonderful university housed in an old Venetian gothic palace and stands on the Grand Canal, between the Rialto and San Marco, in the sestiere of Dorsoduro.

"Viola, I am leaving today," I said. "And I've decided not to go straight to Zurich but drive to one of the Italian lakes and rest up for a few days."

"Oh, that's a good idea," she said as she stood up and went to the bathroom. She came out brushing her hair and held the brush in her hand then opened the doors of the tall armoire, which was all mirrored inside, and continued brushing her hair.

She was much younger than me. But had a look of eagerness, deserving expectation. It was a shame she had such bad teeth. Her hair was short and put to the side and came down above her shoulders.

Both windows were open and the curtains drawn back and the sunlight was bright in the room. I did not feel sleepy anymore.

I started wondering to myself about being alone again. I'm only dangerous when I'm alone, I thought. I don't want to be alone, and the vague sentimental idea of being alone again scared me.

"Perhaps this sounds forward of me, but would you like to join me for a few days? I'm not too sure being on my own right now is a good idea, and I could sure do with the company." I took a drink of my coffee. "I could drive you back to Milan after so you could get the train back to Venice," I added.

"That's a nice idea Harry, but I have class this week."

"So just skip it, it's only for a couple of days," I said, shrugging.

"I don't know," she replied. "It's a little crazy."

"Well, craziness is in the air at the moment," I said and she looked blankly at the window.

"Can I go home and pack first?" she asked with a smile.

"Of course."

"So where do we meet?" she asked.

"We could meet at the bus station in Santa Croce at twelve-thirty?"

"What time is it now?"

"Ten-forty."

"Okay. Perfect."

She stood up from the bed and made a pass at her hair again in the mirror and we said goodbye and kissed on the cheek twice. She left and started off. From the open window I watched her walk through the square, playing with her hair as she did. The light from the hotel shone on the blackness of the gondolas and made the water green. Only tourists and lovers take gondolas, I thought. Expect to cross the canal in the places there are no bridges.

I walked over to the bed and turned off the side lamp and sat next to the wide window that was next to the bed. The bed was back slightly from the window, and I sat with the fresh air on my face.

On the table was an empty bottle of Valpolicella next to the reading light and a glass half-full of brandy and soda. I drank it down and then called down for someone to collect my luggage. The Paris edition of the New York Herald Tribune lay on the bed besides the three pillows.

I settled the bill and made the proper tips. The people of the hotel had put my luggage by the door and then retired. I said my goodbyes and walked out of the hotel lobby. It was really an awfully wonderful hotel.

The streets were dead and pigeons were out in the square. A few children were kicking around empty fireworks and the cafés were practically empty. Outside on the terrace I saw a couple of people drinking still in costume from the night before. They were eating potato chips and talking loudly.

I turned and looked back at the hotel and saw the windows of my room still open. There was no promise or threat of rain, only the same strong wild wind, cold wind from the mountains.

I walked through the city past the Campo Sant'Anzolo with the empty market stalls that still stood from the day before, past the closed shops and down the long narrow street that led to the Ponte di Rialto bridge and over the Grand Canal and into San Polo. Everyone in the gondolas looked cold, I thought.

Every chance I got, I kept sure of looking behind to check nobody was following. The advantage of moving fast through Venice was that you could take in the houses, the minor vistas, the shops and trattoroas and the old places of the city. If you loved the city of Venice, walking fast was an excellent game.

I walked through the close-packed and crowded market that spilled out into several side streets. As I moved I studied the spread and high piled cheeses and the great sausages and inhaling the smell of roasted coffee and looking at the amount of fat on each carcass in the butcher section. A market is the closest thing to a good museum, I thought.

I eventually reached San Croce the gateway to Venice. It was quite empty, except for two policemen stood by the bus terminal. I kept my head down and walked quickly across the street. I checked my watch. It was noon, which gave plenty of time to rent a car and meet Viola.

CHAPTER IX

The Grand Hotel Menaggio is a stone's throw away from the shore of Lake Como. Looking out past the flowery hotel courtyard stood a large iron gate. In front of the gate was a cobblestoned walkway that ran along the banks of the lake and was lined with linden trees and empty flower boxes. It ran past the hotel in both directions and to it's right, less than one kilometer away, was the village of Menaggio.

Sitting outside on the hotel terrace, there was a soft but cool breeze in the evening air and the view of the lake felt peaceful and calm.

There was a private mooring for boats in front of the walkway and had a wooden sign above it, which said The Grand Hotel. A wooden speedboat pulled up on the dock and a man jumped out. He had curly black hair peppered with gray and a sharp angular chin. He wore shorts and a navy shirt and a gold cross-hung from his neck. He got out and tired the boat up securely. The boat was built like a bullet. He walked through the hotel gate and up the path. He gave me a long hard stare but didn't say anything. I gazed passed him and out onto the lake. It was dark now and I ordered another martini. I felt exhausted and in pain.

The view is better in the summer months, I thought as I looked out. The mountains are much more luscious and green and they rise high and dip straight down, almost vertically, into a bright deep blue lagoon. In February it was very different; the mountains were brown and the water was dark.

The waitress came out with another martini and placed some bruschetta down with green olives and artichoke. Taking a leaf at a time, I dipped them, heavy side down, into a deep saucer of vinaigrette.

It was now past six o'clock and Viola had been up in the room for over an hour. I decided to continue waiting instead of going up.

When she eventually came down, she took the chair across from me and gave a smile. She was wearing a slipover jumper and a tweed skirt over thick, black tights and black ankle boots. Her hair was brushed back into a ponytail, which ran down to the middle of her neck. She had been quiet and a little withdrawn, since we had left Venice. Something was going on in her mind.

"It is peaceful here, Harry," she said. "The room is great and the view is wonderful. It was a great idea to come here. Thank you for inviting me."

"It's no problem," I said. She seemed much chirpier than on the drive up. She ordered a Prosecco and bit into an olive.

"Did you know that Lake Como makes the best olive oil in Italy?" she said.

"Really?"

"Yes really, tourists seem to think Como is all beautiful gardens and villas, but it's really a center of manufacturing."

"Interesting."

"Well," she said. "Are you going to buy a girl dinner?" She grinned and I made a point of not smiling.

We drank up and walked out to the street and along the cobblestoned walkway, toward the center of town. The villages across the lake looked like a collection of twinkling dollhouses and the mountains looked like sleepy giants.

As we walked, Viola put her hand on my arm and hooked onto me like couples do. It made me uncomfortable so I stopped for a moment to light a cigarette. She released my arm and I sat down on the small gray stoned wall with my back to the lake, looking onto the center village of Menaggio.

The village itself was small and centered around a main square that had two cafés directly opposite from each other. The buildings were mostly of the same height, perhaps three storey's tall with flat roofs and iron balconies. They were painted in different tones of yellow and brown, much like the colors of Sienna. I imagined in the summer months, these houses became a reddish brown as if almost burnt. There was no central fountain in the square for the young village children to play and no central church, which was unusual. We passed some lovely gardens and had a good look back at the town.

"Harry, is that Bellagio across the water? I say, I think it's Bellagio"

"It's Bellagio."

"Oh it looks wonderful."

"It is," I replied.

"Can we go tomorrow?"

"Sure, but we can even go for dinner tonight. It only takes thirty minutes by ferry."

"Really? Then let's go," she smiled and seemed excited.

It was becoming cold now as we walked and I wished I had worn a jumper underneath my jacket. When we arrived at the small boat terminal at the edge of Menaggio. We were just in time to take the boat. I quickly ran into the kiosk to buy tickets and cigarettes.

As the engines started, we sat back and looked onto the quietness of the dark lake straining to see Bellagio in the distance. Beyond the curve of the lake and on the approach, I could see that the promenade was lined with olive trees.

Bellagio is often described as la Perla del Lago and is the most famous village on Lake Como. It is small and sat on a hillside with historic buildings and cast iron balconies that have maintained their historical ambiance. The village itself is full of small narrow walkways and picturesque stairways rising up on the hill with, many shops, gelato stands, cafés and restaurants. It has stoned walls covered in ivy, and glimpses of marble through open windows.

We got off the boat and smelled the evening air. It was quiet but I had a good time seeing the village again. We walked to the only one of two cafés open for an apéritif. It overlooked the lake. I was happy to see Viola appreciate it. We ordered two large glasses of white wine and a selection of dried meats, cheeses and olives. The wine made everything seem better and I drank it down without remorse.

Only a few other people were inside and I found myself thinking of Cleo. I wished I had come here with her; our conversations had always been deep and meaningful. I looked out of the window, past the road and out over the small garden which belonged to the café. I saw white iron tables and chairs overlooking the lake. In the summer months it was terribly difficult to get a seat here.

"Viola, I'm going for a cigarette in the garden over there," I said pointing to the window. "Would you like to join me?"

"Sure," we put on our jackets and gave a gesture of our intentions to the waiter.

Standing in the garden, I lit a cigarette for Viola and she looked at me very brightly.

"Would you mind very much if I asked you to do something, Harry," she said.

"Don't be silly," I said, smiling at her. "Of course."

"Would you kiss me?" she asked. The very words surprised me, as she had been so quiet since we left Venice. I didn't say anything and gave into the idea and put my arm around the lower part of her back and pulled her close. It started soft, and the wind blew her hair up and it beat silkily around my cheeks. Then it became a hard kiss, tense and strong, and she kissed leaning into me, almost as if she were trying to push me away. It was not pleasurable, and I broke away suddenly.

I breathed in deeply and looked up to the sky and saw that a bird was circling above us and swooping down toward the lake.

"He's found fish," I said aloud.

We went back in, finished our drinks, paid and left and walked up to a pizzeria called Il Grotto, which was located at the top of a very steep cobbled street. We stopped outside and I could tell Viola did not like the looks of the place. Still, I walked inside. It was small and pleasant, and we were the only customers.

"Is there someplace else we can go?" She asked.

"What's wrong with this place?"

"I don't know it's a little strange."

"No," I said. "I've eaten here before and the food is really good. Maybe you would rather go to somewhere else on your own?" she didn't answer.

"Why don't we have any smells from the kitchen to cheer us up?" she asked.

"Because the wind is from the wrong direction," I answered.

She picked up the menu and spoke behind it. "Can we go dancing afterwards?"

"Dancing on a Sunday night?"

"Sure, why not?" she replied.

"Not sure anything will be open."

"Let me ask the waiter." He came over and they began to talk in Italian, and he seemed happy to help. After they stopped talking the waiter gave me a long hard stare and walked away.

"What did he say?"

"He recommended a place close by; he's not sure it's open though, but says it worth a try."

"Very well."

We ordered a liter of white wine, which came in a ceramic jug. As the dinner progressed I could feel Viola was becoming quite drunk. I ordered a liter of water to take away the effects of the wine. The conversation at dinner was excruciating, despite my best efforts. All I could think of now was getting to the dance club, where the music would abandon the need for talk.

I could feel the wine and as we went outside I figured that kissing her again might break the dullness of the evening, although I wasn't very motivated. But when I moved close, she turned away and moved her face away to the side.

"Please don't, Harry," she said. "Please don't kiss me."

"What's the matter?"

"I don't know," she answered. "It just doesn't feel right."

"But you wanted me to kiss you some hours ago."

"I know. Forgive me. Perhaps I just feel lightheaded."

"Do you want to go back to the hotel?" I asked.

"No, let's just walk for a while and get some water."

We walked slowly while taking deep breaths of the cold air. I could see she was now very cold so I put my arm around her, and I could feel that she was shaky.

We went inside and I went over to the bar. It was really very hot and the accordion music was pleasant. Someone was playing the banjo.

The music was loud and it was warm. The room was small but long, with an intimate dance floor in the center and candles on the tables. There were perhaps six people in total, all Italian, all young, and all men. We sat down.

"How are you feeling?" I asked.

"Much better, thank you. I think it was the stuffiness of the restaurant but the walk seemed to help."

"Happy to hear that."

We were drinking white wine, and Viola sat far from me and I felt a little uncomfortable. I looked around the room. At the next table was the group of Italians. I reached for the wine bottle, but she took it first and she laughed.

We sat in silence and finished the wine. Viola asked if I would like a cocktail and then walked over to the bar. One of the Italians and followed her, then seemed to introduce himself. They started talking. I was expecting Viola to give a glance over once or twice but nothing came. When she eventually came back over she brought with her the young man who was dark and tall and handsome.

"Harry, I want you to meet my new friend," she said, sounding like a teenager.

I stood up to shake his hand and he introduced himself as Tomasso from Milan. The music was suddenly turned up by the bar man.

"Signore, would you mind if the lady and I have a dance?" Tomasso asked.

"Oh, Tomasso," Viola jumped in and touched his arm. "You don't have to ask Harry, we are not together. We are just friends."

Needed or not, I gave my blessing and followed up with the fact that I would go outside to smoke.

I went to the sidewalk and down the cobbled steps until I hit the main road, where I lit a cigarette and blew it out into the cold night air. I really didn't want to stay at the club any longer, I thought. Viola was being too strange and I didn't feel like sitting on my own while I watched her with some younger guy. This was not what I had planned when I decided to come here.

I was suddenly very angry. Somehow they always made me angry. I know they are supposed to be amusing, and you should be tolerant, but I wanted to swing at someone, anyone, anything.

Instead, I walked along the street and had a beer at the café next to the ferry terminal. The beer was not good and I had a worse brandy to take the taste out of my mouth. When I came back there was a crowd on the floor and Viola was with the tall youth, who was dancing with his arms up and, carrying his head on one side, his eyes lifted as he danced. As soon as the music stopped another one of them asked her to dance. She had been taken by them. I knew then that they would all dance with her. They are like that the Italians. I stood by the bar and waited for her to come over.

Viola stopped dancing and went over to where Tomasso was stood. I sighed and then went over to the end of the bar to join them. I said my goodbyes and felt little protest from either.

"Will you take a glass before you leave?" Tomasso asked kindly.

"No thanks, I must go now if I'm going to make the next ferry," I said, before turning to Viola. "I'll see you back at the hotel. Will you be okay getting back?"

"Don't worry Harry, I'm a big girl."

"Yes, don't worry, signore, I'll make sure she is fine," said Tomasso.

"Very well then. Have a nice evening."

I took my coat off a hanger on the wall by the door and put it on and walked out and down and onto the main street, past the two main cafés that were still open with tables running out onto the walkway. To hell with her, I thought.

On the dock, the air felt colder than before. There was a strong wind and as I rushed onto the ferry, I ran up the stairs, inside the door and straight toward the electric heater.

When the ferry docked in Menaggio, I walked back through the village and could feel its silence. I could see a stormy night coming over the lake, the darkness had turned gray from the moonlight, and the waves were working hard against the shoreline.

One of the cafés on the square, had closed up and a girl was stacking up the outside tables, and locking them down with cables. I walked quickly along the walkway toward the hotel fighting the cold.

As I got to the room I turned on the light and it felt warm inside. I saw all of Viola's clothes spread across the bed. To hell with her, I thought again, shoving everything onto a side chair. I lay down on the bed and thought about the night, then looked up at the play of light on the ceiling. It was reflected, in part from the lake. It made strange and steady movements, changing, yet remaining.

When I could find no rest I got up and opened the window. I pulled a chair close and sat down next to the heater under the window, which kept my legs warm as the cold air from the lake rushed my face. I sat for a while like this with a whiskey, watching the moonlight hit the roughness of the lake.

After a while I turned out the gas lamp and undressed by the bed. It felt like so much had happened these last days and there had not been a lot of time to really digest it. I lay awake thinking, my mind jumping around. I couldn't keep away from it. I thought about Cleo and the murder. Then I tried to just focus and think only about Cleo, which helped, and my mind stopped jumping around. It started to move in smooth waves of warmth, and then, all of a sudden, I cried.

The sound of stones hitting the window startled me awake. I listened and thought I recognized a voice. Half asleep I had been sure it was Cleo. I looked out and saw it was Viola. It was four in the morning. I dressed quickly and went downstairs, to the back of the hotel where she stood at the door, I opened and she bounced in.

"Harry!" she shouted, "Harry, how are you?"

She was swaying around and finally leaning on the wall to steady herself.

"Harry, are you mad that I didn't come back with you?"

I would have told her to keep her voice down but I knew we were the only guests in the hotel that night.

"Oh, Harry, look at your face, you poor thing."

"Are you coming in?" I asked.

"No, Tomasso is waiting around the corner. He wants me to go back to his hotel, but I came to tell you that I'm going back to his hotel and that I'm okay and that I'm with Tomasso. Oh my English."

"Are you sure? You seem like you should really just go to bed."

"It's fine, Harry. I'm a big girl."

"Okay, where's he staying?" I asked, and upon hearing myself, realized I sounded more like a concerned father.

"At the Hotel du Lac. You remember the place, Harry, we walked past it."

"Yes, I know it."

"Please don't think bad of me or make me feel drunker than I am," she said, looking at me and taking my hand. "Perhaps we shouldn't have kissed today."

"Perhaps not."

"Please don't look at me like that, Harry. Can we meet for breakfast in the morning at nine o'clock, no wait, ten?"

"Sure."

"Let's make it ten-thirty," she said, correcting herself.

"Good night, Viola," I said with disappointment and watched as she walked out the door. I shivered from the cold air.

I went back upstairs and from the open window watched Viola walk to meet Tomasso under the arc of the light in front of the hotel. I turned around and poured another whiskey, flicking off the light but continuing to sit by the window. I felt like hell. How is it that things are much easier to deal with in the light of day, but at night it's when things really set in.

CHAPTER X

THE TERRACE OF THE HOTEL DU LAC was on the main square of the town and the sun was hitting it perfectly. I felt warm and happy to be enjoying this moment on my own. I read the international papers and smoked a cigarette.

"Good morning, Harry," he said, speaking my name in a heavily Italian accent.

"Tomasso, how are you?" I said in a mundane and uninterested manor.

"Fine. It's a beautiful day no?" he said.

"Will Viola be joining us?"

"Oh yes, she will be down shortly. She's just putting her face on. Can you say that in English?" he asked.

"Not really, but I get what you mean," he sat back and rubbed his eyes and tried to signal the waiter.

"Viola tells me you're a writer," he said. "How is the writing going?"

"It's not going for the moment," I replied.

"Oh, that happens to everyone."

"What do you know of it?" I asked, stiffening at his opinion.

"I studied literature at the University of Milan," he said, feeling my coldness.

We sat in silence and he ordered a croissant and an espresso.

I suppose he was nice to look at. I could see why Viola was attracted to him. He seemed to have a good body, and he kept it in shape. He had a funny sort of undergraduate quality about him along with a boyish cheerfulness.

When it came he shoved the croissant down without even taking a breath and spoke with his mouth full.

"Viola is a lovely girl. Don't you think so Harry?"

"She is," I said. Lovely, though, was not a word I would use to describe Viola, but perhaps she was different in her native language than in English. Maybe that was our problem.

"There's a certain quality about her," he said. "I'm sad I must leave today."

It was at this point that Viola came out. She was looking well and fresh.

"Buongiorno, chaps," she said brightly.

"Good morning, Viola," I replied.

She sat down next to Tomasso and rested her hand on his leg.

"Sorry for waking you last night, Harry, I feel awful about it."

"Not to worry, I was happy to know you got back safe. Did you have a nice evening?"

"We did, although I have a terrible headache this morning. Too much drink." She pinched Tomasso's arm. She looked up, very bright-eyed, trying to talk inconsequentially.

"Tomasso is leaving today," I announced.

"Soon actually, my friend should be here with the car any minute, and I need to get my bag and check out."

"Are you sure you can't spend another night?" Viola asked. "We could all have dinner together."

"I would like that too but I really have to get back," I said, but not really explaining why.

"Maybe I'll come back with you?" Viola said. I watched his face cringe and could almost see the working of his mind as he tried to find a valid excuse.

"I really have an early start in the morning and I must prepare. Work stuff. You understand."

"You should go with him, Viola. Don't stay on my account. I'm sure Tomasso can get up early and prepare, no?"

"Not possible, Harry," he said quite sternly. "Sorry, Viola."

"Well it doesn't matter, I promised I would spend some time with Harry anyway. Well, now that matter is settled, what's for breakfast?"

Tomasso stood up and gulped down his espresso. "It was nice to meet you, Harry. All the best with the writing and hope the face heals up."

I smiled and shook his hand without saying a word. Viola stood up and gave him a hug and kiss. They exchanged contact details and a brief promise to meet again and then he was gone. I searched Viola's face for signs of sadness but she was shy with her emotions.

We finished our coffees and walked through the center of Menaggio and up past the shops. I could feel that Viola wanted to bring up last night again but I held her off. The wind was at our backs and it blew Violas hair forward. The wind parted her hair in the back and blew it forward over her face. We looked in the shop windows and she stopped in front of a jewelry shop. There were many good pieced of old jewelry in the shop window and she stood and looked at them and pointed out the best ones.

I went to off to buy the evening papers and sat for a little while in the hotel bar.

I drank a glass of wine slowly, and looked through each of the papers for the last-minute articles that were sometimes put into Italian papers just before they came out. I found nothing more on the murder of Massimo. But then in a small article on the last page of the last newspaper it read:

DEAD BODY IN VENICE. POLICE INITIATE MANHUNT.

I read it rapidly. My Italian was terrible. My name wasn't mentioned and no new information that I didn't already know appeared. I let out a sigh and put the papers down and walked slowly up the stairs and back to the room. I lay down on the bed. Volia came in shortly after.

"I've been looking for you," her voice came in with the door.

"Shall we go downstairs and have a drink?" she asked.

"Can we just relax here for a while?" I replied.

"Sure."

I pulled the chair to the window and looked out onto the dark water. It occurred to me that it was exactly the kind of thing the Italian newspapers loved to write up in their melodramatic journalese. Maybe I should write the inspector and say I had to leave urgently for business reasons. I still had his card. Surly, they would have mentioned that they were searching for an

Inglese. But there was no mention. I worried now for my own safety, and physically I felt sick.

She lay down on the bed and I lit a cigarette. She saw me watching and, after a moment, she raised herself up onto her knees then came over and took my cigarette, inhaled deeply and then collapsed back down.

We sat for a moment, then I broke the silence.

"I figured we could go to an Italian restaurant tonight that I read about in one of the hotel guidebooks," I said. "It's close by."

"When we are in Italy, Harry, we just call them restaurants," she said smiling. "And anyway, I'm too tired to go anywhere on a boat. I could do with an early night to be honest."

"Me too," I admitted.

We sat there in silence, waiting for time to pass. I watched the big sky from the window and waited for it to turn from light to dark. In the back of my mind I figured it had been four days since the murder.

"What's the matter?" she asked, noticing a change on my face.

"I was just thinking about a murder that happened some days ago in Venice." I tried to keep my voice light. "Did you read about it?"

"A friend of mine mentioned it. What do you know of it?" she asked.

"Just what was said in the papers. It sounded pretty gruesome."

"How so?" she asked.

"The guy was stabbed at first and then had his head crushed on the stone floor. I was up by Campo San Lio at the time."

"Is that where the murder happened?"

"Yes."

"Did you see anything?"

"Just the police."

She paused and seemed to reflect and then came over and sat down on the window frame.

"Wouldn't this be just the perfect setting for a murder," she said.

"What do you mean?"

"This hotel. It's so old and feels like it could be the setting for a murder," she said in an ominous tone. "Could be the setting for your next book."

I looked around at the dark room. "Yeah, I suppose the hotel is a little creepy and I think we are the only guests. It's definitely old."

The hotel did have a certain Victorian character and style to it. It was elegant and grand and had a huge ornate staircase decorated with chandeliers. The furniture was shoddy and in need of replacement, but it was comfortable and cheap and most of the rooms had lake views.

"Let's get ready and head to the restaurant," I said. "I'm famished." She looked up at me with very bright eyes and tried to say something, but I said nothing.

By ten-thirty, we were the only people left in the restaurant. The two waiters were standing over against the door. They wanted to go home. The night had been a disaster. We had a lousy dinner and argued throughout over something of no importance. After dinner she mentioned that she wanted to be alone for a while and go for a walk. So I left her outside the restaurant and headed back to the hotel.

I started up the grand stairs as the concierge saw me arrive from his office. He caught my eye and when I stopped he came out. I had seen him before and I was pretty sure he was the proprietor. He had a large stomach and gray mustache. He wore a white shirt that was tucked tightly into his bulging stomach and a waistcoat with a gold watch chain hanging down.

"I say, Signore Von Horn, will you be checking out tomorrow?" he asked.

"Yes I will."

"Will it be early?"

"I don't believe so."

"Okay. We still need some details from you, like a copy of your passport etc."

"Very well, I'll be down in the morning with everything you need."

"Grazie. Bunanotte, Signor Von Horn."

I got to the room switched off the lights so I was not visible from the street and stood by the window, waiting to see when Viola would return.

An hour had passed and I was still alone in the dark, I kept an eye outside by the window. I grew tense and my mind drifted. Outside the noise of a running car filled the streets. The sound of two men talking came up through the window.

I lit the gas lamp beside the bed and I stood up and searched my bag for a distraction. I had been reading a very sinister book that recounts imaginary dark adventures of a perfect English spy in an intensely romantic post-war setting, the scenery of which is very well described. I heard a car drive past again and started to drift. Two Italian police cars with flashing lights scrambled up the drive way of the hotel, and four policemen ran out toward the entrance, leaving their engines running and the doors open. Shouting in the hallway and then a large bang at the door and then another bang, shaking the picture frames from the wall, until the door crashed open. Then I blinked and came to my senses.

I walked over to the mirror by the bathroom and saw that I had started to sweat. I took a long hard look at my face, which was now turning a slight yellow and blue around the eye. I pulled my shoulders back and asked myself to forget. There was no use in worrying.

I looked blankly around the room. It was a very typically Italian way to furnish a room, I thought. Practical, too, I suppose.

My mind jumped around from one thing to another. Now I was dreary at the prospect of going back to Zurich and racked my mind for alternatives, but money was low and I knew I must. I only had eventless and lonely weeks to look forward to now and each day that would go by would only confirm and emphasize the dullness of my existence. I should really start writing again. I now had that familiar feeling of emptiness and lack of purpose, which had plagued me and driven me almost crazy. In Venice it had, briefly subdued, but now, there in that room, the sensation was back only it felt ten times worse.

I smoked about six cigarettes by the time I heard the noise of someone walking through the courtyard. The sound of gravel came up through the window and brought with it the relief that I did not have to be alone with my thoughts any more. She came into the room looking sad and defeated. "Harry, I'm sorry," she said.

"I'm sorry too, Viola."

She came close and we hugged. She was fresh from the night air and her hair was cold and smelled like the outdoors. I loosened myself and rested my weight on her for a moment.

"Can I ask you something?" I said softly. "How does one end up here?"

"What do you mean?"

"I mean, I look at my life, at my fathers' life, at my friends, I look at everybody's life, and I have no clue how anybody ends up where they do."

"You don't have to know, Harry," she said, pushing her hair back. "There's so much time."

"Yes, but I'm talking about my life," I said softly.

"What about your life?"

"It's not right."

"What is not right?"

"I'm not who I thought I was."

Viola took off her coat and led me to the chair by the window. She sat me down and knelt before me to take off my shoes.

"Relax, Harry, and be comfortable," she said, then she stood up and went to the bathroom and I sat there with my gritted teeth. I looked around the room; it looked like a dozen other hotel rooms I had ever stayed in.

Viola returned from the bathroom, dressed in just her bra and knickers, which were both black and both laced. She came over and sat down at my feet with her hands on my knees and stared at me with tremendous eyes, so large and bright. She was lit only by the moon. She moved up between my legs, up to eye level, and came close and kissed me, her tongue slowly searching my mouth. I pulled back for a moment to look at her. She stood up and led me to the bed, and I could see her wet lips glimmer in the moonlight. I undressed while she was kissing me, and we lay down together. I took off the remaining items she was wearing and got on top of her, and after some moments of teasing I entered deep inside. Ecstasy swept across her, and as I moved slowly I could see wave after wave of it. I felt the passion of her arms and fingers searching my throat and my hair, her lips now pressed against my neck, kissing up toward my ear. She suddenly screamed, a piercing shriek that clawed onto the walls of the room. I grabbed her wrists and pinned her down and began to climax. I grabbed the edge of the bed and tightened my grip and let out a violent scream...

For a moment we lay still and motionless, and she looked at me with bloated lifeless eyes while struggling for breath. Then we were still. We were peaceful, and soon we were silent.

I knew it was morning even with my eyes closed from the sound of the passing motorboats and the people on the street. The window still open made me cold. I grabbed the covers and pulled them up and rested for a while longer.

When I eventually opened my eyes I looked up at the white ceiling. Slowly and cautiously I raised myself up and went to the bathroom, trying not to make too much sound. I came back and closed the window and got back into the warm bed.

Viola was facing away from me, half-covered by the blanket. I lay looking out through the window and up toward the clouds that moved slowly in the clear blue sky.

I turned to Viola and drew the blanket down her naked back, ever so slowly, to admire the contours of her shape all the way down to the top of her buttocks. My eyes followed it down past her and onto the bed where, I saw white sheets swollen with blood.

"What the hell," I shouted, jumping out of bed and looking at her. "Viola," I screamed, "Viola?" I leaned over and hit her on her back.

"Viola, for God's sake!" I whispered, but she didn't react.

Eyes wide now, I looked down and saw that the bed was full. It had even seeped down onto the mattress below. I looked at my hand and body and saw that it was covered and dripping with the stuff. "What the hell is going on?" I shouted, at no one, at anyone.

I leaned over again and pulled at her shoulder. She rolled back and her eyes were wide and lifeless. Her stomach was curdled with blood and the sheets down to her waist were drenched and clinging wet to her naked body.

My head began to spin and I became dizzy, and without another thought I collapsed onto the floor with a loud thud.

IN ANOTHER COUNTRY, AND BESIDES

———

BOOK II

CHAPTER XI

I HEARD HER VOICE without looking up. "Can I get you something?"

"Coffee Americano bitter," I said and sat there until the cup arrived. I sat there a long time like that, looking around the café, thinking of the hopelessness of it all. It wasn't good coffee.

I looked around for the girl who had waited on me. She was five or six tables away, serving beer from a tray. Her back was turned, and through a thin white blouse I saw the smoothness of her shoulders and the faint trace of her arms. The coffee began to cool.

From a distance, she was only faintly attractive with wide eyes and an expression of bored aloofness. Except for the contours of her face, and the brilliance of her smile, she was not beautiful. Her lips were heavy and red with thickness. There was something almost Latin about her, South American perhaps, and as she walked her breasts moved in a way that showed their firmness. She ignored me after a first glance and went on back to the bar. I continued to watch her as she ordered more beer and waited as the bartender served it on her tray. As she waited she glanced at me vaguely and then went on.

The coffee was cold and an oily substance had formed around the surface. I looked again for the girl. She was moving about the place like a dancer. She was small and straight-shouldered of perhaps twenty-five. I fastened my stare, watched her movements, turned my chair, and twisted my neck. Unknowingly she had effortlessly become a distraction.

I looked down and opened my bank statement. It showed a balance of 988.60 Swiss Francs. I got out my checkbook and deducted four checks drawn since the first of the month, and discovered I had a balance of 532.60 left. I wrote this on the back of the statement. In disgust, I put it back into my briefcase. It won't be long until I'm out on the street.

Now it was the turn of the gray-haired bartender to look over in my direction. I gestured and he nodded.

I turned to the letter and tensed up and gave out a sigh, and soon looked up and wondered why she wouldn't come over.

Fifteen minutes past until she finally arrived and although I wanted to continue with my arduous stare, I couldn't keep it up.

"Did you want something else?" she asked.

"Yes, another Americano."

"One Americano," she turned away.

"Can I ask you a question?" calling her back.

"Sure," she turned back with a cool expression.

"Are you ignoring me?" I asked.

"How do you mean?"

"I don't know. Just a feeling I guess."

"No I'm not ignoring you."

"I'm just busy."

She could see from my half smile that I was joking. She changed her stance and smiled through the corners of her eyes then she looked around.

"I should get back."

She said nothing more and walked away. She returned to the bar and looked over and I gave her a smile then returned to my letter.

I read it again and felt the restlessness come. To hell with it, I thought and took out a fifty-cent piece, placed it on the table, stood up and left.

I went back the next morning in the hope of seeing her again and to write back to Marie-Anne's letter. She came in around ten o'clock and did not venture near my table, but I was glad. Don't come here straight away, I thought, let me sit for a while and watch. I took out a sheet of clean white paper and pen and sat back with a blank stare.

She walked in my direction carrying a cup on her tray. I wanted her to ignore me some more—I wanted her to give me that rare excitement which allowed my mind to ignore this letter and travel to the infinite loveliness of her strange beauty.

Her eyes were blacker and wider than the previous day and she walked toward me on soft feet, smiling mysteriously.

As she stood beside me, I sensed the slight odor of her perspiration mingled with the cleanliness of her shirt. It overwhelmed me and made me stupid; I breathed through my teeth. My mouth felt dry.

"I took the liberty of ordering you an Americano," she said and placed the coffee down in front of me.

"Sorry if I was rude yesterday. It wasn't the best of days."

"It's no problem."

"I'm Berta by the way." She put her hand out.

"I'm Harry."

"Please to meet you, Harry." She paused and looked down. "What do you have there?"

"Oh, just catching up on some letters."

I tried to hold my stare but blinked, then looked down and around the room. "Well, I should get back," she said.

"Yes, me too."

She walked away without a word. I turned my mind to the letter and wrote:

DEAR MARIE-ANNE,

Thank you for your letter. I'm sorry I didn't write to you before starting the book. I really had wished to write and even tried a few times. I didn't know where to start and the words just wouldn't come. That's why I only mailed you the manuscript.

I'm sorry you felt hurt that I put our experience down on paper. I guess after all that happened I needed to let go of the pain and the hurt of losing you both by writing our story.

Please know that I have mourned you both, and this book was a way for me to finally let go and move on, but to do so I had to go back and give our story it's time. To digest it, to relive it, in order to move past it. I really hope you can empathize and even understand.

If you read the story again you will find that my love and admiration for you both shines through. I hope you can hold onto that and not just focus on the negatives.

I'm hurt when you say that I'm only profiting from the death of our daughter. That's absurd and so far from my intention, you have to believe me. I think if you can read it with an open heart you will feel that it is sincere and it might even help you in some way.

All I ever wanted to be was a great writer and writing is such a lonely life and I must draw from past experience to write something of worth. I know you understand this. You always did and you always supported me.

It's for that reason why I am writing to my publisher today to state that half of all royalties from The Blue Room shall be paid to you.

I want you to please not make any objection to this, and as you say, it's our shared story. As such we should share any good, no matter how small that should come from it. You must let me do this for you. I will send more on the particulars later. You must agree to this, Marie-Anne. Please just take it as a gift without any protestations or bitterness.

I'm sorry this is now a long letter and there are doubtless many things I have left out. I won't tell you how much I miss Catherine. There's not a day that passes where I don't think of her. I pray to God that she is fine and also to make up to you the very great hurt that has been done toward you—you who are the truest and loveliest person I have ever known.

With love,
HARRY.

I sat there grinning wretchedly. Standing at the bar, she watched me leave and could see the hurt in my eyes. There was pity on her face and see could sense regret but I kept my eyes away and walked out onto the street and across to Bellevue.

I was calmed by the sound of street trams and the strange city noises pounding at my ears and burying me in an avalanche of chatter and screeching.

I put my hand in my pocket, lit my last cigarette and walked out over crushed leaves toward Lake Zurich.

It was a clear fresh October afternoon and I sat there on a bench overlooking light green water and snow-tipped mountains, and felt sadness. I looked down into the gutter beside my feet and saw a long cigarette butt. A man and a girl passed me. They were walking with their arms around each other. When they passed and without shame I picked it up and lit it, puffing and exhaling it toward the clear sky.

I stayed there until the cold had taken me and then walked down until a tram came along.

There were two letters in my mailbox when I arrived home. I went up the stairs to the small dirty apartment and put the mail on the table, fixed a drink and went to the bedroom and sat on the bed, loosened my tie, and rolled up my sleeves and opened the first letter. It was brief.

HARRY,

Enclosed you will find a cheque made out to you for twenty thousand pounds on the promised advance for The Blue Room.

DAVID.

P.S. If it sells below estimated amount in the first three months we will take back thirty percent of the advance as per contract.

It slipped from my fingers and did a kind of slow zigzag to the floor. My mouth was open. I picked up the cheque and took a long hard look again and reread the letter once more. "Twenty thousand pounds," I said out loud. I looked in the mirror and shook my fists defiantly.

I picked up the second and opened it with the feeling that perhaps this was even more great news. It was from my editor along with a book enclosed.

HARRY,

Hope you're well my friend. I think I finally got through to David to send you the money. I hope he has by now and you're happy with the amount. Getting him to part with a penny is like pulling teeth, but you know that already.

We are still working on getting you the final proofs of The Blue Room and should be with you next week latest. I think some words should be avoided so that we shall not divert people's attention away from the quality of the book to a discussion of an utterly impertinent manor. The use of the word 'f----' and 'b----' are in my view over used and we simply cannot have these words published. For this book and others you submit all profanity will be blanked out as I have done, but you will see these comments and more in the forthcoming proofs.

The manuscript is an exciting and truly meaningful story Harry and you should be very proud of your accomplishment.

I have also sent you 'Adventures of a Younger Son' which I recommend you read and expect that you will enjoy as it's alive with grand material.

I will be over in the Zurich office in the coming weeks so let's arrange something as we have lots to discuss. Please keep sending more short stories for consideration.

THOMAS.

I went over to the writing table and began.

DEAR THOMAS,

I was very happy to receive your letter and cheque today and also to hear your admiration for The Blue Room. Before this cheque arrived, my financial situation was just rotten. In several ways I have depleted my funds from the first novel Bitter Tulips, and have been living on thin air this last year. It's truly a welcome relief. I even bought a ten-franc lottery ticket the other day with a grand prize of hundred thousand francs, so you see I have many irons in the fire.

Thank you very much for sending me the Adventures of a Younger Son, I look forward to reading it with great anticipation.

I imagine we are in agreement about the use of certain words and I never use a word without considering if it's replaceable. But of course in the proofs I will go over it all again very carefully. I think that words—and I will cut anything I can—that are used in the conversation of The Blue Room are justified by the tragedy of the story. I plan to go over the proofs very carefully. By which date should you have the final proofs returned?

Up till now I have heard nothing about a short story called—Home Town—that I mailed to you sometime the first week of September. Did you receive it? I have another copy, which will send if you did not. Last month I wrote two more stories ranging from 1,400 to 3,000 words. I haven't had them re-typed and sent on, as I was waiting word about Home Town.

The reason I haven't sent more stories for the magazine is because I was so sure you would buy anything that was publishable that my hopes got very high and after I'd tried both a long and short story- and I suppose those stories aren't that pleasant- and in the end, both were not accepted or published it made me feel very discouraged, as I had counted on that as a certain source of income. I suppose I have been foolish not to copy out more stories and send them to you for consideration.

Enclosed is another story. Three Strangers on a Train. I will try and send the other one soon and I hope you will consider both.

Given my new financial situation, I may now plan to go to Paris and work on the final proofs for The Blue Room, as I feel a change of scene will do the manuscript and myself some good. As such it's best to write care of:

American Express c/o Harry Hoffman,
Neugasse 18
CH-8003 Zurich

As I will keep them informed by wire of my address in Paris or where ever I may be as they have excellent mail forwarding services and will re-wire all cables and re-forward letters with no delay. I also will start to look for a new apartment and get out of this filthy mess I've been living in for far too long. So best to always use the American Express address.

I have a grand idea for a novel to write based in Venice when I get some tranquility in the head.

Again, it was very pleasant to get your letter and learn how much you liked the book. I look forward to the proofs.

Yours very sincerely,
HARRY

CHAPTER XII

I SAT THERE AGAIN in that small damp waiting room, thinking of what to say. I took some coffee and it tasted like boiled dirty rags. It was bad coffee.

"Mr. Hoffman," a lady appeared in the hallway.

"Doctor Bussmann will see you now."

I stood up, feeling uneasy. "Please come this way," I followed her down a corridor and entered a sterile room and Doctor Bussmann was sat behind a large desk.

"Hello Mr. Hoffman," I took off my jacket and got comfortable.

"How are you?" he said in a stern tone.

"To be honest, not so good," I answered. "I'm still having trouble sleeping."

"Are you taking the medication I prescribed?"

"Yes, but I think my body has become immune to it or something because it's not working anymore."

"We can put you on something stronger," he said. "And the panic attacks? How are you doing there?"

"They came back."

"As intense as last time?"

"Not really, but I feel like they might."

"How so?"

Not knowing where to start. "Do you remember when I first came here? I was having at least two or three panic attacks a day?"

"Yes, I remember, it was just after you returned from Italy, correct?"

"Exactly," coldness ran down my spine.

"But then I started to write again and my mind felt occupied so I barely had them at all. Now the book is finished and I have more time, my mind is jumping back and forth."

"What is on your mind, Mr. Hoffman?" he asked.

"The book for starters, it makes me anxious. The money I'm now getting from the book also stresses me, and the guilt, I suppose, the guilt of writing a true story from my own life. All these things and other things."

"Harry, I took the liberty of calling on your doctor in Paris, Doctor Bertrand, I believe was his name."

"I didn't ask you to do that."

"Standard procedure. And what I found was a long list of issues dating back almost six years from your Paris days. Confused thinking, false beliefs, hearing voices, anxiety disorders, I mean the list goes on. Your doctor there, Monsieur Bertrand, diagnosed you with minor schizophrenia."

"Doctor, I'm not schizophrenic."

"I'm not saying that, but you sometimes have a failure to understand and grasp what is real."

"Look, I know I've said it before, but I really know a great psychologist," he said. "She speaks perfect English and she's close to here. She's really quite wonderful, and you need to talk to someone about all of this instead of just relying on medication. You have an illness, Harry, and you need to take responsibility for it. You need to wake up."

"I don't think so," I said, shaking my head. The idea made me feel cold.

"So what do you need?" he asked, letting out a deep sigh.

"Valium."

"To prescribe you that, I would rather have you talk to someone first," a frown formed across his weathered face.

"I'm not doing that. Really," I said.

"Harry. Please."

"Look, I need something strong for these attacks and also stronger sleeping pills." Exhaustion started to stir.

"I'm okay with the sleeping pills, I can even prescribe them for you now. But I really think you should have a few meetings with a therapist before we talk about Valium."

"You know I puked on the side street on the way over here? I come in here against every instinct of privacy, of self-reliance, and what do you do? You say, no! You don't help me at all, you push me back on the street, send me off to score crack or heroin. You're ridiculous," I stood up.

"Please sit down, Mr. Hoffman." He took out his notebook and started to scribble. "A prescription for Valium. Take eight milligrams, four times a day, for fourteen days."

"And here is my home telephone number. Call me if you need more, okay?"

"Thank you," I stood up and shook his hand and turned to leave.

"Why is the last client of the day always the hardest?" he said as I put on my jacket. "Because you're tired and you don't give a s---."

I went out to the street and walked down toward Birnensdorferstrasse, passed the tables of Café Uetli, still crowded, looked across the street at the Café Rosa, its tables running out to the edge of the pavement. Someone waved from a table, I did not see who and went on. I walked down to the pharmacy and picked up the medication. The girl behind the counter looked at me with a form of pity. I wanted to get home.

It was around five o'clock and the light was leaving slowly. I walked down Saumstrasse and through the gravelly asphalt of the Sihlfeld cemetery between the ferns and tombstones, and the chestnut trees in the arc-light and the sound of crows. There was a fresh red wreath leaning at the base of a tombstone. I stopped and read the inscription. To Jack, from Mary, all my love. There was a picture of Jack on the tombstone. He looked very fine and handsome.

My apartment was just across the street, a little way down from the cemetery.

There was light on in the concierge's room. She came out as I came in.

"There is post for you, Herr Hoffman," she handed me three letters and some paper.

"Harry, please," I said, with an attempt to smile.

"There was also a young lady here earlier looking for you, but she didn't leave her name."

"Did she leave a card?"

"Sorry, no," she replied.

"Okay, thank you, have a nice evening."

I went up to the empty apartment, still filled with a dozen half-opened boxes, and out to the terrace to smoke. The street was dark and busy with men working on the car tracks by the light of acetylene flares. A night tram went by, running on the tracks and having to stop and wait while the workmen organized so it could pass. It was carrying vegetables for tomorrows market.

I went back in and put the mail on the dinning table, went into the bedroom. I lit the gas lamp at the side of my bed and undressed and showered and took the medicine. I was rubbing down when I heard the telephone ring. I put on the bathrobe and slippers and answered the call. It was the concierge.

"Herr Hoffman?" she said.

"Harry, please."

"The lady is here to see you again. Shall I send her up?"

"Yes, please do." As soon as I put down the phone I quickly dressed and combed my hair. A knock came and I went to the door.

Cleo was holding a suitcase, a big green duffel bag, flowers and to her side stood a little girl.

"Buonasera, Harry," she said in her familiar accent. "Aren't you going to invite us in?" she was holding a great bunch of roses.

"Of course, yes come in, sorry I just got out of the shower," I felt slightly confused. "Please, come in. Excuse the mess and the boxes, I just moved in."

She stepped into the apartment and stood in the hallway, and looked around.

"I don't know whether you like flowers, but I took the liberty."

"Thank you. They're wonderful. I'll put them in some water," I walked to the kitchen and filled a big earthenware jug with water and put the roses inside and placed them on the dining room table. I was now dizzy from the medicine but I let it ride. That's the way it always is, I thought.

"Can I get you anything? A drink perhaps?" I shouted out then came into the hallway. She could tell I was nervous. I looked down at the little girl, and she screwed up her face and hid behind Cleo's leg.

"Would you like a drink?" I repeated. She continued to hide. I turned to Cleo. "What's her name?"

"Liv."

"Oh, that's a beautiful name." I knelt down on the floor to smile at her.

"Sorry, Harry, she doesn't speak English."

"Not a problem. Will orange juice be okay?"

"Yes, that would be just fine."

"I'll fix us a couple of martinis," I said with false brightness, heading back to the kitchen. Sweat was now on my forehead. Cleo was speaking Italian in a high-pitched voice, as people do when talking with kids. When I came back to the living room, Cleo and Liv were settled on the sofa.

"This is a great apartment, Harry," Cleo said, taking the martini and handing the orange juice to her daughter. She wore a black sleeveless dress and looked quite beautiful.

"Thanks. Sorry again for the mess."

"How many bedrooms?"

"Three, plus a dining room."

"It's big for one person, or do you live with someone?"

"No, it's just me for the moment," I said. I did not want to stay myself. I was reserved and formal and tried to ignore the tension. "Tell me, Cleo, what are you doing here? Are you in some sort of trouble?" She was trembling and looking away. I thought she was looking around the apartment. Then I saw that she was starting to cry. I could feel her crying. Shaking and crying.

"I don't even know where to start," she answered. She glanced down at her daughter warily before looking back at me. "Do you have something Liv could read or play with while we talk?"

"Let me think," I said. I went into the bedroom and picked up some blank paper and colored pencils and took the old stuffed donkey I had once given my own daughter, and placed it on Liv's lap. She smiled and took it in her arms. I saw that Cleo had left the room and was now out on the terrace. I brought out two chairs and we sat down together with a feeling of things coming that I couldn't prevent happening.

"It's such a great apartment, Harry. Really," she said.

"Thanks, Cleo. So what's going on?"

"Oh, I don't know, I had such a hell of a time and I just had to get out of Italy. I didn't know where to go or who to turn to. Do give me a cigarette, will you."

"Sure, but why come here? We hardly know each other."

"That's not true, Harry," she said, shaking her head. "I've often thought about you, about how we connected. I've wanted to reach out many times, but I couldn't with all that was going on."

"What was going on?" It felt like she was evading the question, but I could see that she was also very nervous, and I did not want to help her in any way.

She would not look up. "I don't know where to start."

"Start somewhere, please."

"First of all, I'm sorry about how I treated you in Venice," she began. I sat back and opened the cigarette box, handing one to Cleo. She put it on her lips, and I leaned over and lit it. I took one myself and inhaled deeply, letting out a whistle through my teeth.

"To be honest, I was really disappointed," I said. "We had this great time together and I liked you and I thought we really connected. Then you disappeared without a word. Not even a goodbye. I later found out you left with some guy."

"I know, I feel just awful about it. I'm sorry, Harry. I really am." She took a long drag on her cigarette and thought of a better response.

"I'm really sorry" was all she came up with. She raised her head to the sky. "I'm in such a mess, Harry."

Looking over at her I could see she was about to cry again.

"Look, everything is fine," I said, feeling the need to change the subject. "How did you get here?"

"We took the train to Milano and then onto Zurich," she said, her voice straining but her tears at bay.

"And how did you find my address?"

"I searched your book, and the publisher's address was inside, so I just wrote to them saying I knew you, that you had left something valuable with me and I wanted to return it. They gave me an American Express address. When I came to Zurich I went straight to that address and pleaded with them to give me your home address. Was that wrong of me?" She could sense my surprise.

"Of course not. I'm just surprised they gave out my address like that," I said. "But why come here, Cleo? What about friends or family?"

I felt the impulse to keep deviling her. I was angry and blind and unforgiving of what happened in Venice. The fact that she was here now did not alter any of that. But I certainly didn't hate her.

"I want to be honest with you, Harry," she said. "But it's so hard, given my story."

"What story?" I drank my martini down quickly. She put her hand on my arm.

"Don't get drunk, Harry," she said. "You don't have to."

"I'm not getting drunk," I said. "I'm just drinking a little. I like to drink when I know something impactful is coming."

"I don't want to stress you."

"It's fine, Cleo, continue with your story."

"My story." She let out a deep sigh and sat back and looked up to the sky and then onto Liv through the window. "Well, it's certainly a story," she said, turning her eyes toward me so I could see the truth in them.

She did not say anything after that. She just sat there, and I could see tears building up in her eyes and then her eyes became glossy.

"It's tearing me all up inside, I can't even begin to explain."

"Then try saying it in the third person. Tell it as a story…it may help."

"What do you mean?"

"For example, you could start by saying this story is about a girl, and this girl…"

"I'll try." She took a deep breath and began. "Okay, let's say it's a story and this story is about a girl." She looked over at me for approval.

"Exactly." I had the feeling of going through something that had happened before. Like a nightmare of it all being repeated. Something I had been through and now I must go through again.

"And this girl had a husband. And the husband hurt and abused the girl. Until one day the girl couldn't take it anymore and feared for her life and the life of her daughter."

I sat back with wide eyes.

"And after years of living in fear, one morning she decided it was enough and the only way out was to fake her own death and disappear."

"Are you serious?" I paused for a moment, almost enjoying the story. It was lousy to enjoy it, and I felt lousy. "Why couldn't she just leave?"

"Believe me she tried. And every time she did, he found her and made her come back, threatening their daughter's life if she didn't."

"So what happened?"

"She took on a new life under a new name and moved to Venice."

She looked at me with a sad smile. It was clearly very hard for her to have an audience for this. Her vulnerability made her attractive and sweet and sincere. I was reminded why I had thought she was wonderful. And she was wonderful.

"But how did she fake her own death?"

"The how is not important, Harry. What's important is that she left."

"What about her daughter?"

"She left the daughter with her husband knowing only too well that he would not wish to raise her alone and would give her to the girl's parents, which in the end he did."

"The girl then moved to Venice and started her new life." She took a long drag on her cigarette and exhaled with a quick blow through pursed lips. "Then one day, two years later, the guilt and need to see her daughter became too much to bear, so she went back, confessed all, and dealt with the consequences."

"My goodness," was all I could say.

"Yes. It's a sad story but unfortunately a true one."

"I don't know what to say." I swallowed hard.

"You don't need to say anything," she said bitterly. "It is what it is."

"Is Cleo your real name?" I asked.

"No. It's Maria."

"And when we met? You were still in hiding?"

"Yes."

"And your last name?"

"Moretti."

"Sorry to put this on you, Harry."

"It's fine, Cleo, I mean Maria." I gave her a sympathetic smile. "So what happened next?"

She went on. "I went back home to see Liv. It was a great shock to my parents, as you can imagine. Then my husband Roberto found out and came to visit, saying how much he had changed and that he wanted us to be a family again. I just couldn't believe it, Harry. I mean, after everything he put us through, to even think I would be willing to give us another try." She reached into her bag for her long thin cigarettes and placed one on her red lips.

"Then a few weeks back, he started to become crazy again. Showing up at my parents', constant calls, letters, telegrams. He's a complete psychopath. In the end, I just wanted to leave and I found myself here."

"I'm so sorry for all you've been through," I said after a small silence. "It all sounds just horrible."

"It was horrible, Harry. Especially the last weeks. Seeing Roberto again. It was, well. Perhaps you can imagine."

"How is he with Liv? Did you let him see her?" I glanced back into the living room.

"Yes. But supervised with my parents. He's better for sure. They definitely reconnected. He now puts more time and focus on her. I just hope it's for the right reasons, and not just to win me back."

"I guess only time will tell," I said, sighing. "So that whole story about you leaving him and having an affair with Alexander…was any of that true?"

"Yes, that was when I first tried to separate from Roberto. But during my time with Alexander, Roberto threatened to kill him if I didn't come home. And I could see he was serious. So I went back to Roberto for some months, but when things got bad again I started to panic."

"I can imagine," I said.

"I really tried, Harry, I really did," she said, her face a mask of anguish. "I tried so hard to reconnect with him and make it work. Even after all he had put us through for the sake of our family. He told me he had changed and that everything would be better again. But it wasn't. The abuse came again, only some days after."

"Unbelievable." I couldn't think of anything else to say. "So how did you do it?"

"Do what?"

"Fake your own death?"

"Do you really want to know."

"Yes."

Now for the first time she dropped the manner she just had and became almost bright and chillingly cheerful.

"We were on holiday in Sicily," she said. "And one evening I went for a swim and never came back."

"What, that's it?"

"That's it. That simple. Of course, they thought I had drowned. So I made my way back to Bologna where I had left money and clothes in a locker at the train station. One day I will tell Liv, but she is too young now to understand."

"It's just so incredible, Cleo," I said.

"Maria," she said smiling.

"Maria, sorry."

The telephone rang.

"Excuse me a moment." I got up and went inside and picked up the receiver but it was dead on the line, so I hung up the phone and went back out to the terrace. Liv was completely absorbed in her drawings and didn't even notice me walking by.

"Everything okay, Harry?"

"Yes, everything's fine," I said.

"Anyway, what were we talking about?" she asked.

"I think you were talking about Roberto. Did you tell him you didn't love him anymore?"

"Yes, but he doesn't listen, or doesn't want to listen. I think the only way I will get it through to him is to ask for a divorce. But I know he will not make it easy."

"I understand."

"But really, it was too much these last weeks. I felt very unbalanced."

"I can empathize. And how is Liv?"

"She's fine so far, she reacts on me I guess. If I'm unbalanced then so is she."

"Poor thing."

She was nervous again, as I had never seen her before. She kept looking away from me and looking ahead in a blank stare at the wall.

"So what was the turning point?" I asked.

"How do you mean?"

"In a sense of, at what point did you decide to leave Venice?"

"I guess, some months after we met, I had a visit from the inspector investigating Massimo's murder. Remember the inspector, Harry?"

"Yes," I said darkly, remembering all too well.

"He came to see me in Rome and told me they had caught the killer," she said. I reached for the cigarettes.

"Okay."

"But it gets worse," she continued.

"How so?"

"They told me it was Alexander."

"Alexander? Your Alexander? The one from Paris? Are you serious?"

"Yes."

"Oh my God. Do you believe it?"

"I don't know what to believe," she said. "It all seems too surreal. Like a movie, or a bad play."

"They said they found Alexander's skin under Massimo's finger nails, or something like that. I don't know how they can know it from skin. I mean, it could be anyone's." Her face scrunched up in disgust.

"They have new technology these days, I guess."

"Well, apparently some days after he did this he then drove up to Lago di Como with a local girl and murdered her in a hotel room."

I stayed silent.

"It's just horrible, Harry. Although the inspector does seem doubtful it was Alexander. I don't know. They are still investigating."

"Does the inspector know about Roberto? I mean, could it be him?"

"I don't know. I don't want to think about it. It was all too much and I just had to leave."

"I understand."

"He was even very suspicious of me."

"Who?"

"The inspector. He was suggesting I was somehow involved. It's all such a mess," she said, smoking heavily now.

"Let's have another drink," I said suddenly. I went in and took the whole bottle and brought it outside. I poured a little in my glass, then a glass for Maria, then filled my glass again.

"In the end, I just had to get away, away from Roberto and away from everything. And I'd thought of you so many times these past months, and I ended up here. I hope you don't mind. I really could use a friend right now."

"I don't mind at all."

She smiled weakly back.

"Did you book a hotel?"

"I was hoping we could stay with you for some days until I figure things out. I'm too scared to stay alone. Do you mind? I don't want to impose."

"Of course you can stay, if you don't mind the boxes."

"Thanks, Harry, you are so very sweet."

"You can both stay in my room and I'll take the sofa."

"Will your girlfriend mind?" she asked, her eyes worried for a moment.

"I don't have a girlfriend." I could see relief in her expression.

"I really can't thank you enough."

I was now looking at her from across the small outside table under the gaslight hanging from the wall. She was smoking another cigarette and flicking the ashes onto the floor. She saw me notice it. "I don't want to ruin your new terrace. Do you have an ashtray?" She turned away and looked at Liv through the window and we stayed silent. She left like a child to me in that moment. I felt her pain and all she had been through. She didn't deserve any of that. No woman does. I looked at her with admiration, and all the anger I had felt toward her washed away. She was in need of help, and I was in a position to help.

She smiled back and then leaned forward and broke the silence.

"So tell me a little about you, Harry. We've only spoken about me."

"What's to say really?" I breathed in deeply and leaned back.

"Well, how's the writing going for a start?"

"Very well actually. After Com-, I mean Venice, I had some form of clarity and I was able to start writing again, and only very recently I finished my second novel and a few short stories that I hope to be published soon."

"Really, how wonderful. What's the novel about?"

"I have a manuscript somewhere here that you can read. I'm just in the final stages of editing before it gets published."

"What's it called?"

"*The Blue Room.*"

"Nice title."

"Thanks. It's a good book. You are lucky as a writer if you can write truly what you hear and think. And I think I did just that."

"You seem to be doing well for yourself," she said.

"Yes, over the last couple of months, things are starting to come together. I just wish I could sleep. I suffer from insomnia."

"How terrible."

"I'm on medication, it helps, but sometimes I have problems catching up with reality."

"What do you mean?"

I leaned over and drank my glass down and poured out another for Maria. I put my hand on her arm.

"Listen, let me go out pick up something for dinner and some other supplies. You two just make yourself at home and I'll be back soon and we can continue our talk."

"Of course," she said.

I stood up and felt shaky on my feet and as I did so she also stood up and came close. She put her arms around me and whispered, "I knew I was right to come here." I pulled back, smiled, and left.

Downstairs I came out through the first-floor door onto the side street. I walked alone. It was cold and bright in the evening sky, and I gradually digested all Maria had said.

Up the street was a little square with trees and grass where there were taxis parked. A taxi came up the street and I waved toward him before he stopped.

A bicycle cop saw me waving and came over before I could get in the taxi and asked to see some identity papers. I took out my Swiss blue paper, and he gave it a long hard stare and then let me go. I got inside the taxi and told the driver where to go.

The driver started up the street and I settled back and wondered if I was in fact safe to be around. I had been on my own since Como, and there was some safety in that.

Ahead was a mounted policeman in a gray and blue shirt directing traffic. He raised his baton. The car slowed down. I tightened up and clenched my fists and started to sweat.

CHAPTER XIII

Two weeks went by and Maria and Liv were still here. I was not bothered by any troubles and I rather enjoyed having them here. I still had plenty of work to do on the manuscript but we often went to the park together in the afternoons. Liv was fun and beautiful and caring and enjoyed it when I played the goofball. The language barrier didn't stop us from having fun either. The three of us connected and it felt great. Maria told me more about Roberto and I tried to reserve judgment as much as I could. At nights I would sit and read to Liv in English before she fell asleep. I think she liked the new, strange sounds of the language. Then Maria and I would sit out on the terrace, talking and drinking and smoking. I was happy she was there and I told her as much.

I had thought that Maria being around would bring me into great stress and anxiety, but it really didn't. The opposite in fact happened and I didn't feel touched by it at all. I even started to think that perhaps Alexander or Roberto really killed Massimo and Viola. Life felt simpler that way.

One morning I was walking down the stairs to buy cigarettes, I noticed a strange looking man talking to the concierge. He looked up and grinned. He was carrying a briefcase. I met him on the way down and he introduced himself as Romano. He was Italian.

"Hello there," he said in a firm manor.

"Herr Hoffman, this gentleman is looking for a woman and child who he believes is staying somewhere close by." She looked at me with wide eyes.

"Appunto! I am looking for this girl," he pulled out a picture of Maria.

"Have you seen this woman?" he had a big mustache and looked very military in his black suit. The concierge was just behind him.

"I haven't sorry," I looked at Frau Fischer hoping she wouldn't say anything.

"Why are you looking for her?" I asked. "Is she in some sort of trouble? Mr..?"

"It's Romano," he snatched back the picture. "She disappeared some weeks ago and her family is worried. They believe she is here in Zurich," he turned back to the concierge.

"Are you absolutely sure, Frau Fischer? Please look again at the picture," I was stood behind him and she looked at me over his shoulder and I shook my head slowly with wide eyes.

"I haven't seen this woman, Mr. Romano," she said.

"Very well then, if you see anything, please contact me on this number," he handed her a card and started for the door.

"Mr. Romano," I called out and he turned back. "Why do you think she could be around here?"

"What business is it of yours?" He looked on with inquisitive eyes.

"None, I guess, I was just curious."

He turned away and continued to the next building. I could feel that he sensed the tension.

"Herr Hoffman, what is all this about?" Frau Fischer asked with tension in her voice.

"Can I see his card?"

She handed it over. It read.

GIOVANNI ROMANO
INVESTIGATORE PRIVATO
VIA PIEMONTE, 140
ROMA
06 884 3240

"The picture is the lady who is staying with you, no?"

"Yes, but you must not tell this man."

"I don't want any trouble here, Herr Harry."

"There will be no trouble, Frau Fischer, I promise, but please do not call this man. I will handle it."

"But what is she doing here?"

"Really, you have nothing to worry about."

I tipped her two francs and looked at the card again. A postman was coming along the sidewalk. He turned into the open door and handed a packet of post to Frau Fischer, she looked at me in a motherly disappointment and then turned her attention to the postman. I walked out to a nearby café and had an espresso and cigarette and contemplated if I should tell Maria.

By midmorning the air still had a cool freshness to it, and it felt pleasant to sit outside on the terrace of the café. It was past ten now. I finished the papers and was about to go back to the apartment when I saw Maria and Liv walking toward me. They came over and sat down. A cool breeze started to blow, and I could feel that the cold air was coming from the mountains. The waiter came out and asked if we would like to order something. My nerves felt shot to hell so I ordered a beer.

"Are you okay, Harry? You seem a little pale."

"I'm just low energy. Everything is fine," the waiter came with the beer and I paused to take a sip.

"Are you sure? Do you not want us here anymore?"

"Don't be silly; I love the fact that you guys are here. I'm having a great time with you and Liv," on hearing her name, Liv looked up and smiled.

"Come on, Liv, let's cheer up Uncle Harry."

"Uncle Harry," I said and smiled.

"Listen, I should tell you something, before we go."

"What is it?"

"There was a private investigator here this morning asking around for you."

"Are you serious?"

"Yes, he even had a picture."

"What did you say?"

"That I hadn't seen you, so did Frau Fischer."

"Who's Frau Fischer?"

"The concierge."

"Would she say anything?"

"I don't believe so."

"He seemed to suggest that your family had hired him," I passed her his card.

"It's not my parents, this is Roberto," I could feel her body tense and stiffen.

"I figured as much."

"Can we leave and go for a walk? If he's around, I don't want him to see us," she asked.

"Of course."

I finished my beer and paid the bill and we walked to the playground across by the cemetery so Liv could play on the swings. We sat down on a bench and had a cigarette. From where we sat we could see the church in the middle of the cemetery. Maria seeming distracted, made some remark about it being a very good something or another, I wasn't really listening. It did however seem like a nice church.

We decided to walk up and go inside. Liv was on my shoulders and as we entered I put her down and she kept close to Maria. It was calm and dim and dark and the pillars reached from the floor to the high ceiling. There were people praying and the scent of incense came between the tall glass windows.

"Come on, Harry," she whispered, taking my hand. She brought us three to a chair and we all knelt down. Liv was enchanted by the place but kept silent.

"Maria, I don't really feel comfortable here," I whispered back.

"It doesn't matter," she said. "Just try to be calm and still. We will feel better, trust me."

I sat for a moment and felt like I shouldn't be there and that if God was present, I was to him an enemy of the worse kind.

"Maria, I can't be here!" I said, raising my voice this time. A man turned around.

"Please, Harry, just try. For me."

I turned to Liv and she smiled and put her hands together like her mother.

"But I've sinned too much!" I swallowed hard.

"Then ask for forgiveness."

Something in Maria's words touched me—her faith, or her belief in salvation perhaps. I knelt down beside them both and prayed.

I prayed for everyone I knew. I thought of Maria and Liv and prayed that they would find their way and be happy. I prayed that the private investigator would leave town, and Roberto would leave Maria alone and just disappear. I prayed for my own daughter and wished her well and told her that not a single day goes by that I don't think of her. I prayed for Marie-Anne to be able to find some peace and rest wherever she was and then I prayed for myself, for my sins, for Viola, for forgiveness.

While praying, I found that I was getting tired, and all the time I was kneeling with my forehead on the wood in front of me, thinking of myself praying, I was ashamed and regretted being such a bad Catholic and the guilt of being a bad Catholic and the fear of an eternal punishment that would surly await me, then I realized there was nothing I could do about it, at least for a while—well, maybe never. But it was a good religion and I only wished I felt more religious. Maybe I would next time, I thought, feeling the need to leave.

I waited on the steps of the church. The forefinger and thumb of my left hand were still damp from praying so I stretched them out and let them dry in the sun.

That evening while preparing dinner, I found that Maria had taken a bath. She came into the living room smelling clean and wonderfully fresh and her hair was stringy and wet. She sat down.

"Are you okay?" I asked, seeing a frown on her face.

"Not really," she sighed. "My parents sent a telegram, saying that Roberto found where we are and is on his way to Zurich."

She got up from the table and picked up her glass of wine. Her hair was tied up in a knot.

"Join me for a cigarette?" she asked.

"Sure," we walked out onto the terrace.

"I have to keep an eye out," I said, "I'm cooking us spaghetti."

"I'm not really hungry."

"No problem."

"I guess the concierge called the investigator back?" she said.

"I don't think Frau Fischer would do that."

"He could have seen us at the café or at the park. Maybe he even knew already and was just testing me. We really don't know,' I said.

"True."

"Can we go away for a few days?" she asked.

"Running away is not going to help the situation, Maria."

"I'm not running away, I just can't deal with this right now and neither can Liv. We are just starting to become balanced again. I don't want to see Roberto."

"Well, to be honest, I'm also not such a fan of seeing your crazy husband and explaining myself."

"So let's go away somewhere," she said, turning to me with bright, eyes. "We could drive to Lago di Como? It's only a few hours from here, no?"

"No," I said quickly. "Let's stay in Switzerland. Listen, are you sure you want to leave? He will be annoyed as hell that you guys are not here."

"Please, Harry?"

"Very well, I'll arrange something."

CHAPTER XIV

AT SEVEN O'CLOCK the next morning, I put the last of the baggage into the car and went back upstairs to get Liv and Maria. It was a lovely bright day and not too cold.

We started up through the city and out onto the highway with Lake Zurich below us to our left. The country was beautiful from the start.

As we started climbing, we crossed a small bridge and the road winded back and forth on itself at every corner. One really felt like this was Switzerland.

Around us stood tall stretches of brown and green mountains with snow at their peaks, and beyond we could see the road we would follow running up the mountainside. There were many pine trees and far-off forests on the hills building up toward the mountains. As the road climbed higher, the snow appeared and gathered on the trees and along the roadside. We came down out of the headlands and through a dark pine forest until we reached pastures where cattle grazed in open fields and deep, clear blue streams. We crossed another wooden bridge and went through a small village and then started to climb again.

For a while the countryside was much as it had been. We ate sandwiches and drank cold coffee from a flask and watched the country out of the window. The fruits were just beginning to ripen and the fields were full of small dark patches of snow. The pastureland was still green, and there were fine trees, and sometimes big rivers and chateaux off in the distance.

We climbed high and after some time we came out of the mountains and onto a straight road were big pine trees lined both sides. As the road went on I turned to Maria, happy to see her there by my side.

"We are almost there darling," I said.

"Darling?" she replied, turning to me with a strange look.

"Sorry," I said quickly. "I forgot myself for a moment."

"Darling," she smiled. "I like that."

We came into the town on the other side of the plateau, the road was slanting up steeply with pine trees on both sides and then leveling out through the new part of the town. I could see the hotel high up on a small hill overlooking the town of Engelberg. We slowly climbed up and then stopped in front of the hotel.

The Hotel Terrace was situated on a south-facing slope, and had stunning views of the village, Mount Titlis and the Swiss Alps.

"How do you know this village?' Maria asked surprisingly.

"Thomas, my editor recommended it. He used to come here before the war with his family. He is always talking about the place."

The porter came out and helped us with our baggage and there were some kids playing in front of the hotel, their parents watching from above. The air felt cool, the trees were green and there were many different flags hanging from their poles above the hotel.

It was a nice hotel, and the people at the desk were very cheerful, we both had a good small room and it was nice to get into the room after the drive. I had booked two separate rooms that were joined together by a connecting door. Both rooms looked out over the town and had a great view of the mountains and the valley. We washed and cleaned, then went downstairs to the dining room for a late breakfast.

There were two dining rooms at the Hotel Terrace. The one upstairs on the second floor, was a very elegant room with Victorian charm. The other was down on the reception level and was built as the main attraction of the hotel. It had a glass-enclosed terrace with great views. The terrace was not so much of a dining room, more of a place to have cocktails and food, but the temperature was right and we ordered a large Swiss breakfast.

Liv ate well at first but got bored after a while and asked Maria if she could go play in the games room at the end of the hall.

"Go on, sweetheart," she said, and then we were left alone.

"Well," I said. "What do you think?"

"I think it's a nice hotel with great views, but I have a feeling that it was once a really great hotel and over the years they have changed it too much and has lost its early century charm."

"I think you might be right. Still the rooms are comfortable."

"Don't get me wrong, Harry, I'm really grateful and happy to be here with you and Liv," reaching out to take my hand. She held it for a moment. "So what's the plan?" she asked, in an upbeat tone.

"Good question," I reached for the map and unraveled it and spread it out across the table.

"I believe there's a good walk from here that goes through the town and up into a valley," following the route with my finger. "At the end there is supposedly a restaurant we could go to for lunch. It's called Ende der Welt."

"How long will it take us to walk there?"

"Depends on Liv, I guess."

"Well, if she gets tired she can always go on your shoulders. You know how she loves that."

"True," I grinned.

"So?"

"So what?"

"How long?"

"Oh, I don't know exactly," poring over the map for a moment. "Maybe one hour, maybe two?"

"I was thinking it was going to be around four hours or something."

"For sure not."

"Okay, I'll get Liv and let's go."

"I'll meet you outside in some minutes," I said and went back up to the room to get my cigarettes and a flask that I had filled with rosé wine and had put in the icebox to cool. I placed them in my backpack along with my folded-up fishing rod and when I came outside Maria and Liv were playing and running around the courtyard, trying to catch one another.

By noon, the sun was out and it felt quite warm. I took my jacket off and put on my sunglasses. We walked through the town and stopped in some shops, where we bought a pack of cards and a bottle of water. Getting tired, Liv said, "Shoulders, shoulders!" She was raising her hands while looking up at me. I swept down and pulled her up.

We made one last stop in the town for fishing bait as I saw on the map there was a deep stream running parallel to the route we would take. If Liv and Maria didn't mind, we could stop off for thirty minutes to try and catch something. We then started on again, this time with Liv on my shoulders.

At the edge of the town the road stopped and became a walkway over fields that raised up as the ground beneath our feet grew steeper. We were now walking through farm country with rocky hills that sloped down into fields. The pine trees went up sparsely on the hillside and as we climbed higher, there was a strong wind blowing against us.

Out ahead, there were wide gaps cut through the pines, and you could look up at them like avenues and see wooded hills way off.

In the pine forest it was all sandy pine country floor and heather. There were little clearings with houses in them, and once in a while we passed a sawmill.

Hikers had made the walkway over the years, and it had brown grass around the sides that mixed into the fallen pines.

The walkway cleared and opened up and we walked across a nice piece of land that was used as a ski run in the winter months. Past it, in the distance, above where the pine trees started again, there were three large gray mountains with patches of snow clinging to their tops and sides.

We came around a curve and continued on. I saw the start of the stream and watched as it went off into the distance. After what seemed like an hour of walking we found a bench with a view of the three mountains and we sat down and had a cigarette. I had lost the motivation for fishing as I had become tired from the walk. Liv went off exploring in the long grass and Maria and I sat there, relaxing and talking. One thing I really appreciated about Maria was our conversations. I felt she was just so easy to talk to. At times I felt that I could tell her anything, well almost anything. So we sat there talking, overlooking the mountains and watching Liv chase little flies.

We continued up the mountain path until we came to a sign that said Restaurant Ende der Welt, 1km. we were all pretty tired at this point and I could almost taste the cold, fresh beer that would await us. As we came up toward to the town, there was a little stream and a bridge.

It looked like any typical Swiss or Austrian mountain towns. The pine wooden exteriors, the triangular shaped roofs, the wooden balconies with animal shapes carved into their fronts. There was a general store and inn on each side of the street. We walked over to the stream to see if there were any fish. It was clear and fast flowing. Liv, pointed with her finger, if there were any fish in the stream, and I said some, but not many.

We turned up toward the inn and I could see a family walking down toward us. Something about the shape of the head made me look twice, and sure enough, as they came closer I could see it was David.

"You've got to be kidding me," I whispered to myself.

"What's the matter?" Maria asked.

"Oh, I just can't believe it," he saw me too and muttered something under his breath.

"Harry!" he called over, with false jollity.

"Hello, David," I said, calling back.

"What are you doing here?" he asked.

"I guess Thomas also recommended this place to you?"

"He did." We all stood together.

"Who is this?" he asked and looked at Maria. "Did you go and get yourself a family since I last saw you?"

"This is Maria Moretti and her daughter Liv," I said and watched with unease as he gave Maria a long hard stare. His wife was standing beside him.

"I guess I should introduce myself, as David clearly won't," she said brusquely. "I'm Frances and this is our boy, Jonathan, and our girl, Zara."

"Hello, very pleased to meet you all," I said. "It's certainly a small world, isn't it?"

"Too small," David said, continuing to stare at Maria. His wife eventually pinched him on his arm. He winced and looked back at me.

"So, you're going for lunch?" he asked.

"Yes, can you recommend it?"

"Yes. It has good local food and the beer is fresh."

"Great. Well we better shove off," I said, forcing a smile.

"Us too," Frances said, eyeing her husband.

"Nice to meet you," Maria said.

"Yes, nice seeing you David, and nice to meet you Frances," I said. As they were walking away, Frances then turned and waved and then turned away.

"Who is he?" Maria asked as soon as they were out of earshot.

"He's the owner of the publishing company I'm signed with."

"So you work with him?"

"I work with Thomas mainly, who is my editor. Thomas works for him."

"So what does he do exactly?"

"He's the owner and just signs the cheques and drives everyone crazy."

"I see. So what's he doing here if he's based in London?"

"They have an office in Zurich and one in Geneva," I explained. "The Zurich office is new and Thomas told me David is in the process of moving his family here."

We continued up a stone path, past a few houses with families sitting in their doorways, watching us walk toward the inn. The large woman who ran the inn came out from the kitchen, which had a door on the side and as we passed said hello. She took off her wired spectacles, wiped them, smiled and put them on again.

It was getting cold and the sun had disappeared behind thick clouds. The wind had started up too so we decided to eat inside. Soon the wind was blowing hard against the shutters, so we took a seat in the corner.

The place didn't have great light and we squinted at the menus. There was a stone floor, a low ceiling and the walls were all paneled with pinewood. There were pictures on the walls of hunters and a dozen or so stuffed animals on the walls, which fascinated Liv, and was not afraid by them, just curious. A piano stood in the far corner of the room beyond the tables and I asked Maria to go play us something. I knew she played well, but was too shy and refused. There were no other customers. I looked at the menu.

"Are you okay, Harry?" she asked after a while. "You seem a little distant."

"Really?" I said, surprised. "I'm just annoyed that David is here in town, that's all."

"Why?" she asked. "He seemed nice."

"He couldn't keep his eyes of you," I said, surprised by her response.

"I hadn't noticed. Plus, we are not together, Harry."

"Yes, but he doesn't know that."

I sat at the table and looked again at the pictures and dead animals on the wall. There were stuffed rabbits, pheasants—even ducks. There was also a cupboard full of liquor bottles.

The girl brought out three bowls of vegetable soup and a bottle of local red wine. Afterwards, we both had the salmon and some sort of stew. Liv had chicken with potatoes. The old woman looked on once or twice.

"I can really see that he bothered you," Maria said quietly, when we had finished eating. She took my hand.

"Look, we were having a nice time before you saw him, just forget him."

"Of course, you're right."

We got back to the hotel exhausted and went into Maria's room with the intention of playing cards on the bed. We had great fun, mostly because Liv started to make up new rules as we went on and she always seemed to win. We ordered Irish coffees that were sent up to the room and took them out to the balcony, and smoked. When she was fast asleep, we went down to the bar for a quick nightcap.

Together we walked down into the bar, and I quickly noticed that David was there with Frances in the corner. I had a feeling he would be at the same hotel. I should really not go on the advice of Thomas, I thought.

They were not talking and he was smoking a cigar. It was part of his system of authority. It made him seem older and wiser. Maria hadn't noticed them. We sat down at a table halfway down the room.

The barman came over and we ordered an Irish coffee and a whiskey soda for me. We sat overlooking the town, but we could only see our reflections in the windows and the interior of the bar. The concierge came over with a telegram. It read.

FORWARDED FROM:
AMERICAN EXPRESS C/O HARRY HOFFMAN
ZURICH

HARRY STOP IN A SPOT OF BOTHER STOP CALL ME ON THIS
NUMBER TILL TOMORROW STOP ZERO TWO FIVE ONE TWO
FOUR FIVE TWO FOUR EIGHT STOP FINN

I got up and excused myself and went over to the payphone and called the
number. Finn answered.

"Is that you, Harry?"

"Finn, everything okay?" I asked.

"I'm in Amsterdam at the moment," he sounded drunk.

"How is Amsterdam?"

"Not so good to be honest, I'm here following up a story. Thought I'd be
staying longer, but things haven't really panned out."

"Sorry to hear that."

"Got into an awful mess. Really should leave soon."

"Go on. Tell me."

"Can't remember a lot. Tell you anything I can remember."

"Take a drink and remember."

"Right," I could hear the ice knock as he downed his drink.

"Okay. Might now remember a little."

"Met a girl in a bar, cute girl, nice girl, wonderful legs that went all the way
up to her shoulders."

"What's wrong with that?"

"Asked me back to her place she did, went inside and two rather large black
gentlemen were there waiting for me. Took everything, they did. Wallet, watch,
even my belt. Loved that belt. Tried to run, but one of the fellas knocked me
clean out, he did. Woke up on the street, Harry. Horrible stuff. Still all a bit of a
blur. Tight, Harry. I was pretty tight."

"Did you call the police?"

"No. And this I remember clearly. They said that if I went to the police they would kill me. Or something. Maybe not kill. Can't remember exactly. Did I mention I was tight?"

"You did. Go on."

"Oh good, because I was," he said. "I tell you." He continued. "Wrote you a post-card. Remember that perfectly. Did you get it?"

"No."

"You will."

"Anyway, was thinking of coming down to see you for a few days before heading back to the states. Thinking we could go hiking or something with that new car of yours."

"Sure, when were you thinking?"

"I don't know, tomorrow?" he said.

"Tomorrow, that's awfully soon. I'm not there. I'm away for a few days in the mountains."

"Well that simply doesn't work. Need to get out of here."

"Could I just come to your place and wait till you get back? Where do you live again? Geneva?"

"Zurich."

"Same thing. Just leave the key with someone under a stone or something."

"Don't you have to work?"

"Not needed back for a week or two. Paper is going fine. Could take some overdue holiday."

"I guess you could pick up the key from the concierge. She has a spare. I could cable her telling you are coming."

"Do that, my boy."

"Fine."

"So where are you? Still depressed?"

"You're such an s---."

"I know."

"So what do you say?"

"Fine. But I have some people staying with me, so don't go having any parties and getting into trouble while I'm not there."

"Loosen up."

"I'm serious, Finn, and leave my liquor cabinet alone."

"So uptight!"

"I'll be back on Wednesday! The concierge's name is Frau Fischer. Got the address?"

"Best to give it."

"Idastrasse 29. Zurich."

"Okay, very well. See you in a few days."

"Fine. See you," he hung up without saying goodbye.

I walked back to the terrace and could see that Maria had joined David's table.

"Christ," I said to myself and walked over.

"There's our famous writer!" he called out as he saw me approach. "Been thinking up a new story, have we? You really should get started on something new instead of relaxing here in the mountains."

"Hello, Frances! David," I said, trying my best to be bright and normal.

"Hello, Harry," Frances said.

"Maria was just updating us," David said.

"Really. On what exactly?" I asked slowly, glancing at Maria, who was smiling back at me.

"Don't be so uptight, Harry. Loosen up, take a load off and have a drink man. Thought you weren't depressed anymore?"

"Who was on the telephone?" Maria asked leaning over.

"Finn. A friend from New York. I'll explain later."

"But everything is fine?"

"Sure," I said, forcing a smile. "So what did I miss?"

"Maria was just saying how much she liked Zurich and that she'd like to stay," Frances said.

"You'd like to stay longer?" I asked in surprise, and turned my head toward her.

"Well, look here, seems you guys don't talk at all!" laughed David.

"I was meaning to ask if we could stay a little while longer, maybe I could even find a job and a small apartment close by?"

"Yes you should stay," David said with eagerness.

"What do you think, Harry?" Maria asked.

"I think we should talk about it later."

"Well, well, getting all uptight and protective!" David said, who clearly had a few drinks and was still puffing on his cigar. "Is it every day a beautiful woman asks to stay with you?"

"Leave it out David," I snapped back and looked at him and then at Frances. She then tapped David's arm and he sat back.

"Sorry, Harry, just busting your balls," he mumbled.

"When it comes to my writing, feel free," I said heatedly. "But when it's my personal life, please stay out!"

"Oh, you're really so uptight tonight," he replied, rolling his eyes.

"David!" Frances said in a stern tone.

"Well, he is! This beautiful girl just plucked up the courage to ask for help and he blew her off."

"No I didn't," I replied. "Is that what you think Maria?"

"Not at all."

"See?" I said to David.

"Listen sweetheart, if he doesn't want you to stay, you call me and we will sort something out."

"I just said that we had to talk about it privately, that's all," I said firmly and stood up. "Come on, Maria, it's time to call it a night," I waited for Maria to stand up. "Good night, Frances."

"Harry!" David cried out and giggled as we left.

I felt so mad that I took Maria's hand and walked in silence up to the room. I opened the room door and she followed me in. I grabbed a whiskey and cigarettes and went outside to the balcony. The air had changed and I could feel a strong fresh wind hitting my face.

"You're really sensitive, Harry," she said coming up behind me.

"Sensitive…!' anguished by her words. "You have no idea what that man put me through."

"Then explain it to me."

"For example. This book I wrote recently, The Blue Room. As soon as I told him I was working on something new and it was going well, he would send cable after cable pushing me to finish it before a fall release. He drove me crazy with that. He would even call me strange hours in the night to go over the manuscript asking me to change this or that. My nerves were just shot to hell toward the end of the book. I'm sure it showed in my writing. Who the hell does he think he is, he's not even an editor, what the hell does he know about writing."

"Is he really that bad?"

"Yes, and even now he's a nightmare. They are just preparing a marketing push for the book, and he's started to threaten me that if it doesn't sell well I will have to pay back the difference."

"Really? That's not so sweet."

"Honestly, he's just a horrible person and only interested in what he can get out of people and it's all for the glorification of his big ego. The last time we spoke by phone, he said that if the book doesn't do well then he would release a statement to the press saying that two of the main characters in the book were based on the author's real life and they are both dead. He thinks it will create some controversy and help with the book sales. That's my past he wants to put on stage, and he only wants to do it to make money. Sometimes I really think he has no empathy, nor values."

"Sounds horrible."

"He's horrible. I feel sick just talking about him."

"But your ex-wife isn't dead? You told me she's living in Normandy."

"Exactly. Anyway, I don't want to talk about it anymore. And you saw him tonight; he just loves to provoke! He's an antagonist, a pure antagonist."

"Why don't you just leave?"

"I can't, they have options on my next three books. We signed a contract. Plus, I do great work with Thomas. He's really a wonderful editor. The next book I write should be a stinker and then they would surly pass and I would get out of my contract."

"Then do that?"

"Maybe I should. Although, I'm not sure I could do that to Thomas."

"Well for the moment, you should really try and take it—how do you say in English?—On your chin? Is that the right expression?" she smiled.

"Yes, that's right," I said, and with her smile I felt myself starting to relax. It was much better now that it was just the two of us again.

"Give me that thing," she reached for the whiskey flask and took a big gulp.

"Wow. There's a lot of whiskey in that whiskey," I grinned at her. "There's never a dull moment with you, is there?"

"Grazie, signore," she smiled back.

"And listen, you can stay with me as long as you want."

"I already knew you would say that," a small frown formed on her forehead. She looked away from me. "You're too good to us. How can I ever thank you?"

"Don't be silly, I love the fact you guys are at home with me."

"Thank you, Harry. Really."

"So you're serious about staying in Zurich?" I asked.

"Sure, why not?" smiling once more. It's a nice city. I feel safe and I'm sure I could find work and an apartment. Plus I like the idea that you're close by."

She leaned over and placed her hand on my arm. In that moment I wanted so badly to kiss her, and then suddenly a knock at the door came. It was a telegram for Frau Moretti. She opened it and the blood drained from her face.

"It's Roberto," she said. "He's been to the apartment."

I swallowed hard.

"Why is your concierge giving out your hotel details?" she cried, suddenly anxious and worried.

"I don't know, I really need to talk to her."

"He wants me to call him when I get this or he threatens to come out here!"

"Good God. Then you should call him."

"Yes, I will. This could take some time. I'll say goodnight, Harry." She kissed me on the cheek and left the room. I heard her go to the telephone in her room. I turned the gas lights off and undressed and got into bed. I could hear her voice as I tried to fall asleep. I just hoped she stays strong and Roberto wasn't being too hard on her.

Roberto Moretti was an Italian Jew and through his father's shrewdness was one of the richest Jewish families in Rome. He was a playboy in his youth, living from his father's allowance, and he married the first girl that was nice to him. He was married for five years but had no children, and just as he had made up his mind to leave her, she left him first and went off with a stockbroker. Even though he had wanted to leave her, it was still a shock when she said it first—and she did say it first.

The divorce was arranged and Roberto plunged himself into self-pity and expensive girls. With his newfound freedom and money, he discovered a new authority and arrogance. He wasn't particularly good-looking, just tall and wealthy and dominant and a good talker. After years of playing the playboy so well, he was forced by his father to join the family business. So he took the only job possible for good talkers as a sales executive for his father's company. It suited his personality and he was successful, but by that time he had other things to worry about. He had been taken in hand by a lady who was pretty and somewhat the talk of the town.

They had met at a party and she was alluring. Roberto was instantly taken with her. He was sure he loved her, but after some years she became bored with him and Rome and decided that she might as well get what there was while there was something to get, so she urged that they go to New York where she had been educated and to start a family. They stayed for some years and spent the first year traveling and living off Roberto's family allowance.

The lady, who was called Jovanna, found in the end of the second year that she was still not pregnant and that her looks were going. Her attitude toward Roberto changed from one of careless possession and exploitation to absolute determination: she would get pregnant and marry into the Moretti family at all costs. Yet when Mother Nature refused, she resented Roberto and they moved back to Rome. It was then that he met Maria.

Maria at that time was looking for something but she didn't know what exactly. They met at a mutual friend's party late in August of that year, and they got along well at first. He was very open about his situation and played the victim extremely well. He talked about the pressures of coming from money and what the family expected of him. He talked of how Jovanna was treating him badly and how she had come to resent him for not getting her pregnant. Maria saw in him someone to be saved. After a short affair with Maria he separated from Jovanna. Only one month later Maria was pregnant.

Maria, feeling a whole new sense of purpose, realized that even though they didn't have such a deep love connection, perhaps with a child and over time she would feel differently about him. Over the first two years she tried to make it work and he kept disappointing. For Roberto, it was more of a trophy on his arm than anything else, along with the big house, an expensive car, and finally a cute kid—everything that was expected of a man his age. He then lost himself in his arrogance and work and completely ignored Maria and Liv. He became so self-involved that when Maria talked about the possibility of a separation, the violence and abuse came and then kept coming.

CHAPTER XV

IN THE MORNING it was raining and the fog had come over the mountains so we could not see the tops. The town from the courtyard looked dull and gray and gloomy, and the shapes of the houses and trees seemed to have changed. I walked around the courtyard smoking. It was early and the flags hung wet from their poles. I looked up to Maria's room and could see that the curtains were still drawn. Pools of water had gathered around me, and it started to rain more heavily now. I went inside and up to the main dining room for the breakfast service and sat down with a cappuccino and read the Swiss daily papers until Maria arrived. She looked fresh faced and held Liv in her arms.

"Buongiorno," I said.

"Good morning," she replied, giving Liv to me. She sat on my lap and the waiter came over.

"Two cappuccinos and some warm milk with honey, bitte," Maria said.

"Did you sleep well?"

"Liv yes, me not so good. I had intense discussions with Roberto till two in the morning."

"Oh dear."

"I'm sorry, Harry, but we need to go back to Zurich."

"When?"

"Today!"

"How so?"

"Roberto is mad that I'm here with you and threatened to come out here if we are not back tonight."

"What do you want to do?" I asked.

"I'd like to stay but I don't want a drama, especially not for Liv. He really will show up and make a scene."

"Then let him. We can handle it."

"It's not we, Harry," she said firmly. "This is my problem and I need to deal with it. You can support me like you do, but this is really something I need to do alone."

"I understand. So if you're sure, then let's relax, finish our breakfast and leave."

"Thank you. Sorry to ruin our trip. I know it was my idea."

"It's no problem. Where is Roberto staying?"

"The Baur au Lac."

"Of course he is," I said with no surprise.

"It's expensive?"

"One of the most expensive hotels in Zurich."

"Well that's Roberto," she sighed and looked serious. "He asked if we would meet him there, so it's probably best to drop us off as soon as we arrive."

"At the hotel?"

"Yes."

"Are you sure?"

"I'm sure."

We sat there for a while and ate our breakfast in silence. I think Maria was just as disappointed as I was that we couldn't stay for a few more days.

"Listen," I took her hand. "We will go away again. Soon."

She smiled back.

"Perhaps it's for the best," she said. "Did you see the weather this morning?"

"I did, horrible stuff. Raining, windy and gloomy, you name it."

"I like this word gloomy," she crinkled her eyes so they smiled.

"Oh, and I forgot to tell you, my friend Finn…"

"The man on the telephone last night?"

"Yes. Well, he's spontaneously come to town and as I don't get to see him so often, I said he could stay with us for a day or two. I hope you don't mind?"

"It's your apartment, Harry."

"Well, while the two of you are staying with me, I want you to think of it as your apartment too."

"That's a nice idea," she said. "But it's your home and we are just guests."

For some reason, that comment made me sad and I tilted back in my chair, and watched her face. The sleep had made her hard.

"So perhaps I'll take Finn out hiking or fishing or something. But I can stay home if you prefer?"

"No, actually, it's probably a good thing that you go out of town these next days," she let out a deep sigh. "I really need to deal with Roberto. Honestly, I just can't believe he's here."

"Everything will be fine Maria." I said gently. "We won't go far, so if you need me, I'll be an hour away."

"That's sweet, Harry."

We went upstairs and agreed to be packed and ready for noon. I took off my shoes and lay down on the bed. The door to the balcony was open and for a brief moment the sun broke through the clouds and entered the room. A gust of wind blew in and it felt fresh, the type of freshness only rain can bring. A knock came at the door.

"Come in!" It was Maria.

"Harry, what are you doing?"

"What do you mean?"

"We are waiting for you downstairs, it's quarter-past twelve."

"What? I just lay down?"

"You must have fallen asleep! Get packed and hurry please."

I had a quick shower and dressed and packed and went downstairs. The hotel was busy now because of the bad weather. There were children running around everywhere. I paid the bill and asked the porter to bring the car around.

I found Maria and Liv waiting in the bar. When Maria saw me she raised an eyebrow.

"Ready?"

"Yes," I said with a small smile. "Sorry."

The porter brought our baggage to the car just as a bus stopped outside the hotel and many passengers got down, and a lot of baggage was unstrapped from the roof.

We drove out of the courtyard, down into the town and started off. The road was wet and dirty, and the dirt rose under the wheels and clung to the car. The road climbed up into the hills and left the fields below. We turned sharply out to the side of the road to give room to pass a long string of mules, following one after another, hauling a high-hooded wagon loaded with fright and supplies for the town. The wagon and mules were covered with dirt. Up here the country was quite sparse and the hills were covered with a light snow that was being washed away by the rain.

It did not seem very long till we arrived back in Zurich. We hardly spoke a word the whole journey.

When we arrived at Roberto's hotel I got out and helped carry Liv inside. She had fallen asleep for most of the journey. I wasn't particularly worried about running into Roberto, so I walked into the lobby and said my goodbyes. Maria seemed sad and defeated.

I drove home, parked up and went out to the side walk down toward Idaplatz, passed the tables of the café Salon, its tables running out to the edge of the pavement. Someone waved at me from a table, I did not see who it was and went on. I wanted to get home. Idastrasse was deserted, and they were staking tables outside the Italian restaurant close by. My apartment was just across the street, a little way down Idastrasse.

Finn was out on the terrace when I arrived.

"Well," I said. "I hear you had a wonderful trip in Amsterdam."

"Just wonderful," he said. "Amsterdam is absolutely wonderful." We shook hands.

"So you didn't burn the place down."

"Of course not old boy." I was getting some glasses, ice and bourbon.

"You look good, Harry." He stood back slightly and rubbed his forehead.

"Thanks, you too."

"Never too early for bourbon," he said.

"Exactly. Good to see you." We touched glasses.

"I tell you, Harry, this trip in Amsterdam almost killed me."

"Of course it did."

"Experiences like that ought not to daunt you though. Never be daunted myself. Secret of my success, I guess. Never been daunted. Never been daunted in public. That's for sure."

"You'll be daunted after about three more bourbons," I replied.

"But not in public."

"You're probably right."

"Well, anyway, let's eat," I said. "Unless you want to tell me more travel stories?"

"Go on, let's eat."

We went downstairs and out onto the street.

"Where do we go?"

"I know a place."

We walked over the street to Aemtlerstrasse.

"So who's this woman staying with you?"

"What do you mean?"

"Well. You have either decided to cross dress on weekends or there's a woman staying."

"Snooping, were you?"

"Please, there are girls' clothes everywhere."

"Yeah well, I don't want to get into it right now."

"Fine."

We walked on and stopped at one of terraces lining of the Aemtlerstrasse. We had to stand up and wait for a table. Finn ordered a whiskey and soda, and I took a pernod.

"This town is a little boring."

"It's not that bad."

"Been here one night, an afternoon and this morning and it feels boring."

"It's really not that bad, Finn."

"Don't you miss Paris?"

"I was a fool to go away; one's an ass to ever leave Paris."

"Remind me why you left again?"

"I'd really rather not."

"Maybe we should just sit here in silence then?"

"Don't be so bloody dramatic."

We ate lunch at a café on the far side of the avenue. It was crowded with locals. We had a good meal and finished it off with some apple pie.

"I see you're not wearing your wedding ring anymore. At least some progress has occurred since I saw you last."

"When was that again?"

"Perhaps two years ago in New York, you were out there talking to publishers."

"Oh yes that's right. I miss New York."

"You were really in a dark place then old boy. And that story you had me read. Was just dreadful."

"I don't need reminding."

After the coffee and a brandy we paid the bill and went out.

"I was thinking."

"What were you thinking old boy?"

"As I'm already packed and it's not too late in the day, why don't we just head out?"

"Where?"

"Up into the mountains."

"Why not,' he said. "Good idea. Where do you want to go?"

"Depends on how many days you got?"

"Two days," he said. "I already booked the boat."

"Where do you leave from?"

"Le Havre."

"Okay, so we got two days. What about a spot of camping and fishing?"

"Camping? What a novel idea," he said.

"I've got all the gear and we could go up to a lake I know, it's about an hour's drive from here."

"Splendid idea."

We packed the camping gear, some food, three bottles of wine and a bottle of whiskey. I got the rod cases and landing nets and packed them into the car and shoved off.

Finn was in fine form during the journey. He told me a dozen stories from his travels with the paper and they all ended in the same way, with him needing to leave quickly. I mistrusted all frank and simple people, especially when their stories held together, with Finn, his stories were such embellishments of his imagination, that I always wondered why he never tried his hand at fiction. He had a rare quality that I admired.

We parked up and packed everything into two rucksacks and got off with our bags and rod-cases and hiked up a road that turned into a path. When the path ran out it turned into a meadow that led toward a blanket of woods. In the distance I could see the stream I had been looking for as a marker. I checked the map.

"I'm tired, is it close?" Finn asked.

"We have been walking less than thirty minutes and you're already tired! What the hell is the matter with you?"

"It's all this heavy gear!" He stopped and threw everything off his back and sat down. Taking the wine from the cooler, he uncorked it, took a big swig and passed it to me.

"Look, its less than two kilometers to the tree line and then we then just follow the stream down until we hit the lake," I said, trying to show him the map. "There's about another three kilometers to go."

"Fine," he said, ignoring the map.

"Come on."

As we entered the forest, Finn was clearly struggling. He was covered in sweat and panting loudly. We could hear the sound of fast flowing water in the distance. We walked toward it and found a thick, dead tree lying across the stream with its roots above the ground and fanning out into the air.

Finn crossed it first with little problem. I threw over the sack and then came across myself. The trunk was damp from the water and made crossing difficult. The pine trees were big and the foliage was thick and everywhere we looked we saw damp brown and green foliage. The smell of the stream was fresh so I knelt down to touch the water. It was ice cold and I saw myself clearly.

"It's getting late, Harry, we need to get down to the lake soon and set up camp before it's dark."

"Only one kilometer to go," I said, standing up and looking away from the water. "If we pick up the pace we can be there in fifteen minutes."

"Fine," he continued.

We crossed a wooden footbridge, and stopped on the bridge and looked down stream. The trees were high against the sky.

"It's pretty great," Finn said. "I love to get back to nature."

We leaned on the wooden rail of the bridge and saw a crow pass by, it was smooth and black.

"Hey, remember when we were stationed together in Libya, I think around forty-two."

"Here we go."

"And I was sitting outside one of the tents having a smoke and some white dust came over and bunt my eyes and I shouted out gas."

"Of course I remember, back then we thought chemical weapons was just a load of old horses---."

"Exactly, and the gas alarm went off and spread far and wide and soon I think I had everyone in gas masks."

"Our unit was not happy with you."

"It's funny now, but at the time I was scared s---less."

"Remember staff sergeant Jones?" I asked.

"How could I forget?"

"Well, he would be rolling in his grave if he could see you this tired after only a few kilometers."

I thought about the war and all the fun we had.

"Do you remember the time we were doing drills on the beach and there was that one guy, I forget his name and he couldn't swim?"

"Sullivan, one of your lot."

"Oh yeah, Sullivan. Irish chap. We were in the water up to our necks and he panicked and almost drowned, and then that other chap, Walsh, he was called and tried to help, and Sullivan wouldn't let go and almost downed them both until Walsh punched him square on the face and knocked the old bugger clean out."

"Poor Sullivan."

We both laughed.

The last kilometer seemed long and I was also starting to get tired. I could not see the shoreline only the forest but through the trees I could see the tops of the hills that showed white as though they were snow-capped and the clouds that looked like high snow mountains above them. Soon enough we came out of the forest, onto a patch of grass that led to the banks of the lake. The water was very dark, as it always seems at that hour and the dark water made prisms in the water. I sat down and put my sack against a rock and Finn collapsed on the grass in front of me. We stayed for some minutes catching our breath, and then I went down to the lake.

"You sure this place has fish?" Finn asked.

"Dead sure."

We stood and looked out to the lake and Finn blew his breath at me to show how cold it was.

"How about a hot rum punch to start us off?" Finn asked.

"Sure, but it won't keep us warm permanently."

I set up camp while Finn looked for firewood and then heated the rum. I put the sleeping bags outside to sit on.

"That really was a long hike with all that gear," he said from the trees, coming back with an armful of dry dead branches.

"Thought you were in shape," I said, settling myself down.

"I thought so too," he said, still panting, throwing the sticks down in front of me. "It's a good spot here though, Harry."

We sat for a moment next to the fire and preparing dinner. When the meat hit the heat it gave out a loud hiss.

"It's good rum," Finn said, gulping down the last of it from the tin cup.

"Don't get cockeyed."

"You know I will."

The sun was almost gone by the time the meat had cooked, and as we looked over the lake we could see the last light leaving. The stars were coming out and the fire lit up our faces. It felt peaceful.

"My God, it can't be this cold tomorrow. I'm not going to wade a lake in this weather."

"Relax, it's fine. Actually it's unusually warm for October."

He didn't say anything, just took off his glasses and wiped them on his trousers.

"You know, we have some of the best fishing out in the State of Montana. Mighty fishing you did on those trips." Finn said.

"We also have great fishing in the Lake District in the north of England. I used to go with my father."

"You see him much?"

"Never. Afraid, it's just me these days."

"Except for this girl of course? What's the dirt there?"

"No dirt."

"Are you f------ her?"

"Finn!"

"What?"

"No, I'm not f------- her nor have I f------ her."

"But you want to, right?" he said, grinning. "Oh, come on, Harry. I'm teasing. Tell me. What's she doing in Zurich?"

"Well it's slightly complicated, but in a nutshell, we met in Venice over carnival, then I came back to Zurich. I had no word from her and then one afternoon, she just shows up at my door with her kid."

"Typical women," Finn said. I turned to see his eyebrows fully raised.

"She's married by the way."

"Of course she is. And I suppose the husband is sleeping in the next room?"

"Lives in Rome, I think. But at this very minute, he's in a hotel in Zurich."

"Right you are," he said, nodding and clearing his throat.

"Oh, and let's not leave out that I think my crazy boss has a crush on her."

"Seems like you've got yourself in a pickle there, Harry boy," he said with a sympathetic smile.

"That's just the half of it."

He shook his head and blew his breath out to show how cold it was again, and we sat there beneath the dark sky, watching the fast-moving clouds working their way across the lake.

After dinner, I got inside the sleeping bag and lay back next to the fire and smoked and read to keep warm. Only once in the night I heard the wind blowing. It felt good to be warm and in bed.

CHAPTER XVI

"HELL OF A COUNTRY!" his voice came over as I opened my eyes. I saw him standing by the lake in his shorts, apparently contemplating a swim.

It was cool outside in the early morning, and the sun had not yet dried the dew that had come when the wind died down. The early light the sun made in the water, now the sun was higher, meant good weather and so did the shape of the clouds over the land.

"S----, it's freezing," I heard him shout as he dipping a toe in before running back.

"Come on," he said. "Get up."

"What? Get up? I never get up." I pulled the sleeping bag up to my chin.

"Try and argue me into getting up."

"Not a morning person?"

"Not really."

"You slept outside all night."

"Yeah, I must have," my sleeping bag was damp from the wet grass.

"Weren't you cold?"

"I am now, but I guess not during the night, the fire must have kept going till dawn."

"It's really too early. What time is it?"

"Seven-fifteen," Finn replied.

"God, what are we doing up so early?"

"There you go again. And you claim to be writer. You ought to wake up with a mouth full of words."

"Oh go to hell."

We made coffee on the small stove and ate buttered bread. The coffee was good and we drank it out of the pan.

I went over to the lake and tried to dig some worms for bait. The water was clear and shallow but it did not look fishy. On the grassy bank where it was damp I drove my knife into the earth and loosened a chunk of soil. There were worms underneath. They slid out of sight as I lifted the earth and I dug carefully and got a good many. Digging at the edge of the damp ground I filled two empty tins with worms and sifted dirt onto them. I washed my hands and the water was so cold that my hands felt numb. Finn watched on.

"What types of fish are there anyhow?"

"Pike mostly."

"And we don't need a license here?" he asked.

"I told you already, if we use live bait and one hook then we don't need a license."

"Strange rule!"

"So let's go?"

"Do we fish here or take a walk?"

"I think we can walk a bit, but let's keep the camp in sight."

We picked up our rods and the cans of worms and our landing nets and the wine, and walked out along a path out to the far right.

There was dense forest and thick bush along the banks of the lake. Ahead I could see an opening in the trees and as we arrived there was a small, wooden jetty that came out onto the lake. It looked like a perfect place to fish. As we walked out, I leaned over and looked into the water. It was crystal clear. I could see all the way down to the bottom.

We sat down and baited both rods while Finn tied one end of the wine bottle to a piece of fishing line and the other end to the jetty. He slowly lowered the wine into the cold water.

"You sure about this? Won't it scare the fish?"

"I don't think so," I said. "If anything, the reflection from the sun might entice them to come over."

I handed him his rod and we settled back. It was getting warmer now in the direct sun, so I took off my jacket. We both had our legs over the side.

"So how's the expatriate life? You haven't lost touch with the empire, have you? Haven't gone and got all precious? With these European standards? Spending all your time talking and not working? I bet you just hang around cafés, don't you?"

"Sounds like a swell life," I said.

He had been going on splendidly, but then stopped. I was afraid he thought he had gone too far. I wanted to start him again.

"I do hang around in cafés."

"I knew it."

"Cafés are a great place to write. A good cafes keeps you warm on the terraces and the people give you ideas. If I could, I would only write in cafés."

"I do think you're a good writer, Harry," he said. "And you're a hell of a good guy. Anybody ever told you, you're a good guy?"

"I'm not a good guy, Finn."

"You are a good guy."

He stopped.

I picked up my rod that was leaning against a wooden stump on the side of the jetty and started to reel in.

"Anything?"

"Nope," I cast out again with the fishing line and threw a couple of worms. It was a solid but flexible fishing rod. I sat there looking out past the line and onto the countryside.

In Switzerland the land looks very rich and green and the houses and villages seem very well off and very clean. The lake and the hills stretched off back toward the Alps, but you couldn't see the Alps. They were too far away. You could only see hills and more hills, but you could always sense where the Alps stood.

A man in a dark uniform appeared to the far right where the lake curved out. I wondered if it was the grounds keeper. He came out to the jetty and threw his cigarette down.

"Guten Morgen meine Herren—was für ein schöner Tag. Darf ich bitte Ihre Lizenzen sehen?"

"What does he want, Harry?"

"Our fishing licenses."

"But we don't have any."

"Relax, I'll handle it."

"Sprechen Sie Englisch?"

"Nein Deutsch. Wir sind hier in der Schweiz."

"Okay. Okay."

"Wir fishen nur mit Haken und Live- Würmer."

"Lasst mich das überprüfen." He pointed to the rod-case, and I opened it and showed him the one hook and the can of worms.

"Is that all right?" I asked. "Das ist gut?"

"Yes. All fine," he replied in English, tipped his hat, and walked off.

"I bet he spoke perfect English, Swiss prick," Finn said out loud.

"Probably."

"What did you tell him?"

"Just that we are only fishing with one hook and live bait."

"It really is a strange rule."

It was a little past noon now and the sun was hot. There was not much shade. It was damn fine weather and I was beginning to sweat. We had caught nothing. Finn broke the silence.

"I've got to say, Harry, you seem different from when I saw you last."

"Really? How so?"

"How so? You seem much more together. Like back in the old days, in Africa and New York. Before this Marie-Anne business."

He offered me a cigarette and I took one.

"Anyway, I'm glad she disappeared. She treated you like s---."

"I don't want to talk about it."

"I'm just saying, I know lesser men who would not have got through something like that. How you did and came out as you are, I will never know."

I put my hand on my forehead and rubbed it.

"She was such a bitch, and to just up and leave like that after all you both went through. It's unforgiveable."

"Finn, please." I felt dizzy and started to remember. I felt sure I could remember now. You want to remember that? I tried not to remember anything. But there she was.

I could see her face. I could see her face. I could see her gasp for help. I could see my hands at her throat. I could see myself on top of her.

I lifted myself up and tried to stand but my legs wouldn't hold and I came back down.

"Harry," Finn shouted. "Harry!" His words became softer until they were gone completely…

I woke up with my head facing the sky. I sat up slowly and saw that Finn was not there. I tried to stand but my legs were jelly. I must have blacked out. Where's Finn? Oh God, where's Finn?

"Finn?" I shouted. "Finn!"

I looked around and into the water. I looked for blood and tried to gather my senses. I tried to stand up again, but my legs were all shot to hell.

"Harry!" I heard him in the distance and turned toward the camp. Then I saw him. He was running toward me, and when he arrived I grabbed him and squeezed him tightly.

"Thank God, you're okay."

"Me, okay?" he cried. "What about you? You seemed to have passed out. I ran back to get some water. Here, drink this."

I took a big gulp and laid back on the wooden planks.

"For God's sake," I said in a loud and defeated tone.

I turned and looked out onto the lake and then the tree line and up on the tops of the mountains and onto the clouds. They were high and feathered. Suddenly I shivered.

"It's cold."

"No, it's not. Go lie down and come back out when you are feeling better."

"I'm fine."

"You're not fine. Go lie down."

"Okay," I said, nodding slowly. I walked back and got into the hot tent, and it felt good to lie down.

I'm a goner, I thought. Not only that, I'm going mad. How can I stop it? I can't stop it and I can't help it. There's no air in this tent.

I came out and looked at the water. The strange light that the sun made in the water irritated me. I took a deep breath. I wish I could erase everything.

Starting with myself. I looked around on the grass and focused on a single blade. I ought to stop this. Self-loathing never helped anyone.

Finn was eating fruit from a can when I came back out to the jetty.

"Catch anything?"

"Not a damn thing," he sighed. "How are you feeling?"

"Much better."

"Some wine?" he asked.

"Sure, why not."

Fin pulled up the last of the bottles from the water. They looked cold and as they hit the sunlight, I could see the moisture beading down the bottleneck onto his hands. He passed the bottle to me.

"Cheers." I smiled. The wine was icy cold and gave me a chill.

"Sorry about before, Harry."

"Let's not talk about it, Finn. Everything is fine."

I smiled toward him and took a deep breath and rebaited my rod. I walked over to the other side of the jetty and sat down. I placed the rod on the side and took out my book. I was reading *The Fight for Everest* by E. F. Norton. It was about the third attempt for the summit. It was a good book and well narrated. I put my hat on and then the first pike took the bait. The rod moved quickly, and I thought it might go over the side, but I managed to grab it in time and slowly reeled it in. The rod bent almost double.

"Finn!" I shouted. "Come and bring the landing net."

He ran over, flashing the net, unsure of what to do.

"Don't give it to me, for God's sake, put it in the water and try to catch him!"

"Right! Of course."

I pulled the fish in slowly and when he came to the surface he was splashing and dashing around. Finn managed to land him; he was big, of about twelve inches. We brought him up slowly in the net and then I grabbed his tail and threw him onto the jetty. He lay jumping around, compact and bullet shaped with his big eyes staring back at me while I thumped the life out of him against the wooden floor with the quick shivering strokes of his neat and fast moving tail. I banged his head hard one last time until his body shuddered, quivered and died.

"Pretty nice, eh?"

"Yes. Well done," I said and we both sat back with contempt. I wrapped him in ferns and placed him in the rucksack. I looked up to the sky and then out to the fish. I looked at the sun carefully. The wind was rising and the lines all meant nothing now.

It was dark when we came down toward camp, along the path between the trees and ferns. The country was very fine, but we were tired.

We stayed two days at the lake and had good fishing. The nights were cold and the days were mild, and there was always a breeze. It was warm enough so that it felt good to dip in the cold water, and the sun dried you when you came out and sat on the bank. In the evenings we played three-handed bridge. Finn was pleasant and went on like he does. He didn't bring up Marie-Anne again. On the last morning, we woke, packed up, and drove to the main station in Zurich and said our goodbyes.

"Was great seeing you, Finn," I said, and we shook hands.

"You too, Harry." He smiled before turning to walk away.

"Harry!" I heard him call back.

"Yes?"

"I just want to say, this girl Maria and her kid," he called out. "You've done nothing but talk about them nonstop, and I can see how happy you are. My advice to you is to stop hiding, get out there, and tell her how you feel. Who knows? It might be the best decision you ever made." He smiled.

"Thanks, Finn. I'll keep that in mind."

"Well, adios amigo." He raised a hand and eyebrow and with that he was gone.

It was a good morning, there were high clouds in the sky. I felt good and healthy and excited about seeing Maria. You could not be upset about anything on a day like that.

As I stood looking through the two thicknesses of glass, I saw no light on. I went in and saw her bags in the hallway. She was out on the terrace, smoking with her sunglasses on. I came outside, and she threw her cigarette down to the street and put her arms around my neck. We didn't say a word. Just stayed like that for a while.

"You're leaving?" I murmured.

"I have to, Harry," she said.

"No, Maria, please stay," I breathed, inhaling the scent of her hair.

"Oh, Harry," she said softly.

"I have so many things I want to tell you," I said.

"I do too, but now is not the time."

"Where will you go?" I asked.

"Roberto found us an apartment in the center until he finds us something more permanent."

"What?" I pulled away. "You're going back to him?"

She nodded.

"I don't get you, Maria." I shook my head. "You came here to get away from him and now you go back? After all you have put yourself and Liv through with him. To just go back like this."

She looked away. I thought she was looking for another cigarette. Then I saw she was crying under her sunglasses. I could feel her grief. She was shaking and crying. She wouldn't look up. I put my arms around her again.

"Sweetheart, listen, you don't need him," I said gently. "I can look after you."

"But he's Liv's father," she said into my shoulder. "I can't just run away and cut him out of her life. He will always be her father."

She leaned back and lit another cigarette. I watched, feeling helpless.

"You know you have options." I stroked her hair and could still feel her shaking.

"What options do I have?" she asked, her body full of fear.

"You can stay with me. I can look after you."

She shook her head. "Roberto would never allow it."

"What do you mean he would never allow it?" I asked. "It's your life and your happiness."

"You don't know him like I do, Harry." She leaned back from me and took off her sunglasses and looked me squarely in the face. Her left eye was cut below the eyebrow and was bruised black and blue. My heart sank.

"He did that?" I asked. She put the sunglasses back on and looked down and searched for another cigarette.

"What do you want me to say, Harry? That I fell? Hit my head on the sink?"

"That son-of-a-bitch!" I hissed. "Where's Liv?"

"She's with Roberto."

"For God's sake, you can't go back to him!" I cried. The telephone rang. I ignored it while I took a cigarette, but it kept going, and when it stopped it rang twice more.

"It must be urgent, Harry." It rang again. "Please go get it." I picked it up. It was Finn.

"Harry! Why don't you pick up?" he cried down the line.

"Calm down, I'm in the middle of something. Can't it wait?"

"No! I need you here with my passport. I left it in the car. The last train is in fifteen minutes."

"It's really not a good time, Finn," I said, unable to keep the exasperation from my voice. "Can't you catch a later train?"

"Are you joking? No, I can't. It will take you ten minutes here and back."

"Fine," I snapped. "I'm on my way." I hung up.

"Dammit!" I shouted and went back out to the terrace. Maria was looking at me through the window.

"Listen," I said quickly. "I have to go and give Finn his passport or he will miss his train. It's the worst timing, I know. I'll be back in ten minutes. Can you wait? Please wait. I have so many things that need to be said before you go."

"Whatever you have to say, Harry, please just say it now. Roberto is on his way to pick me up."

"Fine," I said. "Here goes." I took a deep breath. "I love you, Maria."

"Oh, Harry," she said. "Now is not the time for all that."

"Please, Maria, we could have had such a damned good time together."

She looked down. I went closer and put my arms around her, then she kissed me and I kissed her. She was trembling in my arms. She felt small. In that moment she felt like a child to me.

"Please stay with me," I whispered and leaned back and looked at her once more. Her eyes were so big and so beautiful. I kissed her again.

"You make me so happy. Please stay with me. The both of you."

"Harry." A tear rolled down her cheek. "You should go."

"Listen, I'll give you some time to think," I said, holding her hand for a moment. "I'll come back in an hour. I hope you're still here."

And with that I got into the car and started to cry. I rode down to the station and dropped off the passport, then walked into one of the cafés and sank down into a high stool. I asked the barman for a whiskey straight. I downed the whiskey and then asked for another.

IN ANOTHER COUNTRY, AND BESIDES

BOOK III

CHAPTER XVII

WATCHING FROM THE third-floor window, the street looked empty and dark. The building across had no lights on and gave the impression of emptiness. Its white wooden shutters were closed and it had a big water stain on its white facade. I could see rain falling underneath the orange colored street lamp that moved with the wind. I switched on the light and looked down so he could see me.

His black car was at the end of the street. He'd been there for two hours now and from a distance it looked like any other parked car. No lights on and no movements. But I knew he was there, just like I knew he was there the other nights.

When she first told me about it six months ago it seemed like a silly crush that any man in his early fifties gets himself into when a younger, fresher, and prettier woman comes along. But this was different. Over the course of the last weeks the dynamics had changed into something else. She had also changed, but I wasn't sure why.

A car drove by and its headlights lit up the inside of the car, and there he was. He hunched forward, looking up toward me with both hands on the steering wheel. I could see his bony face and his cold blue eyes. It wasn't a pleasant face. It was gaunt with deep wrinkles and tired puffy black circles under the eyes. His baldness had made him look older than he was, and he carried a nose that had a broad hump at the tip and the tip bent over. A scar on the top part of his forehead traveled five inches from his right temple. The scar was slightly darker than the rest of his head and looked like a bad stitching job of some sort, or perhaps it had never been stitched.

I stood there by the bedroom window thinking about him and took a sip of whiskey. I wished he would just disappear. It had been weeks now of this incessant stalking and obsessive behavior. She should have never taken the damn job in the first place. He really knew what he was doing when he asked her. I imagined he loved having power over her. I looked down at my hands and wondered at their strength. They say to be strangled is a very painful way to die.

Maria came into the bedroom. "There you are." She saw me at the window and sat down on the bed. "Is he still there?" she asked.

"He's there alright." I looked down at my watch. "It's going on two hours and fifteen minutes. I think it's a new record."

"Have you been standing there all that time?" she asked. I turned to look at her and shrugged, and then looked back outside.

"He's crazy for being there and you're just as crazy for letting it bother you that much," she said and came close and kissed me before taking a sip of my drink.

"It doesn't bother you that he does this?" I asked.

"Yes, it bothers me, but what can I do? I like my job and I need the money."

"Well, it's starting to annoy the hell out of me. I should really go out there and confront him."

"You know if you do that it will just complicate things."

"What I don't get is why all of a sudden he's doing this. Did something happen between the two of you?"

"No, nothing happened. How can you ask that?"

"It just seems strange to me, that's all. Are you flirting with him?"

"I don't think so. I'm just being me."

"You are a little flirty with people."

"No, I'm not."

"Well, whatever you are doing, this is the result."

"I'm not doing anything, Harry. It's not my fault that he has a crush on me."

"Please," I said. "This is way beyond a crush. This is obsessive. Actually it's gone past that and he's turned into a full-on stalker. How do you go to that in the space of six months?"

"I don't know. Ask him."

"You must be leading him on."

"I'm not, Harry. I just don't think he's happy in his own relationship, and perhaps he's looking at me for a way out."

"I'm not sure, Maria."

"Please stop."

"Stop what?"

"Your jealousy."

"I'm not jealous. I'm just sick of it.'

"Well, I'm sick of the constant conversations about it. If you're not pissed about Roberto then it's David." Her voice was raised.

"Okay. Calm down," I said, more to myself than to her.

"No, I won't calm down. I've had months of this from you and I can't take it anymore. I have so much going on, with work, Roberto, and Liv. I can't take it from you as well. You're supposed to be my support, not add to my stress."

"Okay. Relax." I went out of the room and made her a martini.

"Can't you just quit?" I asked as I walked back into the bedroom. She was now lying on the bed.

"No, I can't just quit. How can you ask me that?"

"If money is the problem you can always move in with me."

"Harry, things are complicated enough. Please don't complicate them more," she said. "I need the job and I want to be financially independent. Please just support me. That's all I ask."

"I do support you; I just don't want you working for David."

"Just ignore him. I want to relax tonight and not get into a heavy discussion." She switched on the side gas lamp next to the bed, took her clothes off, and wriggled her way under the covers.

"I'm so tired, Harry. Can we not just go to bed?"

"Fine."

I turned and looked out of the window. It was a black April night, hung as in a basket from a single dull star. The horn of the car came up through the window and was muffled by the cold air. There were street noises in the air, and she changed position. I got in bed and tried to rest, and when I couldn't I raised myself up, walked over to the window, took a breath, and felt drunk on the air. I looked out to the street again. My mind returned to the hope that he would simply vanish.

"Is he still there?" she asked in a muffled voice.

"I think he's gone."

"Good."

"Go back to sleep."

I put my hands out to close the wooden shutters and looked at the moon. It was high and the stars were out. I looked blankly back at Maria in the dark. Everything about killing David started to grip my imagination, and when I looked down to the street, he was indeed gone.

CHAPTER XVIII

THE FOLLOWING EVENING, in the car park of her office, she came around the corner. David was walking with her and they were talking. They both saw me from a distance, and he turned and got into his car and she came toward me, but I kept my stare firmly on him.

The nearness of him almost paralyzed my senses. Maybe it was just the shock of seeing him with Maria, so casual, like he didn't know we knew his obsession. Or maybe it was my own misery that she loved me but still felt compelled to put herself in that type of situation.

Maria got in the car and I had to steady myself. The feeling only lasted for a moment, and then it was gone.

"Hey," she said.

"I'm sorry," I said, shaking my head. "But how can you work with him when you know he's in love with you?"

"Oh, Harry, let's not talk about it."

"Fine."

"Do give me a cigarette."

I lit the cigarette.

We drove out along the long line of trees, which were dark now in the moonlight. Lights of the cars lit up the trees and the road, and to the left was Lake Zurich. The water seemed high from the day's rain. It looked black and still and smooth. I turned to Maria and she was just staring straight ahead, blowing the smoke out the open window. I could tell something was playing on her mind, and I was sure it had something to do with David.

We climbed up the hill toward her apartment.

"Let's drive to the cemetery and go for a walk," she said, breaking the silence.

"Don't we need to pick up Liv from the kindergarten?"

"No, she's with Roberto tonight."

We parked and walked down the side streets, away from the light. The street was dark and wet. We passed the wine shops and bars with light and sound spilling out through their doors onto the street.

"Want to go for a drink?" I asked.

She shook her head.

We walked into the cemetery and from the light of the moon we could see the outline of the mountains in the distance. It was deadly silent and the church in the center was silhouetted against the backdrop of the Uetliberg Mountain.

"Is everything okay?" I asked. I could feel her shivering against me.

"It's starting to get cold," she said.

"Want to go back?"

"No. It's fine."

We walked up the tree line, and it felt strange to be in the center of the city yet still feel the isolation and stillness of the open cemetery. The clouds broke and I could see a few stars coming out.

"Do you love me, Harry?" she asked.

"That's a strange thing to ask," I said. "Of course I love you."

"I love you too, whatever that means in English. I also love you in Italian, against all my judgment and all my wishes."

"What's wrong?" I asked.

"And do you believe in us?"

"Yes, I do."

"And don't you think these last six months together have been amazing?"

"I think they have been the most precious months of my life."

"Me too, I will always carry them with me." She put her head down and we continued walking.

"See that?" she said, putting her hand out so I could see it shivering in the darkness. "I'm like that all the way through these days."

I could tell she had something important to say but was waiting for the right words to come. I stopped and turned to look at her.

"Whatever you have to say, Maria, please say it," I said clearly. "Remember, it's me, it's us. You can tell me anything."

"Oh darling." She put her arms around me and cried.

"What is it?"

"I don't know. I just feel overwhelmed at the moment."

"I know there's a lot going on," I said gently. "You're doing great. I really think you're doing great, and you try so hard to make it right for everyone."

"I know," she said, shaking her head. "But it's all starting to stress me."

"How so?" I asked.

"Something happened today."

"What happened, Maria?"

"David cornered me in the office and tried to kiss me."

"He did what?"

"He tried to kiss me," she said. "He pushed me into a corner and tried to kiss me. I pushed him back of course, but he was very forceful and it scared me."

"I'm going to kill this guy."

"Harry, please!" she cried, clearly in distress. "I don't need that from you right now."

"He knows we are together," I spat out. "I can't believe he did that. I will talk to him tomorrow."

"No, Harry," she begged. "I can handle it. I don't need you getting involved."

I could feel the anger writhing inside me. I waited for it to happen, almost expecting it to come any second. I started to get scared. But it didn't come and we just kept walking in silence. We walked across the gravel and then sat on a bench under the trees.

The trees were black and moved with the wind, and there were no leaves on them. The leaves had fallen early that year and had been swept up long ago.

I turned to look at her but it was almost too dark to really see her face.

"Harry, do you think we rushed into this?" she asked.

"This being what exactly?"

"You and me," she said. "Our relationship."

"You never really choose the moments when you fall in love," I said. "It just kind of happens, and when it does you either embrace it or you don't."

"You didn't answer the question," she said.

"What do you want me to say? I love you, Maria, and I want to be with you." I paused for a moment before going on. "I guess what's more important is how you feel."

"That's what I ask myself." She took a long breath. "I think I need some space, Harry."

"What do you mean you need some space?" I asked. "From what? From us?"

"Yes."

"But, why?"

"Because I'm not within myself anymore," she said. "I came here to find peace, and now I find myself with very little, between you, Roberto, Liv, and David."

She put out her cigarette and looked away. I thought she was looking for another cigarette. Then I saw she was crying. She wouldn't look up.

"I haven't even digested what I went through with Roberto, because I'm so in love with you."

"And what happened today with David has nothing to do with it?"

"No. But, yes," she said. "I don't know. Perhaps it is also that. Being so unclear within myself makes me unclear with other people, and they can perhaps take advantage of that. They read more into things because I'm so unbalanced. I don't know, I feel like there's so much going on that soon my head will explode."

I listened and said nothing.

"And then there's you, Harry," she began in a smaller voice. "I've never had such a love connection with anyone in my entire life. I love you so much, but I just don't feel that I can be with you right now."

"I don't know what to say, Maria." I swallowed hard.

"Well, say something," she said, looking up at me. "Please, say something."

"Fine," I said. "Let's give each other some space so you can digest everything. It just feels like all this is coming out of the blue, and the only trigger point I can see is what happened today with David."

She shook her head. "It's not like that."

"Are you feeling something for him?"

"Who, David?" she asked, her face incredulous. "Of course not. But even this, Harry, this jealousy, it's too much. I can't handle your stress over him."

"I just wish you had never taken that damn job."

"I understand your feelings, but despite what you think I like my job and I know I can handle him."

I could feel her energy level dropping. She looked at me with tired eyes. The moon affects her as it does any woman, I thought.

"So let me get this clear. You want to take a break or break up?"

"What's the difference?"

"My God, Maria." I shook my head.

"What?"

"You're being so cold now."

"I'm sorry, but this conversation is starting to give me headache."

"So that's it then. Just like that, it's over between us? I love you and you love me, but still it's not enough and it's over."

"I'm sorry, Harry."

"Maria, you just can't do this," I pleaded with her. "Especially after everything we have been through. Hell, my life only started to make sense again once you and Liv came into it. Please, don't take that away from me. I don't know what I'd do without the two of you."

"I'm sorry, but I really should go now," she said, the coldness returning to her voice.

I grabbed her hand.

"Please, not like this," I said. I was trying not to let the tears come. "And what about Liv?" I asked, my voice now struggling.

"Well, you can be friends of course." I read her face for any sign of emotion but saw none.

"Friends? I don't want to be friends."

"Look, you can see her again but not right now." Irritation edged into her voice. "I think we all need to have some space, Harry. Even you."

"Please, darling. Don't do this."

She would not look up. I came close and tried to stroke her hair, but she backed away.

"Before you leave, can I ask you something?" Thinking quickly, I searched my mind for anything that would make sense of all this.

"Of course you can."

"Would things be different between us if Roberto wasn't around?"

"How do you mean? I don't know, Harry. You can't say that. He is around, and that's a fact."

"And David?" I asked.

"Harry, please," she sighed. "Please stop these questions. I need to go!"

"At least let me walk you back. It's late."

"It's fine. Let's talk soon, okay?" She kissed me on the cheek and looked at me, then just like that she was gone.

CHAPTER XIX

I TURNED OFF THE LIGHT, got undressed, and sat on the bed. I ran my hands through my hair and looked around the lifeless room. I used to love to take her hair down when she got to bed. She always wore it up, and at night I would take it down. When it was down, I would run my fingers up to the back of her neck and slowly massage her hair. She loved that, and she would keep very still until she dipped down to kiss me. She had beautiful, thick, dark hair and I would watch her play with it and twist it up.

There were parts of her everywhere. From her clothes on the floor to the pictures on the walls, she was still there. How had we come to this point? Everything was going so well. Sure, it was a complicated situation, but we were happy and in love.

My mind was racing and jumping. I tried to fix my thoughts on just one thing. She had such a lovely face and healthy body, and such smooth skin. My legs became jumpy so I lifted them in the air and moved them up and down with my eyes shut. I could picture her next to me now, me on my side, watching while she slept, breathing slowly and deeply, admiring the contours of her face, her cheeks, her eyes, her chin and throat. Some nights I would stroke her forehead with the tips of my fingers while she was still and silent. We used to love touching each other because we were happy. Along with all the big times, we had so many small ways of making love, and we would do it whenever the impulse came. I wanted us to be married and she had wanted it too, but only after she had divorced Roberto of course. We shared the same values and were connected, through and through. We felt each other completely because we were one and the same. What had I lost?

The night went that way. Remembering and feeling. I cannot remember much about the next few days. The apartment felt like a tormented prison of

153

memories. Everywhere I looked there were things we had once shared. I turned to the drink. I even tried to leave the apartment, but when I got to the door I simply could not face it. I could not even go out to buy cigarettes. Hours turned into days and days turned into weeks. In the evenings I would see things. Strange things. I saw my grandmother making tea one night. She didn't say anything, just looked at me the way she always did when she made tea.

Catherine, my daughter, would come on the other nights, but she wouldn't say anything either. She would just sit on the floor playing, sometimes digging for something, maybe a worm. But she was older now, perhaps ten. She was so beautiful. That night she spoke to me.

"It will all be fine," she said. "You mustn't worry, Daddy." Her voice sounded like Liv's voice, but soft and more childlike. "I can see that you worry. You mustn't worry, Daddy. You must stop it. Stop it, please. Wouldn't you like a drink, Daddy? I know drink makes you happy."

"You're right, my snowflake, it does," I said. She handed me a bottle of brandy and I drank it from the bottle and spilled it down my naked chest.

"Oh, it feels so cheerful," I said. "And you're so pretty and wonderful. Thank you for this brandy and for being here." She stood in front of me as I sat on the floor in the hallway in the dark.

I took a big gulp and wiped my face. "It will be morning soon, snowflake. Why don't we go to the park and you can play in the playground or on the swings? We'll have a lovely time. Maybe we will even see Liv. She likes the swings too. And then we could all come home together and maybe you could let me be your daddy again, and you can go to school, and I'll start writing again, and Maria and Liv would be here. You would like Maria, snowflake. She's wonderful. Oh, we would all be so happy, and you will grow up and be so pretty and wonderful."

She didn't answer.

Later I saw her sitting on my bed, and as I looked at her I wanted to touch her.

"Are you mad at me?" she asked.

"Why would I be mad at you, snowflake?"

"Because I left you and Mama."

"Sweetheart, you left because you were sick and it wasn't your fault." I wanted to reach out and take her hand. She looked down to the floor.

"What did you do to Mummy?" she asked.

"Look, it will be morning soon," I said, pointing at the light through the window. "Shall we go to the playground?"

"What did you do to Mummy, Daddy?" she asked again and then began to yell. "What did you do to Mummy? Tell me, what did you do to Mummy?" She kept saying it over and over. It got louder and louder and I shouted: "Stop it. Stop it!"

But she did not stop, and I screamed and ran into the bathroom, frantically searching for my pills. "Where are my pills?" I screamed, seeing my dark self in the mirror.

I found them and took two but could still hear her screaming from the bedroom, so I turned on the shower to block the noise. I got in and sat down, letting the water run over my ears so I couldn't hear the screams anymore. I prayed that calm would soon come and the screaming would stop.

The next thing I registered was the rain. It was raining hard against the window and I was lying naked on the wooden floor. The shower was still running. The rain was coming down heavily on the small balcony, and the wind was strong as it blew against the red shutters. I stood up, turned the shower off, and went into the kitchen and poured myself a glass of brandy. I drank it straight down.

"That was very big one," I heard her say. "I thought brandy was for heroes and brave people."

"It is," I said, turning to look at the small form of my daughter. "And it always makes me happy. It never makes me sad."

I reached down for the bottle and poured another, gulping it down again in one.

"What will you do?" she asked.

"What do you mean?"

"What will you do?" she asked again.

"Nothing, I can't do anything. She won't talk to me."

"She loves you," she said. I started to sob and poured out another glass.

"Go easy on the brandy, you're no hero."

I looked at her and it was not my daughter anymore. It was Viola. She looked just as I had left her; the whites of her eyes were yellow and her lips were black.

"Go away," I cried out, stumbling back and dropping the glass on the floor. I ran into the bathroom and jumped back in the shower until I began to shiver.

A knock at the door came, and I woke up freezing now as the water had turned cold. It was Frau Fischer, the concierge.

"Herr Hoffman! Herr Hoffman!" I heard her shout through the glass-paneled door. "Is everything okay?"

There was a silence. I stayed very still.

"We are getting complaints from the neighbors about your screaming," she called out. "Herr Harry, are you okay?"

I didn't make a sound. No matter how cold I felt I had to wait until she left. I could cut off my tongue, then there would be no sound and I could live in peace here with my daughter. But what if I couldn't cut off my tongue? Would she throw me out?

"We must fight," I said. My voice was trembling from the cold. I got out of the shower and the little girl was again on my bed.

"We won't fight!" she said.

"Why? If we don't fight they will make us leave," I said desperately. "There's two of us now and we must stay strong and not let anything come between us. Not Viola, not David, not Roberto. Nobody. Okay?"

"We won't fight!" she said again.

"No, you're right, they won't get us," I said. "Because we are too brave and nothing bad happens to the brave. Yes, I should drink more brandy and become even more brave."

She disappeared and I held my head in my hands.

"Okay," I said, muttering wildly, shaking with every word. "Yes, well, I know where I stand. I've been brave long enough to know."

"You're a coward," a voice said from the kitchen.

"Who said that?" I cried, not daring to look. When no answer came, I asked again. "Who said that?"

"You're a coward," came the voice once more.

"I'm no coward," I said, shaking my head.

"You're a coward who lets other people take what's yours," said the voice.

I walked into the kitchen.

"No, you are wrong! I'm brave and nothing bad ever happens to the brave. I drink brandy and it makes me brave."

"Brave? You're not brave!" laughed the voice. "You're nothing. Nothing but a coward."

"Who said that?" I shouted. I could hear someone at the door again. I rushed out into the hallway and saw a silhouette behind the glass panel. I slammed my fist against it and shouted: "Nobody's home! Go away." I rushed back into the kitchen and found no one there.

"Who are you?" I demanded. "Where are you?"

"You let people walk all over you."

I whirled around, searching for the source, but found nothing.

"No, I don't," I protested. "I don't make trouble for anyone anymore. I know I made trouble in the past but I'm good now. I've been good, haven't I? Haven't I been good?"

"Yes, and look where it has got you," snarled the voice.

"I made no trouble and I was happy," I said. "I was so happy. And he took it away from me."

"And now you're miserable because you became a coward."

"I'm no coward," I cried. "Stop saying that!"

"Then prove it. Take back what is yours and take your revenge. Become brave again."

"Yes, yes," I said, nodding frantically. "You're absolutely right. I can fix everything and show everyone just how brave I am. But I cannot do it here. I can't think straight with all you people around. And Maria would never take me back in this state. Yes, to be brave again and win Maria back I must leave. I will return stronger and braver than ever before, and Maria will love me and I will get her and my family back and everything will be fine."

My daughter reappeared before me, her face full of fear. "If you leave I will worry about you."

"You mustn't worry, snowflake," I said. "I will go and plan my return and I will be brave once more. I will do it for you, just as much as me."

"Then drink this." She handed me the brandy. "I know drink always makes you feel better."

"Why don't you come with me?" I asked her. "We could have a lovely time. We could go to the south of France and you could play on the beach. You were always so very happy there."

"Where will you go?" she asked.

"I don't know, but somewhere splendid. I'll go now."

"You can't go now. You are too brave and had too many brandies."

"Yes, you are right, I feel too brave; I will leave in the morning at daybreak. But for now I drink."

I don't remember much after that, only registering the cold kitchen floor. I raised myself up and by four o'clock in the morning I packed a bag and headed out. My head was cloudy and I felt nauseous. I had to stop on occasions to get air. When I knew daylight was coming I opened the window and took in deep breaths of the cold mountain air.

The heavy wind had been blowing hard, and it took concentration to stay on the road until I reached the protection of the mountains and the wind calmed down.

When daylight arrived, I was already close to Geneva and I could see the curve of the lake in the distance. I knew that in some thirty minutes I would be close to the French border. I was famished and hadn't eaten anything substantial for weeks. As I looked at my face in the rearview mirror it looked gaunt and my skin almost white. The French do wonderful breakfasts, I thought, with wonderful croissants and delicious breads with jam and butter. My stomach ached.

It was clear daylight when I crossed the border and a fine rain started to fall. The wind had fallen and I could see the tops of the white-capped mountains spreading out into the distance. I checked the map and thought that Annecy would be a good place to stop, but that was another forty-five minutes. I thought about bread rolls and strawberry jam and rich black coffee.

As soon as I entered France I could feel the fog in my head starting to clear. It had been a hell of a few weeks. Yet despite the drunkenness and sadness, one thing had remained. I was going to kill Roberto and David. I just had to figure out how to do it and not lose Maria and Liv in the process.

CHAPTER XX

THE SUMMER OF CAME very late that year, and by early June I was living in a small white-stoned house close to the port of Camargue, a small fishing village north of Montpellier. The summer passed under blue skies, with only the occasional storm as a temporary relief from the heat.

The house was solid and built on a narrow piece of land between a harbor and the open sea. When the wind was low and the air was light, I would walk out to a stoned jetty close to the house and fish for loupé. When the sun was bright I would eat lunch on the terrace, and some nights, if the mosquitoes weren't too persistent, I would also have dinner there. It was a small but comfortable house and I rented it from a retired couple who lived in the house next door.

Even in early June this part of France didn't attract the masses of holiday seekers. The beaches were mostly empty and the sea was full of fishing boats. It was quiet and peaceful.

That morning the sun was high on the window of the bedroom, and the room grew warm. The warmth made me uncomfortable and I slowly woke. I washed and went down to walk on the beach. I saw that Madame Duflow had left fresh croissants and coffee on the patio table along with a note inviting me for an aperitif that evening. I poured the coffee into a plastic cup and took the croissant with me along the path through salt grass that lead to the ocean.

I walked past the jetty and into a small fishing village four kilometers away. There was a pleasant café that served strong espressos and sold the international papers. I sat there trying to read but my mind kept wandering. I felt I had weighed up all the options now and the only concrete solution was poison. It was the only practical way to do it and not get caught.

That afternoon, I started again on my research in the local library. I was always careful not to leave any trace of my readings, but read everything I could get my hands on. Over the weeks I had become an expert on different types of poison, which would be the means by which I would eliminate.

There are many different types of poison, and cyanide was a popular weapon of choice for novelists and spies over the years. But getting hold of the stuff would be practically impossible and would raise too many questions. It was really just a question of which type of poison. But it must be poison. It was only by poisoning that it could look like a heart attack or something and nobody would ask too many questions.

I closed my book and embraced the idea of poison once again. My mind started racing with ideas. Perhaps the trick here was not to examine every little thing too closely, nor debate every option too much, but to go with a gut feeling when choosing action.

Afterward the library, I walked down to one of the cafés that lined the canal close to the lighthouse of the town and sat in the corner with a heavy mug of beer and a packet of pretzels. There salty flavor and the way they made the beer taste were delectable. I watched the afternoon fishing boats return one by one with their sails down and motors chugging slowly by. They headed up the canal, which bordered a small road lined with cafés, and shops and one hotel. It was a quiet and friendly town. Tomorrow I would come here again and fish off one of the main jetties that ran out from the canal through the center of town and out into the sea.

The pretzels were making me thirsty so I decided to stay for another, and ordered a dark beer this time. I was now in the mood for fishing and wished I had brought my casting rod and tackle. The brightness of the road from the café and the glare of the jetty was too inviting. The sun was still high and it felt warm, despite the cool, fresh breeze. A young boy came in front of the café and cast out across the flow of the water from the side of the canal and over the rocks. His bright orange quill float and sand worm flew gently in the air from his long pole into the depths of where he guessed the fish might be feeding. I sat there watching the float.

So there you are. I was sorry for him in a way, but it was not a thing you could do anything about, because right away you ran to David's failings. I could picture it now. Death by poisoning. I really have a rotten habit of picturing death in all its forms.

Madame Duflow had taken away the breakfast tray by the time I arrived back at the house, and had left another note reminding me of tonight's apéritif. I really didn't feel like socializing, but I imagined for her it would be nice, and if I wanted to stay some weeks longer—which I did—I had better try and make the effort.

The mosquitoes were out and I brushed a few off my face as I walked up the dry and dusty white path toward Madame Duflow's house. Madame Duflow was a retired guide for one of the big French tour operators and had spent thirty years of her life traveling the world. She spoke a number of languages and was always polite and hospitable. She had short gray hair and spoke with a slight Irish accent when she spoke English. Her husband had been a professional musician and played the cello. They were both retired and six years ago purchased the two neighboring houses with the intent of fixing them up and renting them out during the summer season. It gave them a steady income and something to occupy their days. She would clean, organize and handle the guests and manage reservations, while Monsieur Duflow would do very little, spending his days fishing and playing bridge with the local fishing croonies.

"Bonsoir," I said as I arrived through the opening of the thick green hedges that separated their garden from the dusty white path.

"Ah, Monsieur Hoffman!" Mme Duflow said with an air of excitement.

"Henry! Henry!" she shouted for her husband. "Monsieur Hoffman est là!" She turned to me.

"Asseyez-vous, monsieur," she said with a smile and pulled out a seat. I sat down and she poured three large glasses of rosé wine. There was a green and black olive tapenade with pieces of torn off bread in the center of the table.

"Venez ici, Henry!" she shouted up to the window once more before turning back to me.

"Alors," she smiled. "How are you, Monsieur Harry? Are you enjoying your stay here?"

"Yes, merci," I said. "The house is wonderful and very comfortable. Thank you for the coffee and croissants in the mornings. It's really very nice of you."

"Oh, do not mention it," she said, waving her hand.

Monsieur Duflow came outside with an unlit thick cigar in his mouth. I stood up and shook his hand.

"Done much fishing, Harry?" he asked through his white beard.

"Yes, I try to fish every day," I said. "In the afternoons mostly."

"Any grande loupé come your way?" he asked. "Where do you fish?"

"Not really," I shook my head, "I only seem to be able to catch small ones, but they're still big enough for a good dinner. I fish out on the jetty close to here."

"Ah yes, that's a good spot," he said. "You can also try the canal. There is good fishing there too. I should take you out on the boat one morning and show you what size of fish our small town can really offer. I don't want you going away with the impression that we only have small fish in our waters!"

"Yes, I'd like that."

Mme Duflow picked up her wine and held it up. "Santé," she said, and we all touched glasses.

"It's the first time we have a writer stay with us here," she smiled and seemed proud. "Tell me, are you working on a roman nouvelle here at the house?"

"Not really," I said, "I'm down here more on a fact-finding trip."

She seemed disappointed.

"Would you like to set one of your stories down here in the south?" she asked.

"It's possible, yes. It's really inspiring country."

She seemed happier.

"What do you think of the wine here in France?"

"It's lovely," I said.

"You know, there wouldn't be any vines in France if it hadn't been for America."

"How so?"

"Back in the 1860s, a beetle killed almost every vine in France. Then they found out that some American vine was resistant to the bug, and they brought over millions of vinestocks and grafted the European vines onto them. There you go—the basic history of modern wine in thirty seconds."

"Very interesting."

Monsieur Duflow abruptly changed the subject. "Is there good money in writing these days?"

"There is if you can write well."

"And can you?" he asked.

"What?"

"Write well?"

"I try my best."

"So have you published anything?"

"Henry, I told you this already," his wife scolded him. "You really never listen. Harry gave me a copy of his last book. I'm really enjoying it, Harry."

"Thank you," I said, and quickly tried to change the subject. "This is good wine Madame Duflow. Is it from the region?"

"Mais oui!" she smiled. "It's actually from my cousin's vineyard. It's close to Nîmes. About an hour's drive from here."

"It's okay," said Monsieur Duflow with disinterest. "I'm more of a cognac drinker." He leaned in. "When I want to get drunk, I don't want to spend all night trying."

"Oh, shut up, Henry," Mme Duflow scolded him before turning back to me. "Excuse my husband."

"I would really like to visit a vineyard while I'm here," I said. "Does your cousin give tours?"

"Normalement, non," she said. "Mais, I could call her and ask."

"That would really be something. I've always wanted to see the wine making process."

"It's no problem. She used to run tours but stopped a few years back after a man collapsed and died in the middle of her tour."

"Heart attack?" monsieur asked.

"I told you about this," she snapped at him once more.

"How did he die?" I asked. She leaned forward and took a piece of bread and topped it with the green tapenade, ate it and sat back.

"He died from carbon dioxide poisoning, CO_2," she said, shaking her head. "You see, my cousin makes mainly rosé wines and the methods used are different from red wines."

"So how did he die, exactly?" I asked.

"From visiting the tanks when there was too much CO2 in the air from the fermentation."

"I understand very little about fermentation or the winemaking process."

"Let me explain. So we cut the grapes, yes?" she began. "We cut them from the vines and bring them back to the château and press the grapes for their juice."

"That I understand," I said. "And when you press them is it still done with your feet?"

"Non, monsieur," she tutted, shaking her head. "Most vineyards these days have modern presses, except maybe those in Champagne. So then, once pressed, the juice from the grapes gets decanted for one night and then put in big tanks with yeast inside. That's when the fermentation process happens."

"And that's how it becomes alcohol?" I asked.

"Exactement," she nodded. "The sugar from the juice with the help of the yeast turns it to alcohol, and when it's turning there is a lot of CO2. Let's say you have breathing problems, it's not advised to go and visit these tanks when the wine is in the fermentation process."

"And that's how this tourist died at your cousin's vineyard?" I asked.

"Oui," she sighed. "My cousin has a fermentation room with about twelve large tanks. It's damp and has very little air inside. He was asthmatic, and during the days when they were changing one or two of the tanks, by taking the new wine out and removing the yeast which had fallen to the bottom, the CO2 was at its most deadly."

"But isn't CO2 impossible to smell?" I asked. "How could you know it's at a high and dangerous level?"

"Some of the more modern vineyards have fans inside the tanks," she said. "But what's dangerous for one person is quite different for someone else." David was asthmatic, I quickly thought to myself.

"So when is the CO2 at its most deadliest?" I wondered and sat up straight.

"As I said," said Mme Duflow. "When they start emptying the first few tanks and remove the yeast. The air is heavy and it smells very strange, almost like a mixture of sweet grape fruit and alcohol. It's really a very strange and unique smell."

"But I guess more and more vineyards these days are modernizing so the risk is less and less?" I asked.

"Not really," she shrugged. "Vineyards tend to stick to the old fashioned ways of winemaking and they reject much of this so called technology."

"Could you please call your cousin and arrange a tour for me tomorrow?" I asked.

"It's a bit late to call now," she said. "But I will call in the morning. What time would you wish to visit?"

"Anytime," I said.

CHAPTER XXI

IT WAS STRANGELY EASY to forget any morals when plotting a murder. I imagined David in the tank room; the sound of his voice in my ears was exactly the same as I had remembered it. I could even smell his overpowering cheap cologne. I could picture him taking an interest in the tanks and listening attentively, but finding it strangely difficult to breathe and then a sudden drop to the floor. There would be some coughing, crouching, suffocating and then a half-baked attempt at resuscitation by me; Then gone, dead and silent.

I was still pondering all this as I drove closer to a village close to the vineyard. There was a long avenue of plane trees formed a graceful natural entrance to the village. They had been planted, like every other plane tree in Provence—if one believed the stories—by Napoleon, to provide shade for his marching armies.

I parked in the shade and strolled into the main square. It was like every other Provencal village in the area. A café, a tabac, the Mairie, and a fountain. The only obvious addition was a small restaurant, the tables under their umbrellas still filled with people lingering over a shady lunch.

Leading off the square were narrow, shadowy streets, little wider than passageways. I could see signs hanging over the doors of the bakery and the butcher's shop and, on one corner, another sign with peeling, sun-bleached paint and an arrow marked Notaire pointing up the street. I looked at my watch, and saw that I had half an hour to kill before the appointment at the vineyard.

The sun beat down, so I took my thirst into the café, nodding at the group of old men who had paused in their card game to inspect this new stranger in their town, and ordered a pastis. The woman behind the bar waved an arm at the shelf behind her. "Ricard? Casanis? Bardouin? Pernod?" I shrugged, and she smiled at my confusion. "Alors, un Ricard." She poured a generous shot into a glass and placed it on the pockmarked zinc bar next to a jug beaded with moisture. I added water and went to sit at a table on the terrace, where I was joined by the café dog, who put his head on my knee and stared with large, soulful brown eyes.

I took a first sip of the cloudy liquid, sharp and refreshing with the bite of aniseed, and wondered why it tasted so much better here than the few times I'd had it at home. The heat, of course; it was a warm-weather drink. But it was also the surroundings. Pastis was at its best when you could hear the click of boules and the sound of French voices.

Looking across the square, along the walls on the village side all was dusty, the wriggling vines, the lemon and eucalyptus trees, the casual wheelbarrow, left only a moment since, but already grown into the path.

I watched the last customers leaving the restaurant, flinching at the heat and adjusting their sunglasses before ambling off in a slow, post-lunch waddle to deal with the business of the afternoon. I finished the drink and stood up. It was time to go.

It was ten minutes to eleven now and the sun was at its hottest. I came down a white road across a hill and ahead I could see a large stoned building with a tiled roof. It looked like any typical farmhouse of the region. It was whitewashed with variant colors that had faded over the years and gave it a very rustic feel. It had old, light blue wooden shutters on each side of the windows and there were newly planted trees on each side of the road that led to the house.

The road was bumpy and uneven and I had to slow down to stop rocking around. I could see in the distance two men in the front courtyard fixing up a tractor and black smoke was rising from the engine. There were vine trees all along the side of the driveway that lead up to the house and went off in the distance. I rolled down the window and slowed down to take a better look, the warm, heavy air hit me instantly.

The vine trees were small and stumpy with black roots and green leaves. They seemed to have already been harvested as I saw no grapes hanging. They were all set apart in straight lines and separated wide enough so a small tractor could drive up. The ground around the vines was covered in what appeared to be loose white limestones.

I continued up in front of stone pillars, crumbling and stained almost black by two centuries of weather, that marked the entrance to the dirt road leading down to the house. The name of the property could just be made out etched into the stone, the letters soft and fuzzy with lichen after their prolonged battle against the elements. I drove on, through rows of well-kept vines, and parked under the plane tree—a huge tree, pre-Napoleonic—that shaded the long south wall of the bastide. In contrast to the clipped and orderly vines, the garden was in a state of some neglect, as indeed was the outside of the house.

I entered the courtyard and pulled up next to the tractor and killed the ignition. I took out a pencil and a cheap lined notebook and put them into my pocket. The notebook was full of notes on poison and a half-written letter to Maria. I made a note in my head to burn the damn thing before returning to Switzerland.

A lady came out of the house and walked over to the car as I was getting out. She wore a big smile and had a tanned face, which was burnt dark from the sun, and long gray hair that was tied up in a bob.

"Bonjour," she said brightly.

"Bonjour! Je m'appelle, Harry."

"Yes, I know," she replied in English. "My cousin called this morning and told me all about you."

"Ah, okay. Great," I said. "Yes, Madame Duflow is very nice. Thank you so much for taking the time to see me, Madame?"

"Annette, Madame Annette," she said with a nod of her head. "It's no problem. So, welcome to Château La Canorgue."

"Thank you."

"I hear you are interested in the vines and the wine making process."

"Yes," I said. "Very much so. But I know nothing, and this will be my first time."

She smiled. "Okay, then let's get started. Follow me, please."

Her eyes gleamed restlessly in the sun, as she wiped her palm on the seam of her trousers.

We walked behind the main house to another even older building of about the same size. The building had thick stone walls, and as we entered it was very cool and cold and there were crates of bottled wine everywhere.

"These will be shipped to Paris this evening," she pointed.

There were tables around where wine tasting took place and thick chairs that were worn out. We walked into another room where wine casks were piled high. The light came in from the door and Mme Annette brought out two bottles of wine and two glasses. She uncorked the bottles and poured wine into each glass slowly, explaining the flavors and differences between each vintage.

I held the glass up to the light, allowing myself to have an optimistic moment to contemplate. I sniffed, gargled and shuddered, and immediately spat before rubbing my teeth with a finger to remove what felt like a thick coating of tannin. The wine was one step up from vinegar, enough to kill the liver. Awful.

"No good?"

"Not to my taste no."

"Perhaps it was a bad bottle. Try this," she handed me another glass, which tasted much better.

It was still a very hot day outside but the coolness of the building made me shiver.

"What do you think?" she asked.

"Yes, I like it very much," this seemed to please her greatly.

The proprietor came in and Mme Annette introduced him as her husband. He was a short, middle aged man, heavily built and square in the face. We shook hands and his hands were thick and looked tight and bloated.

"Would you like to see the fermentation room?" he asked.

"Yes please," I answered with enthusiasm.

"Okay. Follow me," he said in a very thick French accent. I started to walk, but he pointed at the wine.

"First finish your wine, monsieur," he insisted. "But please, do not rush it. I will go for a cigarette."

I took the glass and raised it to my lips. Mme Annette smiled and left the room. I walked around the big, cold cellar, holding my glass from the stem.

There were a few posters on the wall explaining the region's different type of wine production and the difference in grape types. Around the tables there were a couple of glass display boxes filled with old corks and plastic grapes.

I walked over to the wine rack and examined the bottles. There was a scattering of regional reds and whites—some Châteauneuf-du-Pape, a few cases of Rasteau and Cassis, but the great majority was the wine of the property, decorated with a florid blue and gold label. I picked up a bottle, and took it over to the upended barrel that served as a cellar table, where there was a corkscrew and a none-too-clean glass.

I heard the door open and a gust of light and wind lit up the room before disappearing again as the door closed shut. My eyes took a moment to readjust. The owner came in.

"Monsieur?" he called. I came out from the shadows.

"I was just admiring your wine collection," I said.

"Ah oui," he muttered, seeming not so interested. "So allons-y. We go to the fermentation room. Have you finished your wine?"

"Yes, I have."

"D'accord, follow me then."

We walked to the dark side of the room and he pulled on a large, red wooden door that slid off to the left, making a loud screeching sound. He then walked into the darkness. The lights came on with a large hissing sound, one after the other, and finished at the end of the long hall. To each side of the walkway there were large wooden barrels placed one on top of the other, stacked three barrels high. I counted at least fifty. In the center of the walkway between the barrels, stood a thin light wooden table.

"This room we use for maturing le vin," he said. "And we must turn the barrels from time to time."

"It's a wonderful room for wine tasting," I said brightly.

"Oui, mais, not these days," he sighed. "Madame Annette does not have the patience any more for that, and I certainly don't want to be entertaining the foreigners."

"Please through here," he grumbled.

We walked toward another sliding door in the center and to the end of the great room and it again opened to the left. As we walked in the smell hit me and almost took my breath away. He switched the lights on and turned to me, grinning like a little fat pumpkin. I noticed one of his front teeth was missing and the rest were brown and decaying.

"Something wrong?" he asked, still grinning.

"No. I'm quite fine," I said, screwing up my face. "It's just the smell is quite overpowering."

"Mais oui."

Around the room stood six large steel tanks with small wooden ladders propped up next to each one. The tanks were painted red and stood on four small steel legs that were painted white. The tops of the tanks seemed to be open from what I could see, and at the bottom of the tanks there was a small dial and faucet. The legs were rusting around the bottom and in the corners. My breathing eased up now and the smell was becoming less intense.

Monsieur Annette explained the process as Mme Duflow had done the previous night. I asked to climb up the ladder and take a look inside.

"Of course," he said. "Be my guest. But please only for a moment. We've had too many people fall off those ladders over the years and some never got up again."

"Why is that?" I asked.

"The CO2, monsieur," he said. "It's very heavy up there."

"I see," trying to sound only mildly curious. "Would you say here at the top is where it's the most deadliest?"

"Mais oui," he said. "So come now. Have a quick look and get down."

He was right. When I arrived at the top I felt dizzy almost instantly. There was not much to see either, only a thick layer of white foam. I quickly came down and could feel my legs shake as I descended the ladder. I asked him about the cleaning process of the tanks and how all that worked, but as I heard his response, I started to lose focus. I sat down for a moment on the floor.

"Ca va?" he said brusquely. "Let's leave now as you're starting to lose your color."

We walked out and I felt I had seen enough, if only for the sake of my health. I was back in my car after saying goodbye to Mme Annette and then out onto the dusty road in less than ten minutes. I felt nauseous and tense. Despite the overwhelming evidence that my plan had taken a big step forward; I still couldn't shake my own lousy feeling. The nausea stayed with me.

I drove back through Uzès and across a square with a great cathedral and stopped the car to stare. It was magnificent to look at the great dusty walls and to think of going inside, to imagine its smell.

I stepped out of the car and spent the remaining of the morning calmly, lonely but very pleasantly in which I wandered around the small Provencal town, stopping here and there for an hour or two in a café or a restaurant and read the newspaper.

In one of the shop windows stood a tall picture of a sailboat and one of a beach. It made me think of the ocean. I stood back and felt the humidity along with a sickening feeling of returning home.

CHAPTER XXII

THAT AFTERNOON I CHECKED to the Hotel Cézar near the Théâtre Antique d'Arles. It was a moderately priced hotel in the center of Arles.

Sundown was the hour when the French and everybody else in the town gathered at the sidewalk tables of the cafés. They were freshly showered and dressed, staring at everybody and everything that passed by and eager for whatever entertainment the town could offer. I walked around the center wearing only shorts, sandals and a light linen shirt. I had spent the afternoon wondering the city streets and writing in one of the cafés by the colosseum. It was the first time on this trip that I had really put pencil to paper and it made me feel exhausted. Writing always made me feel exhausted.

Still, I walked along with certain casualness and kept my head up for the benefit of the people who stared at me from the cafés. I had fortified myself with two espressos and one brandy. Now I was playing the role of an athletic young writer, who had spent the day honing his craft.

I made it back to the hotel, collected the key and went up to the room to collapse on the bed. I put my head down, happy and utterly satisfied with the city and the afternoons writing. When I felt myself falling to sleep, I jolted myself awake, got up and went to the basin and splashed my face.

I could start to feel the magic returning within me, and it remained throughout. I had a drink from the mini bar and smoked on the terrace, then showered and changed. I felt in good humor that night. I had felt in good humor since I arrived. It was Arles.

The next morning, I went out for a stroll. I walked with my head up and a smile on my face. I had slept well, and figured it was the atmosphere of the town. It reminded me of Paris, but there was something else, a mixture of things. Perhaps it was the Italian, Roman influence in the architecture or the Spanish influence on the food. I wanted to let the atmosphere seep in slowly, so I bought a local paper and sat down in one of the cafés at the Place du Forum. Feeling relaxed, I ordered a café au lait.

I could see myself here, I thought. I just needed to find an apartment in the center, near the Arles Amphitheatre would be great. I could stay for a while, though I didn't plan to stay for months on end, especially in the winter. But Arles seemed exciting. I felt excited.

"Yes, I live in Arles now, and keep an apartment," I said to myself.

By late afternoon, I left Arles and made my way back to the small house by the sea. I had just stepped out of the car when I almost squarely bumped into Madame Duflow, who seemed to be hovering around the house for some reason.

"Ah, Monsieur Hoffman! There you are!" she said awkwardly.

"Bonjour, Madame Duflow," I smiled easily.

"American Express came with some mail for you this morning," she said.

I opened the door and put the letter on the table and noticed that Mme Duflow had followed me in.

"Madame Duflow, I have decided to move on tomorrow," I told her.

"Oh dear, so soon?" she said with an air of friendliness. "Where will you go?"

"Arles," I said.

"Are you staying with someone?" she asked.

"No, just in a hotel," I took a glass of wine and walked outside. A moment later I heard her cork-soled sandals trotting after me.

"Why the rush?" she asked. "You should stay till at least to the end of the week, no?"

"No. I'm sorry," I said. "I really need a change of scene."

"So how long are you staying?" she asked, her expression downcast.

"Where?"

"Here."

"Ah. Just overnight. I'll be going to Arles tomorrow. Probably in the afternoon."

"Oh, I won't be around," she said.

"Well, I hope it's okay that I leave like this," I said, clearing my throat. "We didn't agree on anything permanent, at least that was my understanding? I will of course pay you till the end of the week."

"It's fine. I just enjoyed having you around."

"Merci. I also enjoyed being here."

We said our goodbyes and I told her I would come visit again and we arranged that I would drop off the key in her mailbox before I left in the morning and went upstairs and laid down on the bed. I awoke suddenly and remembered dreaming that I was in another village and on another bed and it was very cold. I rubbed my eyes and raised myself up and realized my right arm was asleep because I had rested on it and used it for a pillow.

By eight o'clock that evening, I was pottering around the house, but the suitcase was packed and all that was left was to sort out the fishing gear. I took a chilled bottle of Tavel wine from the icebox and poured myself a large glass, and sat outside with the last remaining light of the day. I'd forgotten the letter from Zurich. I opened it and it was from Maria. It read:

Dear Harry,

I don't know how to start this letter, so I'll start with saying I have decided to take an apartment in Venice for a month, just to have a change of scene and get away from Zurich and be by myself with Liv.

It was really all too much these last months. Liv, you, Roberto, David. Too many energies and I just couldn't handle it in that moment. I'm so sorry I hurt you, Harry, and we left as we did. I was too much in my head and lost, and unfortunately we all suffered the consequences. Part of my unhappiness wasn't with you or our love. On the contrary, it was more just the situation. My going away now doesn't solve anything of course, but it will help me discover how to feel and how to handle things and let go of others. One thing I have realized during this time apart from you is that I still love you my darling.

With you out of the picture these last weeks, I tried to reconnect with myself and what I have been through. And by going through this process, my love for you only grew. I hope you can understand.

As for us, I now need time and space to digest and go through that process. I know it's something I have to go through alone. These last days, I went through my life three times already and as my love for you is within me and I carry it around every single moment, it can't harm anything if we don't see each other for a while.

I do hope you understand and if you don't, well—that's the risk I take. I don't want to lose you again darling, so please stay strong for us.

As for David, well, he really has started to scare me. He has tried too many times and it's getting tiring. We went out for lunch together on my last day before coming to Venice and he pushed me into the cloakroom and tried to grab at me. I pushed him back of course but he really frightened me. Even now, in Venice, he does not stop.

He wrote this morning saying he will come. I know this is not easy for you to hear but I want to tell you everything and be so completely honest with you, as we always have been. I just wish he would stop all this. But he does not listen. What would his wife think, if she knew? Poor woman. When I return I will start to look for another job as you once suggested, but my fear now is that my leaving will not stop him in his obsession.

Liv talks about you often and still sleeps with your donkey every night. I just want you to know that we both miss you dearly and dream of a day soon when we can all be together and live our love once more. I love you my darling.

MARIA.

I could feel the tears as she wrote it. I felt happy and relieved that it had come from her and I wouldn't have to go on a crusade to win her back. She loves me and everything is fine.

On the thirtieth of July I wrote to Maria and told her I was in France after some time alone on the coast and that I had left Zurich almost six weeks ago. I thanked her for the honest letter and told her that I understood her situation and reasoning completely. I told her that I loved her and missed them both deeply, and despite how we left things, when she was ready I would very much like us to be together again. I had mentioned I was not yet ready to come back to Switzerland and decided to take an apartment in Arles for some more weeks, but had not yet found a suitable place. I finished the letter with words that flew straight to the heart.

> *I miss you more than you can imagine, and the idea that we won't see each other for several more weeks gives me a heavy heart, but I understand the necessity of space and the time apart. I know that in the end it will bring us closer together. Please give my love to Liv along with a big kiss. I love you my princess.*
>
> *HARRY.*

It was a letter full of love and good humor and it felt good to say these things. It was a warm and compassionate letter, but said essentially nothing about David.

I found a large apartment on Rue Genive in Arles on the banks of the Rhône, five minutes' walk from the Place de la République. The apartment had a large living room, a bedroom, a kind of sitting room, kitchen, and bath. It suited the respectable neighborhood.

The first night in a new bed always took some adjusting. I no longer dreamed of storms, or women, or Viola, or great occurrences, or fights. I only dreamed of new places now and Maria was always there.

The first thing I thought of when I woke up was Maria. I reached for the telephone and realized I didn't have her Venice number. I had a terrible feeling that she was in trouble of sorts. I went upstairs to the kitchen and opened the door to the terrace. The hot early-morning air rushed into the cold damp house.

I dressed and put on one of my new light traveling suits, and walked out into the early morning and headed to the shop on the corner of Rue Genive.

It was a nice morning. High white clouds hung in the blue sky above the houses. It had rained a little in the night so it was fresh and cool in the shadows and hot in the direct light. I felt good and I felt healthy and happy to be here in Arles on this summer's day.

I bought a couple of local newspapers, coffee, filters and a pack of cigarettes.

In the distance I could see a line of stalls where the brocanteurs had set out this week's priceless relics—old linen, crockery, ragged posters, café ashtrays, chairs on their last legs, amateur Cézannes, the contents of a hundred households.

I walked down and saw more stalls sprawled along the bank of the river, some laden with cheese and flowers, others with olive oil and herbs, cheap clothes and sturdy pink brassieres and corsets that only seem to be sold in provincial French markets. I remained silent, taking in the colors, the smells, the good-humored jostling of the crowd, and enjoying the lightness of Arles.

I got back to the apartment with some olives and sat out on the terrace waiting for the coffee to be ready. I sat there with the sun on my face and smoked a cigarette. I closed my eyes and felt the sun warm my face and thought about Maria and Liv. Then my eyelids became warm, and after a while I could only see red. Tomorrow, I thought, I would commence my tourism of the city properly, but this moment was glorious. I stared over the balcony onto the dusty arches and façades and rooftops that have stayed the same for hundreds of years.

I smiled to myself, then focused on the day's problem I had yet to solve. How to write my experience into a fictional novel. I got up and went downstairs to the bathroom and took a long hard stare at myself in the mirror. My posture looked terrible. I straightened myself up and gave myself a long, hard full-teethed smile. There you go, Harry. Much better.

Now, for sure, there was a danger in doing this. But what had I always said? Risks were there to make life more interesting. However, am I really willing to risk everything for a book? Reality and fiction do come very close, but do they actually touch? If I did write this, the Italian police would have a field day, especially the inspector. He would certainly wonder what the hell I was doing and it would most definitely give him the motivation to come after me. But that's why murdering David had to be so flawless and so perfectly executed. It would have to be the definition of a perfect murder. Even though I would not kill him with my bare hands, I would put him in a situation that would almost certainly result in his death. That way the evidence could never come back to me. There would only be speculation and these events would then simply inspire a story.

I took my hat off, ran my hand through my hair, giving myself another big-toothed smile. I could write about the murder in Venice, about Maria, and I could even write about murdering Viola if I did it in an intelligent way.

Hiding behind fiction creates a respite from the truth and by simply changing the names and storyline; I could make it into whatever I wanted. The idea gave me goose bumps.

The possibilities were speeding through my subconscious and I could already feel the story start to take shape. I went back out to the terrace and picked up a pencil and started to write. It began:

My name is Harry Hoffman and I am writing this story, not—as I believe is unusual in these types of cases—from a desire of "confession" being a Roman Catholic; I feel I must set things out as accurately as possible, not for the good of some future generation or from any other moral urge, but because I believe it is a good story that must be told.

I did not want to tell this story in the first person but I find that I must. I wanted to stay well outside the story, or better still, bury it deep inside so that I could not be touched by it ever again. I did not want to run through the emotions and hurt for a second time, by trying to handle all the people in it with some form of irony and pity that is so essential to good writing.

I even thought I might be amused by all the things that are to happen, but I made the unfortunate mistake for a writer of actually having been the main character of the story. So it seems that this is not going to be splendid and cool and detached after all.

Yes, I could feel the words being written already. Of course, I would have to change my name to something else.

I lit another cigarette and pondered that and the word murderer. It's funny to think of oneself as a murderer. It's not something you ever set out to be.

I took a shower, dressed and strolled out into the afternoon sun. Across the plaza was a great cathedral influenced by the Romans. I remembered reading about it in a guidebook. I walked in and thought about going to confession. The coolness inside brought a welcoming relief from the outside humidity. I stood there in the entrance for a moment and felt uneasy. I'm a terrible Catholic, I thought. I decided in that moment confessing my sins in French would be practically impossible and therefore the whole idea was not as interesting as it had sounded in my head some minutes before.

I walked over to café Bistrot Arlesenne. It was happy hour and leather-faced men dusty from the fields were lined up at the bar of the café, loud and talkative, their accents as thick as the smoke from their cigarettes. I ordered a Ricard and found a seat in the corner, feeling pale and foreign. From where I sat, I could see a game of boules in progress, the players moving slowly and noisily from one end of the court to the other. The sun slanted across the square, painting the stone houses with a coat of honey-colored light.

One of the players was about to throw. His feet together, knees bent, brow furrowed in concentration, and pitched his boule in a long and deadly arc that knocked aside two other boules before coming to rest within a hairbreadth of the small wooden target ball, the cochonnet. Voices were raised, shoulders were shrugged, and arms spread wide in disbelief. There seemed to be no immediate prospect of the game continuing.

At the table in front of me was a family of four. Both parents each had one of the children sat on their laps. The young boy must have been around five and had long curly hair. He was silent, watching his baby sister across the table, who was stood up on her mother's knees, poking at her face. The parents were not talking, just sat in front of each other with two glasses of red wine, both untouched. The father smelled the little boy's hair. They seemed like a sweet family, and wondered where they came from. As nobody was talking, I couldn't know for sure. Perhaps Italian, as the mother had thick dark hair and wonderful bright eyes and dark olive skin. The father threw me off a little. He was fair, which explained why the little boy was so blond. I felt a faint sadness now and wondered what their story was and how they met. I imagined the man was me and the girl was Maria, and there we were, here in Arles, on a family vacation. The only difference would be that we would look happier together and be enthralled in some deep and interesting conversation.

The waiter came out wearing a thick dark blue apron, picked up a metal stick and stuck it in the canopy, winding it slowly down to give some shade from the sun.

The café was now getting busy. Another waiter came out from inside, carrying more comfortable dark brown wicker chairs and marble-topped tables and arranging them neatly in the shade. I kept my focus on the family, watching the kids play, and suddenly missed Liv terribly. Why was life so damn difficult, I wondered. Why couldn't everything just be simple? Why did the David's and Roberto's of this world have to exist?

I got up and went to the bathroom, locking the door behind me. I looked in the mirror and could see I was shaking. I ran to the toilet, opened the lid and threw up. I crouched down for a minute, until the feeling had left and then slowly came back to the mirror. I rested my hands down and slunk over the sink. I was still shaking after several minutes. There remained only one more step, I thought. But was it true? Did I really need to murder David to have what I wanted or was it just a fantasy, I had cooked up in some dark moments of despair? Was it really necessary to sin again? To take a life? I fell down to the toilet and threw up again, but this time not getting there quick enough. I lifted myself up straight and ran the tap. What a mess. A knock came and the door handle went down with an impatient squeak.

I looked at myself. I was now sweating uncontrollably and felt faint. I splashed my face with water and then took some paper towels to clean myself. A knock came again.

"Ça va monsieur?" it was the voice of the proprietor.

"Oui, ça va, un instant s'il vous plait," I called out and straightened myself. I took a deep long breath and unlocked the door, and headed back outside. I sat down at the table and there was a glass of water waiting for me. The young family had gone and that somehow made me angry. It was really hot, even in the shade, and I could feel myself getting agitated.

I sipped the water slowly and managed to keep the vomit from coming back. I wondered what I should do; what should I do. It had all started to feel like one of those stories told by someone else, or better yet, one of my own imaginary fears, which were never based on fact. Perhaps in a couple of weeks I would feel some form of shame that I could have even conceived of it all. "Why is it so damn hot!" I said out loud. A few people turned and stared, but I didn't care. My mind was racing. I wondered why this gray-templed, seamy-faced, baldheaded man annoyed me so much, to the point that I wanted him dead. I knew why: it was his presence, negative energy and aura that sank like claws into the nerves of my shoulders and the shoulders of everyone else around him.

I ordered a brandy and took a sip, looking out to the plaza. I wondered if in another few months my nerves and patience would be able to bear the likes of people like him and if I should just drop the whole stinking idea. I sat there, setting my jaw firmly together, flowing and listening and concentrating. Perhaps I should just let it all go and not let things rattle me so much, causing me to act on my fears in so much as a blink of the eye.

CHAPTER XXIII

FIVE MORE DAYS passed calmly. They were solitary but agreeable days in which I wrote in the mornings and rambled about Arles in the afternoons.

One gloomy day, I took a visit to the colosseum. It looked like a smaller version of the one in Rome. I sat there inside and took out my notebook and sketched the view for no particular reason or purpose. I signed and dated it and put the notebook back into my pocket.

This day I felt alone. It was not like the sensation of Paris where you can be alone, yet not lonely. I had imagined by coming here that I would have had a bright new circle of friends with whom I would create new ideas, attitudes and standards and they would be far better than my own. I realized now after almost two weeks here that this illusion would not be the case, and I would continue to keep a distance from people.

Over the past days, I had started to research vineyards in and around Switzerland, and from the information I had found in the public libraries, I had narrowed my search down to just three. I had even called ahead to say I would be passing through on my way to Zurich.

I walked mechanically down the hill from the colosseum, narrating to myself the story I would create to get David and Thomas to join me at the vineyard. I imagined writing an invitation to them both on nice thick white paper and thanking them for the success of The Blue Room. To show my gratitude and appreciation, I would tell them, I had arranged for the three of us to spend the day and night at a vineyard with all expenses paid by me.

I walked to the American Express Bureau. There was a cable waiting for me. It was from David.

FORWARDED FROM:
AMERICAN EXPRESS C/O HARRY HOFFMAN
ZÜRICH

HARRY STOP SALES SLOWING DOWN ON BOOK STOP NEED
YOU TO DO MORE PRESS STOP WE ARE WAY BELOW TARGET
AND WILL RECUPERATE TEN PERCENT OF ADVANCE FROM
YOUR ROYALTY ACCOUNT STOP DAVID

I felt a tingling at the bottom of my spine, and it worked its way up to the top of my neck. I walked through the narrow streets and sat down in the corner of a café terrace that overlooked the train station and stared at the vagueness and emptiness of the grand station. I was thinking of nothing and felt nothing, except a faint, dreamlike sense of loneliness. Even Maria and Liv seemed far away, and what they might be doing in this moment seemed unimportant to me.

The waiter came over, smiling, and I was forced to smile back politely and order a drink. I lit a cigarette and as I fixed myself and lifted it to my mouth, I could see that my hands were shaking. A crazy wave of hate, impatience, and frustration swelled within me. It was hampering my breathing.

It was a sensation of an impulse caused by anger and disappointment, and it was an impulse that in the past, usually vanished immediately and left me with a sense of remorse. Now I could only think about the event, every minute, every second, and I wasn't ashamed anymore. I hated David and however I looked at what would happen, that failing had not been my own, only the result of his inhuman behavior.

In the beginning I had offered friendship and respect, everything I could have offered to a colleague. And he had responded with ingratitude, hostility and zero respect toward me or the woman I love. I was sick of debating it now and I would kill him one way or another.

After this acceptance, the simple idea of committing the crime, the danger of it all, even the inevitable craziness of it all, made me more enthusiastic. The how was clear, and the why was even clearer. I just had to make sure that everything was perfectly planned. I smiled largely to myself, amused at this reflection. The man sitting across from me at the next table looked over with concern.

Horizons had all but shifted now. And I felt it. For months my horizon had been absolutely limited to the idea of killing David, and the summer had all been about that. Now the idea was complete, it was all I needed. It was in that moment I realized my time here was done. I had discovered my exit and it was time to go home. I thought for a moment to drive up to Paris, but then decided against it, as it was too long of a drive.

The light had changed and I had missed the change. I took a drink and lit a cigarette and missed Paris.

Paris was a big part of my life and I had enjoyed spending these last month in France and this reflection, in this moment, made me realize just how much. It was such a wonderful country.

Life seemed so simple in that moment when I had found the summer light leaving. It was time to go and I walked around the town and said my goodbyes to the owners and staff of the cafés and a few other village acquaintances I had made during my stay. To all of them I gave the same story that I was here looking for material for my next book. I said that without a doubt, I would be down here for a visit with Maria and Liv before long.

I went back to the apartment and took a very long but cool shower. I had begun to get a reasonable tan and my short bearded stubble had blackened. I looked healthy and this trip had really straightened me out.

I got out naked and dripping wet and opened one of the windows, dislodging an indignant pigeon, and heard the distant tolling of the church bell summoning the villagers to mass, an interlude of piety before the indulgence of Sunday dinner.

With that thought, I began to compose the invitation letter to David in my head and carefully memorized it. When I went out to the terrace, I sat down and almost immediately wrote a draft straight off.

Dear David,

Hope you are well and that you and the family are settling into life in Switzerland. You will be happy to know I've been in the south of France the past months working on material for my next book. It's coming along nicely and steadily and I'm up to almost eighteen thousand words. Writing just over thirteen hundred words a day for the most part. It's becoming somewhat of a murder mystery.

While on my trip I visited a good few vineyards and châteaux and it got me thinking that given the success of The Blue Room and the efforts you and Thomas have put into getting it there, I would like to invite you both for a weekend away at one of the châteaux I visited. One in particular is beautiful, and close to Geneva. I will take care of all expenses of course. We will drink great wine; tour the winery and have fun I imagine. I would be grateful if you accept this invitation and we spend some time together, I would also use it as an opportunity to discuss my next book.

I propose the last weekend of August. We would fly down the Saturday morning and stay the night. Please let me know if this date works for you. I have also written Thomas the same. Sending you and the family my kindest regards and keep me posted on the date.

HARRY.

I felt sick and fake reading it over. I went inside and laid down. I decided it was probably too long and too nice, so I rewrote it to a less personal and less enthusiastic letter, more like my normal correspondence with him.

That evening, I went out for a stroll. I felt good and light and kept my head up. I also wore a bright smile on my face. I walked past a shop window and saw my reflection. I was astonished just by how much straighter I was standing and what a difference it made. It was one of those few times that I felt pleased with myself that I'd finally made a decision of action.

Everybody in Arles that night looked like a professor, student or lawyer. It reminded me of a conversation I once had with a man from Marseille. He told me that Arles was very up itself in a haut-bourgeois sort of way. But I didn't agree. There was a feeling of elegance here. It was a southern town underpinned by Spanish, French and Latin vibes that seemed to flow through the narrow streets, squares and comes out in an entire civilization of cafés, bars and restaurants.

I strolled down an avenue, lined with trees dotted with fountains and edged with small roman style houses. I stopped in at the café insisting my order to the waiter who was, impassive and bored, put two beers on another table and waited to be paid, his eyes focused on something far away, perhaps his retirement. He glanced down to assess the size of his tip, acknowledged it with an almost imperceptible tilt of the head, and moved off on feet toward me and I ordered and he nodded.

Finally the wine arrived in a big glass along with a small complimentary dish of olives. I sat back and calculated in my head just how much I'd spent on this trip. I had a feeling it was all starting to add up. It was a pity I hadn't written to Thomas sooner to tell him how far along I was with the new book.

I knew I was entitled to an advance on each book, but because I hadn't sent them anything or even told them I was in the midst of writing a third book, how could they send me an advance? I couldn't even remember how much the advance was, but I'm sure it would cover the cost of this trip.

Evening had given way to night, and the café was lit only by the flicker of candles on each table and the line of colored bulbs that had been strung along the front of the café entrance. Most people were sitting over coffee, smoking, chatting quietly.

I paid for my wine and walked slowly back to the apartment in the last of the evening sun, making a note to write to Thomas that night. I wouldn't mention the vineyard trip, just enquire about the advance and send him the first three chapters.

When I got home, I ran upstairs and got into the warm bed and tried to catch some sleep. The bed felt wonderful. Then sleep arrived.

As I approached the apartment I was standing looking on from a far. It wasn't a dream ahead, it was solid street that I could walk on, the buildings that could be touched—if I got that far.

The police were waiting outside the house. It felt like Zurich. David was there pointing. I saw three of them, standing with folded arms, looking at me. I turned and walked slowly toward them. I wouldn't cause any trouble, I thought. There was a big newsstand behind the policemen, it had large black text hanging from its top:

FAMOUS AUTHOR ATTEMPTS TO KILL PUBLISHER BUT
FAILS. MANHUNT INITIATED.

I was woken by a banging of the door. I jumped out of bed dripping with sweat and grabbed a t-shirt. I felt rotten and the arm I had been lying on hung uselessly at my side. It was the postman with a letter to sign. I stood there in the cold kitchen and looked over the box. It was from David with an itinerary for the book tour.

Anger rose in me. I did not know why, but that particular morning I felt uneasy and frightened. I stood there and made myself a coffee. I started to shiver. Perhaps it was just the hour. It was barely dawn after all. The apartment looked gray and horrible in the morning light. I put my coffee down, ran upstairs, and grabbed my things. My mind was blurred and tired, and it made me feel more frightened and uncomfortable. It was time to leave. I needed to go home. I needed to go back to Zurich. I left a note for the landlord, and by seven-fifteen I was already in my car and pulling out of the driveway.

CHAPTER XXIV

ON THE DRIVE I thought about the vineyards I would visit and the Swiss wine, which I knew very little about. What I did know was that it was often light, fresh and easy to drink. I knew from my research that most of the wine was grown on the slopes of Lake Geneva. I pulled out the notebook from my bag and flicked to the names of the vineyards. I just hoped at least one would be as I had imagined. I checked the map and concentrated on the road for the next few hours.

It was a hell of a long drive, and by six o'clock in the evening I was close to Geneva and the sun was out briefly, between showers of light rain. The hills around Geneva seemed very fertile and rural, almost entirely removed from the modern, almost sterile city that lay just a few miles away. As I came into the wine country, the rolling landscape was completely blanketed by luscious vineyards broken only by rustic villages of quaint stone cottages, which seemed to house only farmers and vintner families that have been producing this under-appreciated wine for generations. I thought about the vineyards in France I had driven by these past months and how Swiss vineyards, in comparison, were much unlike those of its neighboring country.

I had read that the vineyards in canton Geneva made up Switzerland's third largest wine producing area and it covered three different regions. The one I was interested in was called Arve et Lac, which was on the left bank of the lake, stretching between the Arve River and a strip of land sandwiched between the Arve and the Rhône.

My first stop was at the Château du Crest in the village of Jussy. I had picked it because of its vast estate and beautiful looking château. As I pulled up into the driveway, I felt in awe. It was completely grandiose and fitted exactly with what my imagination had been serving up these past weeks.

I got out of the car and stretched my legs. I felt exhausted now. I would make this quick, I thought, as I walked up the path. The entrance to the vineyard was through a very tall building with three floors and long, high roofs with pointy spirals lifting up into the sky. It was like something from a fairy tale, an authentic knight's castle, with white limestone for the façade and sandstone bricks for the spirals.

By now it was turning gray, not quite raining, but it had rained, and would probably rain again. I knocked at the door and a lady answered. She had remembered me from our telephone conversation. We headed outside and she closed the door behind. She told me all about the history of the château, the vineyard and the surrounding farm land. I asked her to spare me the talk on the wine making process, as I wanted to enjoy that upon my return. She was, however, extremely eager to tell me that they grew eighteen different varieties of grape on the estate. As she spoke I was studying her with inquisitive eyes, which I could feel made her slightly uncomfortable. When she spoke, she lifted her eyebrows high, which put wrinkles into the thick, weather-torn skin. She had very wavy brown hair, with curls over the forehead. I could imagine she had been rather pretty back in her day.

We quickly toured the winery and the fermentation room. I didn't go inside but saw it from a distance because the smell was too overpowering.

She closed the door and we went outside, back to the main reception, where she poured us both a glass of rosé wine. I drank very little and spoke very directly about my wishes, dates and price-range. She regarded me for a moment in silence and then I took a moment to brace myself, hoping that she would be able to accommodate the three of us soon.

"Okay, we can do it end of August," she said. "For one night, with a tour of the winery."

I breathed more easily now and carefully turned my neck, twisting it to release the tension. In that moment I felt almost affectionate toward her. I knew, however, that she had only given me this deal hoping that I might be writing a book on the subject, and she then asked if that was the case, it would please her greatly if I used the full name and address. She wrote it down for me: Château du Crest, Route du 40, Jussy, Switzerland.

I was suddenly aware now that it was raining, and a thin gray sheet of drizzle was now lapping at the old windowpanes. The views out across the vineyard to where the château stood was now totally invisible. I said my goodbyes, shook her hand and ran quickly out to the car. I started the ignition and pulled out. I looked at myself in the mirror again and could see a small smile on the far side of my mouth.

CHAPTER XXV

IT WAS ELEVEN in the evening when I arrived back in Zurich and as I started up the stairs, the concierge knocked on the glass door of her lodge. She unlocked the door and as she came out she looked almost frantic in her appearance. She had today's mail in her hand.

"Herr Harry," she seemed relieved to see me. "Where have you been? We have been so worried."

"Good evening Frau Fischer," I said. She held the entrance door with one hand, while I brought in my bags.

"I was in the south of France, working on my book," I said. "Is everything okay?"

"Oh, I'm so happy to see that you are okay," she said.

"Has something happened?" I asked.

"Well, it's just, how can I say," she murmured, looking around to find the right words. "You were behaving so strangely the last time I saw you, shouting and screaming, I was afraid something had happened to you. And then you just disappeared without a word. I didn't know what to think!"

"Don't worry," I said firmly. "I'm fine. And I'm sorry about all that."

"Yes," she said, nodding with relief. "But please next time tell me before you go away for weeks on end."

She seemed genuinely worried about me and I thought it was sweet.

"I will," I promised her. "And apart from that, is there anything else?"

"Yes," she said warily. "There was another Italian gentleman here looking for you some weeks back and then again two days ago."

"Did he leave a note?" I asked.

"Yes, on both occasions. Here you go."

"Thank you. Did he mention what he wanted?"

It was probably Roberto, I thought, looking for Maria.

"No, but he seemed very insistent on speaking with you. Didn't seem like a nice man. He had an air of… how do you say… arrogance around him."

It was definitely Roberto, I thought.

"Okay, thank you." I started up the stairs.

"Herr Harry," I turned and she had her cheek in one hand, and rocked her head up and down, looking frantic again.

"I must tell you something, Herr Harry."

"What is it?"

"The gentleman," she said in a small voice. "The one who was here. The Italian man. The second time he came he asked me to open up your apartment. He was from the Italian police you know. Oh, I didn't know what to think! I didn't know what to do! And he insisted. Said something about if I didn't he would charge me with obstructing the course of justice, or something. So I panicked and let him in."

I looked at her and slowly closed my eyes.

"I'm so sorry, Herr Harry," she stood with her eyes fixed on me, waiting for me to speak.

"Did he take anything?" I asked.

"No. I made sure of that."

"It's fine, Frau Fischer," I said gently. "You did the right thing."

"What's it all about?" she asked. "Are you and the girl in some kind of trouble?"

"I'm not sure, but don't you worry. Everything is fine. I'll call him and straighten the whole thing out. Do not worry."

I gave her a reassuring smile and went up to the apartment, opened the door and put the mail on the table. I took off my shoes and got into my comfortable slippers. Slowly and carefully I walked into each room, flicking on the light and looking around like I was searching for an intruder. There was a misty air in the place and one could feel it hadn't been lived in for most of the summer. I went into the dining room and took a martini bottle from the cabinet. I poured my drink long and walked around, opening up the windows to let in some air. I walked out to the terrace and took a cigarette.

"Scheisse," I said to myself. What the hell was the inspector doing here in Zurich. Had he found something? I went into the bedroom and undressed slowly, sitting on the bed. I felt tired and pretty damn rotten. I lay face down and stayed like that until I found the energy.

I sat up and took my dressing gown from the back of the door and went into the hallway and picked up the folded piece of papers and letters. I hated to be back, I thought. The place felt so empty without Maria and Liv.

I took a chair at my writing table and looked at the two handwritten folded notes and today's mail. I read the first one.

SIGNORE HOFFMAN,

It is quite urgent that I meet with you to answer some important questions. Your presence would be appreciated tomorrow at Café des Amis at two o'clock. Failure to present yourself will cause us to take certain measures, which will be inconvenient to the both of us.

INSPECTOR MARINO.

I suddenly had the desire to grab my unpacked luggage. I wanted to vanish. I unfolded the second note. It read:

SIGNORE HOFFMAN,

Having spoken to the concierge in your building, it seems as though you have vanished. I'm here till Wednesday 19th. I request to meet you on the 19th at your apartment. Failure to be present this time will force me to involve the Swiss authorities and have you sent to Venice at their earliest convenience.

INSPECTOR MARINO.

Obviously he had something on me. The Italians didn't just summon a foreign national with words like that, especially that last paragraph. It was a plain threat. I stood up and looked around the room blankly. I caught sight of myself in the long, freestanding mirror in the corner of the room. The corners of my mouth were turned down and my eyes looked anxious and scared. I took the next letter. It was from France. To my surprise, it was from my ex-wife's mother.

HARRY,

    What is the meaning of this letter? Are you trying to hurt us? It's sick how you write knowing our daughter isn't here anymore. I think you have gone mad by what you write. Please don't write such letters again.

                                      CLÉMENCE.

What the hell was she talking about? That family is completely mad. I tore up the letter. I really didn't want to be here anymore. Emotion and fear now showed in my posture as I looked in the mirror again. I became twice as frightened. I took out the last letter.

MY DARLING,

    I'm coming to Zurich in the next days and I will call in and see you if that's okay. Your last letter indicates you should be back by then. Miss and love you.

                                        MARIA.

A very cheerful feeling ran through me and I started to relax. I stood there looking in the mirror. Everything is fine, Harry. And then I said it out loud to remind myself.

The next morning, the first thing I thought of was Maria and it gave me a sense of purpose. I would meet the inspector tomorrow and be calm and cool and detached from it all.

I made some breakfast and ate it slowly and with pleasure, before smoking a couple of cigarettes on the terrace with an espresso. By midmorning I had only good thoughts and decided to continue with my plan. Today I would send off the invitations to David and Thomas.

I moved through my routine of showering, shaving and afterwards I felt clean and changed. I was just about to take another cigarette, when the apartment telephone rang. It was Frau Fischer.

"Guten Morgen, Herr Harry," she said in a worried tone. "The Italian gentlemen is here to see you."

I cursed under my breath. I thought he said he was coming tomorrow.

"Very well," I said, clearing my throat. "Send him up."

A minute later, I heard footsteps out in the hallway and a knock at the door. I took a deep breath and opened up.

"Buongiorno," the inspector said, looking exactly like I remembered.

"Hello, inspector," I said formally. "Please come in."

He walked in with his hands behind his back and his head down.

"When did you arrive back?" he asked straight off.

"Last night. Can I get you anything? Coffee?"

"I'm fine, grazie," he said walking into the living room and settling himself down on the sofa. "Tell me, Signore Hoffman, where have you been these last months?"

"I was in the south of France," I said, before adding, "writing a book."

"Ah yes, how splendid," he said. "And what is your new book about?"

"I'd really rather not say. It's in the process and is evolving all the time."

"You won't tell me what it's about? Not even the general plot?"

"I'd rather not," I shook my head. "I don't like talking about my work until it's completed."

"How strange," he said then stood up and walked around now, entering the hallway again.

"Is there a reason why you are here in Zurich, inspector?" I asked following him.

"Yes, now that you mention it," he said, turning around.

"And what would that be?" I asked.

"New evidence has come to light, in regards to a murder in Lago di Como. Have you ever been to Lago di Como, Signore Hoffman?" he wiped the dust off a picture frame with his black leather gloves and looked it almost like it was a crime scene.

"Yes, many times," I answered. "It's lovely down there."

"Indeed. And have you ever been to the town of Menaggio?" he asked.

"I don't recall so, no."

"Well, let me try and refresh your memory," he said. "You stayed at the Grand Hotel Victoria, once in 1954 and then twice in 1955. It seems very strange to me that you don't remember the name of the town that you have stayed in so often."

"Oh, MEN-aggio," I said, changing the way it was pronounced. "Yes, of course. Sorry, I didn't get it from the way you pronounced it. Yes, Menaggio. Beautiful town."

The inspector's lips pressed together softy under his thick and bushy mustache so it seemed as if he was smiling.

"Did you know that there was a murder in Menaggio that same February you were in Venice?" he asked.

"No I wasn't aware," I said. His smile had now thrown me off a little.

"Well, I was there recently at the Grand Hotel Victoria and the strangest thing happened," he said. "The receptionist there remembers someone matching your description and said you were there that particular February and even more strange was that exact same somebody who matched your description was there the night of the murder. Don't you find that strange, Signore Hoffman?"

I stared at him and his eyes rested on me without moving.

"Well, inspector. I can assure you, I wasn't there," I straighten myself.

"But you were in Italy that February, correct?" he asked.

"Yes. You know that because we met in Venice."

"Ah yes, you were in Venice for carnival," he was watching me very closely now.

"Correct."

"And tell me, how did you come back to Zurich?" he asked.

"By car," I answered.

"Yours?" he asked me.

"No, I rented one."

"Do you remember what date that was Signore Hoffman?"

"I can't remember," I shook my head. "I'm sorry."

"That's okay. We can check with the rental companies," he paused and walked back into the living room. "And may I ask why you left Venice so suddenly? Do you remember that I asked you to tell me before you leave? I even had your passport. It seems very strange to me that you would just leave without your passport, Signore Hoffman?"

I shook my head.

"Sorry about that," I shrugged. "I just felt the need to leave. I was going to write to you, but… I started a new book just after and I put my full attention on that."

"Ah yes, your book," said the inspector. "I read it of course. *The Blue Room* is its title, correct?"

I tried not to show my surprise.

"Correct," I said. "And how did you find it?"

"Very strange, signore," he said, shaking his head.

"Okay." I let out a small laugh. "That's a new reaction for me. What was strange about it?"

"Well, you write about your ex-wife and daughter like they are still alive," he said. "But they are not!"

I took a deep breath and looked off to the corner of the room, trying to think of something else. He continued to watch me.

"Look," I said quickly. "Are you accusing me of something, inspector?"

"Let me tell you what I see," he said slowly, in a loud voice. "I see a pattern emerging."

"A pattern?" I replied.

"Yes, a pattern. It seems to me that death follows you around, signor Hoffman. Starting with your ex-wife and child. Then an unexplained murder in Venice and then a few days later, in Lago di Como at a hotel that you frequently visited."

"That's not a pattern, inspector," I said firmly. "That's a coincidence."

"Perhaps," he nodded.

"Anyway, I thought you caught the person who murdered that man in Venice?"

"And how would you know this?" he asked quickly.

"I keep up with the Italian papers."

"Why?" he asked.

"They spark ideas."

"What a strange answer," he frowned. "Well, it's true. We did catch the Venice murderer. And he was also placed at the hotel in Como on the night of the second murder."

Both murder had caused a lot of interest in the Italian newspapers, I thought.

"Well there you have it," I said, shaking my head in disbelief. "The next thing you will tell me is that he has blonde hair and blue eyes."

"Yes that is also true," said the inspector, watching me as closely as ever. "He does have blonde hair and blue eyes."

"Of course he does," I now saw myself and the whole scene in my living room from a distance. I watched myself and corrected my stance and made myself look more confident and relaxed.

"You have been very clever, Signore Hoffman," he said. "I start to wonder to myself if I should start digging around on your ex-wife's disappearance. I wonder what I would find there."

I sat down and crossed my legs.

"Inspector, do you have any concrete evidence linking me to these murders?" I asked.

"No, I haven't just yet," he said, looking away. He ran his fingers through his hair and seemed to be irritated. "But like all killers, in the end something always shows up."

He smiled a broad smile that showed his tobacco stained teeth.

"Well, until that day," I said flatly. "And if you have nothing more, I would kindly ask you to leave."

"Va bene. I shall be in touch."

The inspector put his notebook away in his pocket.

"Before you go, may I ask if you have my passport with you?"

"Si, signore. But perhaps I will hold on to it for a little longer," he tapped his top left jacket pocket.

"Interesting," I frowned. "Perhaps I will go talk with my very expensive lawyer and see what he has to say about that."

He took a long hard stare at me and waited for a moment and then pulled out my passport, and handed it over.'

"Signore Harry," he said. "Do you mind if I call you Harry?"

I didn't respond, simply giving him a dead look, twitching up my mouth to give the vague impression that all of this amused me. He came close so I could smell the tobacco on his breath.

"Let me be as direct as I can be with my English, in order not to waste anybody's time. I believe all this to be of your work," he said. "I believe it is only a matter of time before something more concrete comes up," he tilted his head to the side and gave me a long hard stare.

I looked over to the door and moved my head toward it.

"Very well. Till next time," he said.

I followed him out to the door and opened it to let him out. As I did, Maria walking up the steps. It could not have been worse timing. There was nothing I could do so I straightened myself and felt the adrenaline rush through my body down to the tips of my fingers. The inspector walked past me, out into the corridor, and spotted Maria.

"Signora Tremonte," he said, his face full of surprise. "Cosa sta facendo qui?"

"Hello, inspector," she replied in English. The inspector looked from her to me, almost flustered. "I would ask you the same. I'm here to see Signore Hoffman," she said, and he turned to me.

"Like I said. Very strange, signore," he said, and with that he walked down the stairs and out of the building. I began to breathe again.

"Is everything okay, Harry?" Maria asked, seeing the grave expression on my face. But it was done now, and there was no undoing it.

"What's the inspector doing here?"

"Everything is fine, I'll tell you later," I said, taking in every inch of her and kissing her firmly on the lips.

"Where's Liv?" I asked.

"She's with my parents."

"Get in here," I said smiling, taking her by the arm and pulling her inside.

CHAPTER XXVI

THAT AFTERNOON A BIRD flew into the bedroom through the open window. It then flew into the living room and out onto the terrace. The bird had not frightened me, but I did jump out of bed to make sure it had left the apartment. I got back to bed and pulled myself close to Maria. She was warm, but fresh, and felt so lovely in my arms. I put one leg over hers and rested my head so that my cheek was touching her forehead. I realized in that moment just how much I had missed the touch of her naked skin. Lying there she looked like an angel to me. I lay there thinking about every inch of her, her movements and how her body was more beautiful than any piece of art. Making love to her was one of life's precious gifts, I thought and closed my eyes and tried to relive the experience once more before she woke.

A breeze came suddenly in through the open window and brought with it the sound of the street below. She moved and then stretched and opened her eyes.

"Hey, my love," I said.

"Hey," she smiled sleepily. "Oh, I must have fallen asleep."

"Me too, it really is just too peaceful here with you."

"I know," she said. "I've missed it so much."

I kissed her forehead.

"A bird flew in while we were asleep," I told her. "It woke me up and then went out through the terrace."

"Really," she laughed. "What kind of bird?"

"Not sure. A small one, maybe a swallow," a breeze came in again with the warm air. "Mmm. It feels like such a lovely temperature outside. We should go out for an early evening walk," she said.

"That's a great idea."

We dressed and headed out. It smelled like a summer evening on the street and we walked through the plaza, past the restaurants, bars and shops with their steel shutters down, and up toward the cemetery.

"I'm not sure I want to go in there," I said coldly.

"Why? We used to love walking there together," she said, looking up at me.

"Well, that was before you took me in there and broke my heart," I said, frowning sadly.

She took my hand in hers.

"Come on," she said. "I have something important to say to you."

The sun was starting to set by the time we entered and we walked together, along the gravel path that was lined with trees and the names of the dead. She turned to look at me, saw me smile and then smiled back. We continued like that, arm in arm.

"When we die would you like to be buried together? Like some of the families here?" she asked.

"If we were a family," I said. "Yes, I would like that very much."

"Well, that's what I wanted to talk to you about, Harry," she said. "I've realized these last few months just how much I love you and how much you mean to me. I really would like to spend the rest of my life with you."

"I feel the same, Maria," I said, squeezing her hand.

"That's good," she smiled, and I saw a new light in her eyes. "Because I'd like to start a family with you some day."

"You want to get pregnant?" I asked, taken aback by her words. She laughed.

"Not right now, but some day, yes."

"Well when?" I asked with excitement.

"Soon," she smiled and softly hit me on the arm.

"I just love the idea," I pulled her close and gave her a gentle kiss.

"I really think you are a great father Harry, the way you are with Liv just melts my heart."

"Thank you, sweetheart," I smiled. "Does this mean you are coming back to Zurich?"

"Not for the moment no. I still need to first go back home and deal with Roberto and my family."

"How so?"

"It's time for me to start living the life I want for myself and not what others expect from me," she said, looking up into my eyes. There was a strength there I had not seen before. She went on. "I want a life with you and Liv, and to have that I have to make things clear for everybody."

"I understand," I said.

"Will you wait for me, Harry?" she asked.

"Of course I will, darling," I said. "Do you even have to ask?"

"Then it's decided then," I kissed her once again and we both smiled as we kissed.

We walked down the gravel path and down below the gardens which were now beautifully in blossom. We continued past the trees and the big stonewalled entrance and back out onto the road.

"Can I ask you something?" I said as we walked.

"Anything."

"How are things going with David? Is he still bothering you?"

"Yes, but you have to let that go, Harry," she said firmly. "Let me handle all that."

"I try, but it's not easy. He's still my publisher, you know, and he puts a lot of crap on me, especially when we were together."

"Well, I don't love him and I don't want to be with him, I want to be with you."

"That I believe, but it just bugs me, that's all," I said. "Did he come to Venice in the end?"

"Yes, and we met once," she sighed. "He told me he would leave his wife and kids to be with me. But I was really clear with him, and in the end that's all I can do."

"Do you think he got the message?"

"Perhaps, but I think he chooses not to listen, like other men I know only focusing on their ego."

"So he's still trying?"

"Will you stop?" she asked, with a plea in her voice "Yes, he's still trying, but I don't give him anything. I don't respond him. He will lose interest soon."

I took a deep breath and let out a sigh.

"I wish something terrible would happen to him," I said quietly.

"Don't say that, Harry." She shook her head. "You don't mean that."

"Don't I?"

"No, you don't."

We walked in silence, and I thought she was still holding something back about David. There was something she was not telling me and it irritated.

"Anyway, tell me what the inspector was doing here?"

"He just came to give back my passport."

"He came all the way from Venice to give you back your passport, I don't think so, Harry."

"Well, he did. He mentioned that he was in town on some other business. I don't know Maria."

"Are you telling me the truth? He didn't ask about Massimo or me?"

"Not one word."

CHAPTER XXVII

THAT NIGHT, IN THE BEDROOM with our clothes thrown over the floor and the window open, we could feel a summer storm coming. The rain came as we made love.

I got up and took a glass of water. The apartment felt pleasant and cheerful, and with the lights out and the stormy air rushing through the rooms. It felt good to get back beneath the soft smooth sheets of that comfortable bed, knowing she was there. It was a feeling of being back together, like home. All the other things that had happened since our parting didn't matter anymore. They felt unreal somehow.

That morning, as the sunlight came through the windows, it slowly rose up onto her face and she looked as beautiful as she had ever been.

She left a little after ten o'clock. It was a hard goodbye because I didn't know when I would see her again. But I felt confident in us and that everything would work out fine. I felt proud of the journey she was about to undertake and I knew that she was doing it for us as much as for herself.

I thought long and hard on what Maria had said about David. I wondered to myself if killing him would really be such a smart move to make—especially with inspector now on my case. Yet the more I thought and tried to rationalize everything, the more I just wanted to do it for me more than anything else. He had crossed me and now there was no turning back. And then, after all this rotten business, we would forget and then start over.

I walked to the post office and sent off the invitations. I strolled back and began whistle and stopped for a drink along the way.

I didn't know what time I got to bed that night. I remember undressing and putting on my dressing gown before standing out on the terrace. I knew I was quite drunk. I smoked one last cigarette and came in. I put on the gas lamp next to my bed and got in. I took the pillow Maria had slept on and it still smelled of her. I turned off the light and tried to dream of Maria.

Four days went by and still no word from David nor Thomas. So I settled back into life in Zurich. It was hard knowing that Maria was not around, but knowing she was out there, fighting our cause, gave me peace.

In the mornings I would have a coffee on the terrace and read the daily papers that Frau Fischer would bring up and leave outside my door. She was very sweet like that. Afterwards I would take my notebook and pencil and write in a café close to Limmatplatz, then after, if the writing had gone well, I would reward myself with a brandy and walk along the Limmat River, through the city and out onto the lake. It was a good walk in the summer months. Along the banks were the after work swimmers, distressing. Further down, toward the city, there would be the fishing crowd, hoping for a catch for the evening supper.

Along the promenade next to the lake, there was an orchestra playing next to the water, the sound was soothing. Even when it was getting late in the afternoon, people were still out lying on the thick, green grass, tanning away and then jumping off the rocks into the fresh coolness of the water. I watched with envy.

Day's passed like this for over a week and still no word. In my eagerness, and with one week to go, I had called the airline to make all the necessary arrangements and two days later I received the tickets and confirmation through the post. I had never flown on an aeroplane before, always choosing rain travel for its convenience, safety, ease and comfort. I had heard that they were stating to run direct flights from Europe to New York now.

On that particular day the sun was hot and had a certain early-morning smell and quality to it. I decided it was too hot to write, and I would spend the day at the lake. I packed my swimsuit and wrapped it with a comb and towel and walked out into the morning sun.

As I walked over the Bellevue Bridge, I could see the green and white-topped mountains beyond the lake. The sun hit the water, making it look like tiny white light bulbs, flashing and dancing and making a show just for me.

In the distance, I could see people already in the water, out by the harbor. There were not many sailboats out on the water this morning, but the ones that were there, had anchored and I could see people swimming by the boats and diving and breaking smoothly into the water.

I found a good spot on a grassy bank, under a sycamore tree, and placed down my towel before walking over to the water. It was fresher than I had imagined. I dived in and swam down and deep under the water. By the time I came to the surface the chill had gone. I swam out to a wooden raft, and pulled myself up and lay there on the hot wooden planks.

There was a couple on the edge. The girl had undone her strap and was browning her back. The boy next to her was lying face down and they were talking about something that made her laugh.

I lay on the raft until I was dry from the sun, then I dived back in, swimming down as far as I could with my eyes open looking for fish. It was green and blue and dark and I saw only blurry shadows, which could have been anything. I swam to the shore and came out of the water besides the harbor. I lay on a hot rock until I was dry, and then walked back to rub myself down and lie on the thick grass.

Around noon and after three or four swims I decided it was time for a drink. I walked around the harbor under the cover of the trees to a café. There was a man playing an old piano on the sidewalk and I stopped for a moment to listen. The piano had small wheels on the bottom so he could move it to wherever the crowds gathered. It sounded out of tune, but in a nice way and as I passed by, I put ten cents into his hat.

I sat out on the terrace and enjoyed the fresh coolness of the shade, drinking a glass of pineapple-juice with shaved ice and then a long whiskey and soda. I watched people passing by and listened to the music. Later, when it got too crowded, I decided to go home and walked back along the promenade and followed the shore of the lake into a fertile region of pasture farms and low hills, steepled with châlets. The sun swam out into a blue sea of sky and suddenly it was a Swiss valley at its best, pleasant sounds and murmurs and a good fresh smell of health. Then through the city, where I was glad the cobblestones clicked once more under my feet and in-between the beer halls and shop windows which had bright posters presenting the Swiss defending their frontiers in the war, with inspiring ferocity young men and old men glared down from the mountains at Germans; the purpose was to assure the Swiss heart that it had shared the contagious glory of those days.

In Zurich there was a lot besides Zurich, the roofs upled the eyes to tinkling cow pastures, which in turn modified hilltops further up, so life seemed like a postcard heaven.

As I arrived, Frau Fischer was washing the floor.

"Ah, Herr Harry," she said.

"Hello, Frau Fischer." I smiled cheerfully.

"You received a cable this morning. Let me get it for you," she propped up the mop and went inside, coming back moments later with a blue colored envelope.

"Here you go," she handed it to me.

I picked my finger along under the fold that was fastened down and spread it open so I could read it while I slowly walked up the stairs. It read:

FORWARDED FROM:
AMERICAN EXPRESS C/O HARRY HOFFMAN
ZURICH

THANKS FOR THE INVITE STOP MYSELF AND THOMAS BOTH ACCEPT STOP WILL FLY DIRECT FROM LONDON STOP PLEASE CABLE ADDRESS STOP SEE YOU THERE STOP DAVID

I turned and said thank you to Frau Fischer and read the message again. I then took a shower and went out to buy cigarettes. I had really taken too much sun, but one can only know that after a shower. My back and neck was red and my blonde hair seemed sunburned.

Five more days, I thought. What the hell am I to do for five more days. I decided to eat at a restaurant that night. It was an Italian restaurant on a side street close to my apartment and just off the Idaplatz. There were lots of people eating outside on the terrace. It was full of smoke and everyone seemed joyful and happy. The food was good and so was the wine.

The next days were quiet and uneventful. The days were hot and the evenings cool. I played and replayed everything over in my head and on the Friday morning I was packed and ready to go.

It was a fine morning to fly. There were high white clouds above the mountains. It had rained a little in the night so the air was fresh and cool on the streets. I felt good and healthy and excited by the time I got to the airport. I sat in the airport lounge and had two large whiskey sodas before boarding the plane.

I sat there looking out as the four small, squared-ended propellers turned slowly one by one and from the window I could see them becoming four whizzing pools. The hum of the jets rose up and made a smooth whine. The plane jolted and I held on tight to the armrests. We wheeled out to the shimmering northwest runway of Zurich airport and it felt like I was sitting in a very expensive mechanical toy.

There was a pause, then the engines turned into a loud banshee scream, and with a jerk the plane started hurtling down the runway. I grabbed tighter onto the arms of the seat and closed my eyes as we climbed steadily and quickly. I sat back and prayed.

Ten minutes later, the pilot announced we had reached twenty-five thousand feet and were heading southeast. The scream of the jets had now died down into a low whistling sound. I unfastened my seat belt and lit a cigarette, breathing in some relief.

The plane moved steadily on above the whipped cream clouds that looked solid enough to land on if the engines failed.

The drink cart came by and I put my book aside and ordered a whiskey straight. I sipped it slowly while gazing down onto the cool mirror of Lake Zurich and beyond, and as the pine tree forest climbed up toward the snowy patches of land, I could see the scoured teeth of the Alps and it reminded me of the last skiing trip I had in Austria.

My thoughts were then interrupted by the stewardess asking everyone to remain seated and fasten their seatbelt and as she spoke the plane dropped suddenly and soared up again.

The sky outside had quickly turned a dark gray and fear started to set in. The plane felt suddenly small and frail. Perhaps the twenty-five of us wouldn't get to Geneva after all. I cursed myself for not taking the train.

A sudden flash of lightning flung past the window and I could feel the sweat on my forehead and the palms of my hands.

Crash! Again. I gulped down the whiskey in one go and I could feel we were now in the belly of an electrical storm.

I closed my mind to the hell of noises and violent movements, trying to focus on Maria. Her lips, her eyes, her love were all there with me. When that passed, I tried to focus on a single stitch on the back of the seat in front.

Crash! We jumped again. This was intolerable.

Then, almost at once, it got lighter in the cabin and the rain stopped. The noise of the engine settled back into normality. I heaved a deep sigh of relief and reached for my cigarettes. My hands were shaking as I lit one. It steadied out and the journey became smoother.

When the plane started tilting its nose down I knew we had began our decent. I could see Lake Geneva in the distance once we had dropped below the clouds. Then there was a slight thump as the tricycle landing gear extended under the aircraft and locked into position. Slowly we turned left and then dipped and skimmed down toward the runway. I closed my eyes and then a soft double thump came and the raw sound of reversing propellers. Thank God, I thought.

I climbed out of the plane with a handful of other pale-faced, silent passengers and walked straight over to the lounge bar, where I ordered a shot of vodka, drank it, and then immediately ordered another.

CHAPTER XXVIII

WHEN I ARRIVED by taxi, I was greeted by a neatly dressed concierge in straight trousers and a collared shirt and tie and he was very polite and helped me with my baggage. I asked him if my party had arrived, to which he said they had not.

It was hot outside but cool inside. I took a quick walk round the bar while Maurice the concierge arranged the key. The hotel had an almost sleazy, yet romantic faux-Victorian quality to it. It held two stars from the Michelin Guide, with only ten rooms available and one suite on the fourth floor.

I followed him to an old rope and gravity lift, which made a huge screech when the doors were opened. I said nothing and proceeded down the corridor. It was large, wide and high ceilinged, and there were rooms on each side of the corridor. Naturally, since it had been somewhat of a nobility house many years ago, there were no rooms without excellent views. Except, perhaps those that had been made for the servants.

Maurice unlocked the door and swung it wide. It was a room with a high, dark but well mirrored armoire, one good ornate wooden bed and a large chandelier.

While I put my things down and inspected the room, Maurice opened the windows and a warm north wind came into the room.

"I have brought you some Campari bitters and a bottle of Gordon's Gin. I know how the English like their Gin," he smiled.

"Very nice of you Maurice."

"Shall I make you one? Or perhaps you would like a glass of wine."

"Wine will be fine."

He opened a chilled bottle of wine from the small cool box and served up a glass and then placed it by the window and then asked if there was anything else. I asked him to call me when my party arrived. I took a taste of the wine. It was delicious.

I stood in front of the dark wooden framed mirror and took off my jacket and unbuttoned the collar and relaxed my tie.

"Well here we are. No turning back now," I said to myself and then walked over and picked up the wine again. I sat by the window and didn't unpack.

The telephone rang and I stiffened.

"Oui? Hallo?" I said.

"Monsieur Hoffman, your party has arrived."

"Merci, Maurice," I said.

I jolted myself, gulped down the wine, fixed my tie and walked down the staircase slowly and watched my footing on each step. When I arrived, Maurice pointed toward the bar and I walked in with my shoulders back and my head held high, carrying a smile on my face.

"Gentlemen," I said happily. Thomas jumped up straight away and embraced me.

"Hello, Harry," he said in an almost fatherly manner. Thomas had always been like that with me. He was a good man. David stood up and we shook hands and smiled.

"How was the flight over?" I asked and took a seat.

"Awful. Just awful," yelped Thomas. "Hell of a storm. Hell of a storm. Both of us pale as ghosts, I tell you."

"That's not true," David said, shaking his head.

"When did you arrive?" Thomas asked.

"Oh, just twenty minutes or so before you."

"It's awfully nice of you, Harry, to arrange all this," Thomas said. "We were saying on the way over how neither of us has done something like this before."

"What, fly?" I asked.

"No, come to a vineyard," he said.

"Well good, I hope you can both enjoy it," I said in a light voice.

"Very exciting," Thomas said in his most English manor and rubbed his hands.

"How's the book coming along?" David asked.

"Very well," I said. "Around fifty-thousand words now."

"That's wonderful," Thomas said. "Bravo."

"So what's it about?" David asked. "I read the three chapters you sent Thomas, but didn't really get it or it didn't allude to what type of story it was. And why the hell did you write it in the first person? You even used your real name."

"Yes, but it's very well written, David," Thomas jumped in.

"To be honest, I'd rather not go into too much detail just yet," I said.

"I'm afraid if you want the advance you cabled Thomas for, then I think you must," I looked on and gave him a long hard stare.

"David, you have to understand and respect the creative process," Thomas said. "If Harry doesn't wish to discuss it because it will help the book's progress, not to discuss it, then you have to respect that."

"I understand that, Thomas," he said in a small voice. "But he's asking for a lot of money based on only a few chapters and something we know very little about."

"Yes, but..." Thomas began, but I stopped him with raised hands.

"David, I don't wish to get into this now," I said lightly. "I invited you both here as a thank you. Can we please try and enjoy?"

I leaned forward and took a hand full of salted nuts from the table and put them in my mouth one by one.

"What I can say is that it's a thriller, about lost love and one man's desire to reinvent himself—no matter the cost."

"That's disconcertingly vague," David raised an eyebrow.

"Can that be enough of business now?" I smiled. "Let's order some wine."

I made a hand gesture to Maurice and he came over.

"Maurice, three glasses of that delicious white wine from earlier please."

"Oui, of course monsieur," said the smartly dressed young man.

David was looking at me now with a different expression. It was something like surprise. His freckled, bloated face stared over at me, looking so damned superior. In my surprise at his rudeness, I couldn't find a single thing to say.

"So Harry, what's the day's program?" Thomas asked, sensing the discomfort.

"That's a very good question, Thomas," I said. "Madame Bonnet, the proprietor, said we would start with a lunch out on the terrace if the weather was good, which it is, and then we will commence the tour and wine tasting. In the evening there will be a dinner and most likely a morning handover. What do you say? Sound good with you two chaps?"

"Splendid," Thomas said.

"And you David? Are you going to relax and enjoy a little?" I asked.

He smiled and leaned over to pick up his glass.

"Yes. Cheers," he said, and we all touched glasses.

David & Thomas started in a conversation about an issue with the London office and I sat back uninterested. I looked at David and wondered what he would do differently if he knew he only had some hours left on this earth. Would he be a little kinder? More compassionate? Probably not. The knowledge of what would take place that day stirred inside me and I went cold and rigid. I sat there and said nothing, only smiling occasionally and nodding.

Sitting opposite him, I couldn't help but stare at his bony, arrogant face and his boated hairy hands with a small signet ring on his left finger. Frustration swelled within me, and thought of him in Venice, sitting across from Maria in some piazza and declaring his undying love for her. Hatred and impatience swept over me and hampered my breathing. I started to sweat under my clothes and felt almost afraid of what I could do at any moment and realized then that I couldn't be around him any longer. I knew that even if the CO_2 didn't kill him, I would find another way. I couldn't stop myself now. I had come too far, and this story needed an ending.

Mme Bonnet came in smiling and introduced herself and told us about the itinerary for the day and that lunch would be served in thirty minutes time. David & Thomas went to their rooms and settled in and I stayed at the bar and ordered a dry martini. Once they had left, I sat by the window and gazed out on the rolling countryside and felt much better. My only wish was that we didn't have to have a lunch together. I wanted this to be over already.

They came downstairs wearing more relaxed clothing and we went into the dining room, through the patio doors and out onto the terrace were a table had been set with white linen and silver cutlery.

We sat down under the shade of a large tree and I said very little, which led to Thomas asking if I was okay. I said I was fine and we ordered and they discussed the possibility of buying the floor above in the London office, now that they were enlarging the team. They discussed that in detail, slowly. There was nothing for me to add so I just kept quiet and listened.

The waitress came out carrying three steaming plates of spaghetti, small salad bowls and a plate of bread. I began and in the corner of my eye watched David slowly turning his fork round and round before thrusting a neat mass of spaghetti into his mouth and it made my stomach turn, and I felt like vomiting. I took some water and paused from the food.

The luncheon couldn't have gone worse on my part. I was detached, and clearly not motivated in the conversation. It seemed to everyone that I was in a foul mood of sorts. After the food was cleared, the coffee arrived in a shiny silver pot with three small espresso cups.

"So tell me, Harry. How are you doing with the break up and all?" David asked, smiling. "Got yourself back on track? All that stuff is always good for writing, no?"

"Break up?" Thomas asked.

"Oh, didn't Harry tell you? He broke up with his girlfriend some months back," David declared.

"The Italian girl from the Zurich office?" Thomas looked at me.

"Maria is her name," I said. "And you must be misinformed as we are very much back together."

"What?" he cried out. "How is that possible?" David sat up and straightened himself and I felt a heavy breeze come sharply and the rough familiarity of his ways.

"What do you mean how is that possible?" I asked in a stern, almost surprised, tone. "Just because you worked with her David, doesn't mean you know anything about her."

"I know things," he said, quickly nodding his head. "Me and Maria share a lot."

"Well, I guess in this situation, that's clearly not the case is it?" I said.

I could feel his jealousy and hatred for me as he searched for something to say.

"When was all this decided?" he asked.

"With respect David, it's really none of your business," I said to him with a smile.

Thomas could now feel the tension and sat back with clenched teeth not knowing what really to say.

"So will she be coming back to Zurich?" David asked, still sat up rigidly.

"Yes, in some weeks, but we are now talking about moving to Paris."

"You can't possibly just up and leave to Paris!" he said.

"Excuse me?" I said in surprise.

"I don't think it's really any of our business where Harry chooses to live," said Thomas quietly.

"Thank you, Thomas," I said.

David drank his espresso down in one go. He took a napkin and wiped his mouth and looked around the room and then looked carefully at me. It was sordid how he was behaving now.

"Paris will be wonderful for you to write," Thomas said in his gentle diplomatic way. "I personally think it's a splendid idea, Harry."

I smiled at Thomas, grateful for his support, and he smiled back under his thick white and yellow discolored moustache.

Just then, Mme Bonnet came outside on the terrace and asked if we were ready to start the tour.

"Actually, I'm not feeling so well," David declared. "I need to lie down for an hour or two. I will join you both later."

I completely froze and my heart took a sudden leap.

"What?" I cried, louder than I meant it to sound. "David. Please. You have to join," I said in a hasty manner.

"Yes," said Thomas, frowning. "We have come all this way. You must join."

"I'm sorry. I just need a moment," he said, throwing down his napkin. "I'll join you on the tour later."

"Okay, please, when you are ready, speak with Maurice and he will bring you to wherever we are," said Mme Bonnet.

We all stood up and David hurried quickly off back inside. My guess was that he wanted to place a long-distance call to Maria and find out if there was any truth in all this.

"Please gentlemen, this way."

It was hot and we stood there watching and wondering. I couldn't believe he had left. Why did I have to open my mouth about Maria?

We started with a walk through the vines and the country around felt big and warm and the land was green and had fine and healthy looking vine trees and the grape berries were green and hard to the touch and in the distance, past the rolling hills of the vineyard, were big trees and small Swiss-style cottages, which bordered the lake on both sides.

As we walked she explained the different types of grapes and how and when they are harvested and it was all very interesting and I tried to concentrate, but I could not and it was almost two o'clock now and there was still no sign of David and soon we would be done here and walking toward the winery and I had to stall the tour somehow.

"Madame Bonnet," I called out. "It's such a lovely day, do you think we could go up to that high point and perhaps open a bottle and take a moment? I imagine the views from there are spectacular?" I suggested, pointing to a ridge high above where we stood.

"What a wonderful idea," Thomas said instantly. "You are full of good ideas, Harry old boy."

"Well, I hadn't planned on it," said the vineyard owner. "But yes, I guess it would be okay."

"Great," I said "I tell you what, I will run back for my camera and a chilled bottle of wine and come straight back."

"Jolly good," said Thomas.

I walked away, hearing Thomas in the distance start up a conversation as he always does "You know, during the war...." I was happy he was here, but sad I must put him through all this. It won't be easy on him.

I walked back as slow as I could, figuring that I had at least bought us an extra hour. I moved through the rows of vines, my feet kicking up puffs of dust. The soil was thin and dry, marked by a network of fissures, but the vines looked healthy enough, with bunches of grapes beginning to form in pale clusters. Bending down, I picked a couple of grapes and tasted them: bitter, and filled with pits. It would be weeks before they would be juicy and swollen with sunshine, and probably years before they would become drinkable wine.

As I entered the hotel, I asked Maurice if he had seen David. He just shook his head, so I proceeded to ask for a chilled bottle and a bucket of ice.

Knowing damn well I hadn't brought a camera with me, I went straight to David's room and knocked on the door. No answer. I then proceeded to try the handle and it creaked open. I walked in.

"David? It's Harry." I called out but he wasn't there.

Walking around the room, I looked through the contents of his open suitcase sprawled across the bed. Messy slob, I thought. The smell of cheap yet potent cologne still lingered in the air. I went into the bathroom, searching for the light and then BANG! I jumped around and the door had closed with the wind. I walked quickly toward the door and stopped when I noticed a picture of Maria on his bedside cabinet. Pausing, I shook my head in disgust.

Where the hell was he, I wondered as I rushed down the stairwell and walked into the bar and picked up the bucket and headed out through the terrace doors. I should have checked the payphone in the lobby, I thought. He was probably talking to Maria at that very moment. I was so infuriated at the idea of this, my blood started to boil. How the hell would he have her number in anyway? That son-of-a-bitch, I thought, cursing under my breath.

Thinking all this and walking back with my head down, I could feel myself starting to lose it. I could not stop thinking about that picture in his room. That son-of-a-bitch, I thought once more.

I headed down a hill and up toward the meeting point, although I wasn't quite sure if I had taken the right path and was beginning to sweat and the dry heat of the day was heavy and I took my hat off and wafted it over my face and looked around, searching for some way to try to catch my breath. Just then an old bearded man with a long, sunburned face and clothes that looked like they were patched together from old potato sacks came over. He was carrying a long stick and he looked tired. His head was hanging down.

"Bonjour, monsieur."

"Bonjour," he muttered back.

I tried to explain in French that I was lost and was looking for my friends, using hand gestures. He seemed to understand as he then pointed to my left and up onto the plateau.

"Ah. Okay. Merci, monsieur," I said, realizing that I was slightly off course.

Climbing up the hill the heat with a heavy bucket of ice was painful. I stopped and took out a handful of ice and cooled down my face and neck and it was at that moment, as I approached the top when I could hear David's voice. I asked myself if it was really him, or just my mind playing tricks and I got to the top and he was stood there next to Thomas.

Thomas applauded as I approached.

"You made it old sport! But look at you, you're soaking wet. Take off that jacket and sit down."

I walked over to David and tapped him on the shoulder.

"Feeling better?" I asked, almost out of breath.

"Much better, thanks," he said, and smiled like he knew something I didn't.

I took of my jacket and felt the breeze hit my wet shirt and it cooled me and I stood for a moment looking back on the château and its surrounding land with the wind to my back.

Out toward the lake there were flat green fields with cattle grazing beside nice farmhouses and low roofs and the land looked fine and rich and green and the houses and villages looked small, well off and clean.

Thomas opened the wine and poured us all a glass, including Mme Bonnet, who refused, and then explained more about the surrounding land and the wine we were drinking.

We stood there, high up on the hillside, surrounded by small, waist-high vine trees sat on a rocky lime stone floor. The valley below and the hills stretched off back toward the lake, which was glistening in the sunlight and you could almost see the boats on the water, but it was too far away and we finished the wine and crossed back down the hill and up toward the house and I told Mme Bonnet that I had bumped into an old bearded man, and she told me that he works the land here and has done for many years.

We finished the wine and walked down and out and around the house and to the entrance of the winery, and my heart beat faster and my palms were getting sweaty, and I wasn't sure if it was from the heat or from the nerves.

We entered the tasting room and it was cool, so cool that I could feel the sweat on my forehead turning instantly cold and uncomfortable and the room was dark and the only light was from the outside door. It was small and dim, dominated by a long mahogany table. Arranged along its polished length were shining rows of glasses, silver candlesticks with lighted candles, and a trio of open, unlabeled bottles, each identified by a hieroglyphic scrawled in white chalk. Ornate copper crachoirs had been placed at either end of the table in readiness for the ceremonial spitting that would take place later on, in the course of the tasting.

"It will take a moment for your eyes to adjust, let me find the light," said Mme Bonnet.

The lights came on with a large click and hiss and then she placed six different bottles on the counter along with a large wooden spit bowl. She then commenced to explain the wines and we started tasting them one by one, but drinking it down and never spitting it out. My body was tense and I said very little. I wished I could snap out of it. I needed to start playing the role of a happy, fun and playful writer. I readjusted myself and began.

"I'd like to say a few words, if you gentlemen don't mind?" I said and raised my glass.

"Oh, how splendid!" Thomas said cheerfully.

"I'll start by saying thank you to you both for taking the time to come here, it means a lot and I know you're away from your families on a weekend. I do really appreciate that, along with all the work you do for me."

I took a pause, reflecting on what to say.

"Thomas," I began, raising my glass to him. "You're a funny chap and without your keen eye for detail and your valuable, insightful feedback and suggestions, my work wouldn't be half of what it is. I consider you a great colleague and a true friend." He smiled and tilted his glass.

"And to you, David!"

"Go easy there, old boy," Thomas shouted with a smile and swaying a little side to side.

"To David," I laughed at Thomas. "For listening to Thomas! For publishing my first novel and taking a chance on an unknown and unproven writer," I paused and felt false and swallowed hard. "Thank you for giving the books your full attention, and marketing them on their merits. I hope YOU enjoy the tour," I felt sick.

"To colleagues and friends," Thomas quickly jumped in, and we all touched glasses.

Before drinking David now inspected the color against the flame of a candle. He gave a slow nod of satisfaction, then lowered his head, swirled the glass, and brought it to his nose, closing his eyes as he inhaled. 'Quel bouquet,' he murmured, just loud enough to be heard.

"Okay, gentlemen, if you would finish up and follow me to the next part of our tour," she said and slid open a big green door that I had seen some weeks back and turned on the lights. I took a deep breath and looked over at David, his eyes were bloodshot from sun and wine.

As we entered, we stood listening to Mme Bonnet explaining more, and I scrambled everything out and just kept looking past the wooden barrels and out onto the green door at the end of the hallway.

David started to cough, and I looked at him with wide eyes and hesitation. Surely not now, I thought. We aren't even close. He tapped his chest.

"Are you okay?" Thomas asked.

"Fine, just the air in here is dusty," he said.

"Do you want to get some air?" asked Mme Bonnet.

Oh God, I thought.

"No, let's continue," I jumped in.

She looked at David and he gave a nod. "Very well, please follow me."

We walked down slowly and I could now feel my heart pounding against the wall of my chest and it gave me a nauseous feeling and she slid the big green door back on its sliding wheels and we walked in. The smell was overpowering.

"Oh dear, I do say! That's quite a stench!" Thomas yelped out and held his nose, and I was standing behind them, next to the door, watching with great intensity and patience, and Mme Bonnet started to talk about the fermentation process but I didn't listen. I just watched and waited.

The scene dissolved in swirling yellow-grayness; the color of the walls, the four of us, all started to dissolve. I saw David smiling at me, dressed in his light corduroy suit that he had worn all day but his suit was now soaking wet, the tie a dripping string. David came over at me, "Harry, wake up! I'm all right! I'm alive!" I squirmed away from his touch. Then I heard David laugh at me, his dark, deep laugh. "Harry!" The timber of the voice was deeper, richer, than I had even been able to remember it. "Harry!" David's voice shouted, ringing and ringing in my ears as if it came through a long tunnel.

I blinked and snapped back to reality, slowly, as if I was trying to raise myself out of deep dark water. I was sweating uncontrollably now.

I looked around the room, looking for David in the yellow light under the high lamp, in the dark corner by the tanks. I felt his own eyes stretched wide, terrified, and though I knew my fear was senseless, I kept staring everywhere for David. Now you are getting confused in the head, I thought. You must keep your head clear. Keep your head clear and know how to suffer like a man.

Thomas was now curious about the faucets on each of the tanks and asked if he could turn one and see what came out, and they both walked over to the closest tank and bent down and fiddled with it, and David started to cough and looked at me and then put his head up and raised his eyes wide and started to cough again, and then he started to sway. Surely it's not going to be that easy, I thought, and he bent over and coughed more violently, his pale brows lifted up, and looked at me. His blue eyes were wobbling.

Go down, you bastard, I thought. Go down! He reached out his hand, with his death within him, and it slipped toward me, and I knew I needed to react, but I didn't react and just watched. In that moment, in that look, he knew. I gave him a violent smile and then he looked down, keeled over, and hit his head on one of the tanks.

The edge had cut a deep gash above his right eye, and it filled quickly with a line of blood. I stood there and watched and Thomas pushed me out of the way as David was mumbling, coughing, glowering, and losing consciousness.

Mme Bonnet reacted quickly and pulled him out along with Thomas. His body was now relaxed and limp. Everything sounded like a muffled noise to me, like when you have water in your ear. There was a patch of blood on the floor and it smeared along a line in the direction of where he lay.

"Close the door," Mme Bonnet shouted to me. But I didn't react. Thomas jumped up and slid the door shut.

"What's the matter with him?" Thomas asked, panicking, desperately grabbing at David's shoulders.

"It's probably the CO2 from the tanks," she said, distraught. "We just changed them this morning." She looked in my direction. "Why wasn't I told this man had a breathing condition?"

I looked down at David. "Is he dead?" I asked coldly.

"No," she said. "I can still feel a pulse, but it's faint."

I crouched down, watching for a sign of life. I was too afraid to touch him or his wrist to feel for myself.

"We need to get this man to a hospital," she said.

"No!" I shouted. "He's way too fragile to make it to the hospital. Let's get him upstairs and onto his bed and then call for a doctor."

"Very well," she nodded. "Let's get him up."

Thomas and me carried him outside side by side, letting his feet drag on the floor to relieve some of the weight. He was heavy and his sweat and odor overwhelmed my senses.

We got him into the lift and onto his bed while Mme Bonnet ran off to call the doctor. We were both pouring with sweat, and David was losing a lot of blood now from the heavy gash in his head. I got a towel and placed it on his head, putting pressure, while Thomas felt his pulse.

"How is it?" I asked.

"It's getting stronger, Harry," he said, nodding with relief. "I think he is going to be okay."

"Thomas, go into my room and into my suitcase," I said quickly. "I have an asthmatic inhaler. Go bring me that, it will help clear his lungs of the CO2."

"What will you do?" he asked me, clearly panicked.

"Just go, damn you!" I shouted.

I suddenly knew what I had to do. As soon as Thomas had left the room, I took one of the pillows from behind his head and looked at him one last time and without a second's hesitation I raised myself up and bent over and put it firmly over his face, hard and tight. I pushed down and put all my weight and strength into it. Sweat was pouring over the pillow.

"I can't find it, Harry!" Thomas shouted from down the hallway.

"It's there, just keep looking, dammit!" I screamed back as I continued to force down on his face.

David twitched and then made a violent movement and raised his hand and grabbed at my arm, but he had no strength to stop me. My left hand started to cramp up. It hurt like hell. Then his arms dropped slowly down and stillness came.

I stayed for a moment and looked at the vain in my arm. It was pulsating. I took the pillow off slowly and threw it on the floor. I looked at my hands they were shaking and my left hand had cramped almost shut. I rubbed the cramped hand against my trousers and tried to gentle the fingers. But it would not open.

I was terrified that he might only be pretending and suddenly his arms would come up and try to choke me. But he remained still. After a moment I felt his wrist for a pulse and it was gone. He was gone.

I looked at him and turned my eyes slowly to the corner by the door and imagined Mme Bonnet or Thomas standing in the doorway, having watched the whole rotten thing. But she was not there. Nobody was. I felt sudden disgust and helplessness. Thomas came running in, out of breath.

"I can't find it, Harry," he cried. "I checked everywhere."

"It doesn't matter now,' I shook my head and put my cramped left hand behind my back. "He's gone."

"Good God!" he cried, staring down at the lifeless body. His eyes were wider than a man's hand with three fingers spread wide, and his eyes looked detached as the mirrors in a periscope or as a saint in a procession.

Mme Bonnet came rushing in moments later. She looked at Thomas and he looked down, shaking his head slowly. I stood up and wobbled across the room to sit down on the chair by the window. I opened it and breathed in the fresh air; I breathed it deep into my lungs and rested my eyes absently on David's limp, dead body and blood soaked face, and my stomach contracted and puked into the bin and my left hand still cramped closed. If I have to, I will open it, whatever it costs.

I looked over and saw the pillow on the floor was covered in blood. Nobody had seen it yet. I stiffened and quickly stood up and walked over trying to conceal my hand to pick up the pillow. I turned it around and walked over to the bed.

"What are you doing, Harry?" Thomas asked, looking horrified.

"I can't look at his face any longer," I said and placed the blood-soaked side of the pillow over his face with my good hand.

"Don't do that!" Thomas said grabbing my arm.

"Please, leave it," I said, my voice shaking with fear, though it must have sounded like grief. "I can't look at him like that anymore."

"Christ Almighty," Thomas said and walked over to the room's mini bar and poured us both a large whiskey and handed me a glass.

"Drink this!" my hands were shaking as I raised the glass and gulped it down. You only had to look at David's hands to know that this had truly happened and it was not just a dream.

When I had seen him fall, I reflected and hung motionless before he fell, I was sure there was some great strangeness to it all and I could not believe it. I had come down so fast on him and without caution.

I walked out of the room and into my own and sat on the corner of the bed, not really knowing how to feel. It was done and I felt the adrenaline leave my body and when it left, I felt exhausted and frail and drained and full of resolution but had little hope.

"We should really call his wife or something," I muttered to myself, dropping down and passing out on the bed.

CHAPTER XXIX

I WOKE UP around seven o'clock in the evening and walked out to the hallway and into David's room. The door was still open but the body was gone. I sat on the bed and looked around. The blood-soaked pillow was now dry and dark red. Maria's picture was still in front of me on the nightstand. I looked at her for a moment and gave a half-defeated smile.

Below the picture was a torn off, folded piece of paper. I picked it up and unfolded it. It was an Italian phone number and I figured it must have been Maria's. I went over to the desk and dialed the number. It took a moment to connect.

"Pronto," an old lady's voice answered.

"Buonasera. E Maria la?" I said in my worst Italian.

"Who is this?" she responded in English.

"Ah, hello," I said. "My name is Harry, Harry Hoffman. I'm a friend of Maria's."

"Hello, Harry," came the voice. "Yes, we know all about you. My name is Valentina. I'm Maria's mother."

"Please to meet you, Valentina," I said. "Is she around?"

"No, she left this morning."

"I see. Do you know where she is heading?"

"I think you will find that she's on her way back to you."

"To Zurich?" I asked.

"Yes!"

"With Liv?"

"Si."

"She should have arrived in Milano now for the night," she said. "If you wish to call her, which I'm sure you do, the name of the hotel is Principe Di Savoia."

"Thank you so much!" I said.

"No problem, and Harry?"

"Yes?"

"Be good to her. She has sacrificed a lot, and she deserves to be happy."

"I will. Thank you."

I waited for Maria's mother to hang up then I pressed down on the receiver with my index finger and dialed information.

"Bonsoir. Le numéro pour the Hotel Principe Di Savoia á Milano, s'il vous plait," I said, waiting for the connection. "Oui, connect merci," it connected and rang.

"Buonasera. Maria Moretti, per favore," I said to the receptionist. The number rang.

"Pronto," came her voice.

"Maria?" I said.

"Harry?"

"Yes, it's me. How are you?" I asked.

"Is everything okay?" she asked.

"Oh sweetheart, everything is fine. I just needed to hear your voice."

"Oh, darling. Hello. How did you know I was here?"

"I called your mother and she gave me the name of the hotel."

"Ah, okay," she said. "Well, it's lovely to hear your voice. Although you sound stressed."

"I'm fine. I just miss you."

"I miss you too darling. Where are you?"

"I'm in Geneva at some hotel," I sighed.

"What are you doing there?" she asked.

"It's a long story, I will tell you later."

"Okay."

"Listen, I was thinking, it's only some hours to Milan. What do you think about meeting somewhere halfway? And then finding a hotel for the night? Before heading back to Zurich in the morning together?"

"I think it's romantic!" she laughed down the line.

"It's okay for Liv?" I asked.

"She's still awake and she would fall asleep in the car."

"Okay, sweetheart, head direction Geneva, and let's meet halfway in a town called Aosta. It's in Italy."

"Yes, I know it, but where shall we meet there?" she asked.

"I remember there's an arch in the main towns square. Like the one in Paris, but smaller. Let's meet under there?"

"Okay, my love. See you there." She hung up. I took the picture and number and went back to my room to pack my things.

I took my bag and walked quietly down the stairs and into the lobby. The hotel was deadly silent. I looked around and then walked out into the parking lot. Mme Bonnet's blue Citroën was in the corner under a large tree. I tried the handles but it was locked, so I picked up a rock and smashed the window without hesitation. I wiped away the shattered glass on the seat, got in, and ripped off the cover below the steering wheel and fixed the wires and the car engine made a few chugs before starting.

"Harry? What are you doing?" I heard a voice from an upstairs window. It was Mme Bonnet.

"I'm sorry, Madame Bonnet, but I have to go see about a girl. I'll send the car back in some days." I put my foot down and sped off down the gravelly path.

———————

Thirty minutes in, I pulled off to the first gas station to get some air and clear my head. It was becoming too hard to continue, and as I entered and walked past the shops and into the toilets, I headed straight to the sink so I could splash cold water on my face and neck. I took a long deep breath, water dripping from my skin. I rose up slowly to look at myself in the mirror. I was almost white.

"Well, there's a mirror," a voice came out of nowhere.

"What?" I looked around then realized I knew the voice.

"What about the mirror?" I asked.

"Clean that mirror," the voice replied, and I tried to make sense of it but couldn't, so I ran the water and washed the mirror with my hand, and it sounded odd and felt strange, but I knew in that moment that I had to clean the mirror. It was just something I had to do.

It felt like that water was everywhere. It was above me, below me, and all around me. I could feel water entering my body at the roots, washing me clean and then keeping me dry.

A man entered the bathroom and looked at me, and I followed his eyes scornfully and could see his look on me and it wasn't courteous. He was being rude and it infuriated me. I pulled myself up and looked at him again through the mirror and then laughed out with an insane, almost deafening tone, letting it quietly drift off.

It was clear that this had rattled him. He turned around and walked hurriedly out of the bathroom. I watched him leave and then went back to the mirror. Sweat glistened on my forehead.

"I think we better get out of here," I said grimly into my ear and steered us both out toward the parking lot.

Back in the car, I tried to make light of the situation with a smile and lifted my face to the rearview mirror and gave myself a grin before giggling back.

It was dark and cold and I wished I could shut the window. I climbed up through the town of Cluses and then on into Chamonix. My hands were freezing and I had to keep rubbing them on my chest for warmth. The thought of seeing Maria made me determined to forget the cold. I followed the moonlight with my eyes onto the sharp and steep mountains. They were high peaks that dominated the night sky.

The road climbed steadily through a forest and around a large mountain before dropping down into Italy. There were barns, cabins and meadows at the edge of the woods. The valley was deep and as I came down the road I could see a small lake at the bottom. The wind blew hard and I felt a chill all the way through, but I didn't mind the harshness of it all because I knew I would be warm and safe soon enough. As I got closer I felt invigorated. I eventually saw a sign for Aosta. The road was now hard and the Citroën did the best it could. My arms ached from the hardness of the steering wheel.

Along the road was an old stone château sitting on a ledge of the side of a hill with a terraced field of vine trees. The road went down very steeply onto a new paved road, which lead to Aosta.

As I entered, the town was dark and still. I drove around and followed the signs for the center, and when I made the last corner the arch was in sight and beneath it was a car with its headlights on. I stopped the car in the middle of the road and flung open the door and stepped out without turning off the engine. Underneath the arch I could see a silhouette.

I started to run and so did she, and when we reached each other I picked her up and spun her around and kissed her. At first her mouth trembled under mine, and then, as the passion and excitement took control, her mouth yielded into a kiss without end. She looked at me and I looked at her, and from the light of the car I could see that she was crying so I kissed her once more.

IN ANOTHER COUNTRY, AND BESIDES

BOOK IV

CHAPTER XXX

She turned on the lights and searched for something in one of the unpacked boxes. I lay in bed and watched her move around the room.

"You know, you really should take it easy," I said.

"What?" She didn't look up from her shifting.

"There's not too many heavily pregnant women moving around like you do, especially lifting heaving boxes," I said, half-amused, half-worried.

"I'm not lifting," she said. "I'm just organizing."

"Well, take it easy please."

"I just want to get things organized a little for when my parents arrive," she said.

I looked at my watch. "What time do they get in?"

"Six o'clock. What are your plans today, darling?" she asked.

"I'll go to Le Rostand and read over the manuscript," I said, eying the thick pile of unorganized paper on the floor.

"Okay, but please be back before seven," she said, throwing the pillow at me.

"Look at you." I grinned at her. "You're about to pop any minute. Come lay with me for a moment."

She came over and sat on the bed next to me. I pushed her hair back behind her ear.

"You know this might be the last day we can have sex while you're still pregnant."

"Oh, really?" She smiled. "Is that a fact?"

"Yes, it's a fact." I smiled back. "Plus, Liv isn't awake yet, and you know how sexy I think you are with that big belly."

"Really? I feel like a big bag of flour."

"Don't be silly. You're beautiful."

She scrunched up her face and lifted her nightdress over her head. She climbed on top of me, and her swollen belly touched mine as we moved slowly and passionately, her hands pressed down on my waist. I lay my head back but kept my eyes on her.

The autumn weather sent a breeze in through the open window and we climaxed at the same time. She turned over and we lay together on our sides like spoons. It felt warm and peaceful, and in that moment the three of us felt very close.

I showered and then wrote a little note for Liv. She loved receiving letters. I wrote that I would see her after kindergarten and drew a little picture of a monkey. She loved monkeys. I placed the note next to her bed.

It was seven-thirty by the time I got out into the morning sun. I walked down Rue d'Assas where a good smell of fresh bread lingered in the air, and then on to the corner of Rue Auguste Comte where I entered the Luxembourg gardens. I could smell the fragrant flowers even before I entered. I walked through the lush gardens and out toward the Grand Bassin where just yesterday Liv sailed a tiny sailboat with the other kids. I walked past the palace and through the trees and toward a small gazebo bandstand.

The morning joggers were out now, moving steadily around the outskirts of the park and through the trees. The leaves had started to come down and litter the gravel paths. Looking up, I saw that the trees seemed almost bare. There really was so much to be said about these gardens in the early-morning light, but everything would sound exaggerated until one actually lay eyes on them.

I walked over to the Pavillon de la Fountaine, which was a small brasserie in the park with round green metal tables and chairs nestled between the tall bare trees and a brown leafy floor. I remembered in the summer months one would have to search out a table which lay between an opening in the trees to get the sunlight, but the leaves had all but fallen now and lit up this usually shaded paradise. I took an espresso and asked the waiter for today's Le Monde. It wasn't bad to be back in Paris, I thought. Everything felt new and fresh under the trees. I took my first cigarette of the day and sat back.

The park was coming to life, and the men in suits with briefcases walked past on their way to work. Children played on the graveled walkways with their mothers or nannies watching on before taking them to school. People were out walking their dogs and everyone seemed happy.

I finished the paper, paid and left, and walked out of the gardens and down to the café Le Rostand. This was a pleasant café. It was clean, always friendly, and had a great terrace. Back in the day, I had written most of my first book here. You could always order very little but stay all day and they didn't mind. I ordered a café au lait and took out the manuscript and settled in.

The book was coming along nicely. I just had the ending to work on. I hadn't sent it yet to Thomas, thinking it might upset him at the moment, given all that had happened. I decided I would wait a few more months and edit it myself the best I could. I'd written all about Maria, Roberto, and David, but needed to change the names and add a thick layer of fiction to hold it together. It was a good story, in my opinion, and I was proud of it. Maria had been trying to read it now for some months, so I gave her pieces of the puzzle, but it didn't seem to hit home just yet. Perhaps she was just more focused on being pregnant.

The sun was shining directly on the terrace and looked inviting and decided to go outside and work. I sat down on a round table, which overlooked the boulevard and the gardens. It was nice to be outside and work in the open air with the fallen leaves blowing along the sidewalk.

A manuscript, pencil, marbled-topped table, a café, and the smell of the morning were all you needed to write well in Paris. Although I had found that you could never write about Paris in Paris. But today I will try. Here goes.

A tall French girl sat down at the table next to me and ordered an espresso. I raised my head slightly and looked at her above the rims of my glasses. I saw that she looked over and smiled. I thought I should ignore her and see if I could continue. And I did continue.

The day passed quickly as it always does when one works well. In the early evening, I rewarded myself with a brandy and cigarette before it was time to head back home. The park was closed by the time I shoved off, so I walked up and around the outskirts.

Maria's parents were there by the time I got home. They were here for a week to look after Liv while we focused on the pregnancy. That evening, we spent the night eating and drinking and talking, and everybody was happy and excited.

The following morning, Maria woke me around four o'clock.

"Are you okay, darling?" I asked.

"I don't know," she murmured. "I have some pain."

"Do you think it's time?"

"I'm not sure," she said quietly. "Can you go get my mother?"

I got out of bed and put on a T-shirt before knocking on the spare room door. I could hear Maria's father snoring intensely.

"Valentina, Valentina," I said quietly until she opened her eyes. "Maria needs to see you. She thinks it might be time."

"Okay. I'm coming." She switched on the side lamp, put on her glasses, and came out.

When we reached the bedroom, Valentina began to speak in rapid Italian.

"Mama, please in English, so Harry can understand," Maria mumbled.

"Okay, okay," Valentina said quickly. "Are the pains coming regularly?"

Maria nodded. "About every fifteen minutes."

"Harry, you had better go call the doctor," her mother said. "I think maybe it's time."

I went out into the hallway and made the call. The doctor, half awake, was of the same opinion as Valentina. I hung up the phone. I was still very sleepy.

"He says we should go to the hospital and he will meet us there," I said, attempting to take control of the situation. "Why don't you both get dressed, and I'll go get the car from the garage then let's meet downstairs in ten minutes."

While Maria slowly dressed, her mother arranged the hospital bag and baby things. I went outside and down the stairs.

I had the car serviced some days ago and hoped there would be no problems. I got to the garage and it started with one turn.

"Beautiful," I said out loud.

It was cold inside and I could see my breath in the air, and the heat from my body made the windows steam up. I drove out and up the ramp only seeing partially. Beyond the car windows I could see that the night was clear and the stars were out. As the tiredness passed I became excited.

I saw them waving in the distance by the entrance of the building and flashed the headlights and pulled up, jumping out quickly to help

Maria into the car. I closed the door and we started up the hill as quickly as possible.

"Where's Leonardo and Liv?" I asked.

"They will join us in a few hours," Valentina said. "Don't worry, Harry, they will be there."

"Yes, but I wanted Liv to be there with us," I said.

"And she will be," said Maria. "But the baby won't just arrive. It will take a few hours. So they have time. And you know she needs a moment to wake up. Please relax."

She stopped talking and let out a long murmur.

"Oh, that was a strong one," she said. I put my foot on the pedal and ran a red light.

Arriving at the American hospital, we went in and I carried the bags. There was a fat woman at the front desk who wrote down Maria's name, address, age, and doctor's name. A nurse soon appeared.

"I will take you up to your room, and your doctor will be here shortly," she said in English.

We went up an elevator and down a long hall. The hospital was deadly silent and the hallway was dark until we started walking and the automatic lights hissed on, slowly one by one. Maria was holding onto my arm tightly, walking one step at a time. We got into the room and closed the door. She undressed and got into bed. She was given a plain light blue square-cut nightgown that looked very surgical. Her mother pulled a side chair close and held Maria's hand. The nurse knocked on the door and came back in.

"Are we all fine and comfortable?" she asked.

"Yes, perfectly fine. Thank you," Maria said.

"We don't get many Italians having babies in this hospital," said the nurse, smiling. "You are Italian?"

"Yes, but my partner, Harry, is English."

The nurse looked over to me and I gave her a smile. The nurse had a nice face and seemed very kind.

"Tell me, nurse, when is the doctor arriving?" I asked.

"Do not worry, he's on his way. We have plenty of time, so please relax. How are the pains?" she asked Maria.

"They're getting closer and stronger," Maria gasped. "About ten minutes apart."

"Let me see." She held Maria's wrist and felt her stomach and then timed them. Maria looked over at me and smiled.

"Okay," said the nurse, nodding. "They are coming along nicely. I don't think it will be too much time before we start prepping."

Maria's mother stood up and said she was going to the bathroom. I sat down and held Maria's hand, then the nurse left too.

"How are you doing, sweetheart?" I asked.

"I'm fine. I'm starting to get excited," she said.

"Me too." I grinned.

It was dim and cool in the room. As she lay on the bed I could see the big mirror on the other side of the room but could not see what it reflected. It did not smell like a hospital, I thought.

"Harry, there's something I want to ask you about," she said, closing her eyes against the pain of her contractions. "Because it's bothering me."

"Sounds serious."

"Well, when I was unpacking yesterday I found a little black notebook," she said, watching me. "And inside it had all this stuff about David. And, well, it's really troubling me."

I stiffened up.

"Maria, I can explain," I said quickly.

"Then please do," she said. "Because if I didn't know any better, it sounded like you planned the whole thing."

"Maria…" I paused and had something on the tip of my tongue to say, but nerves got the better of me. I looked up at the ceiling.

"Did you?" she asked.

"Of course not." I shook my head. "He died of CO2 poisoning. Please let's discuss this when you're back home. Now is not the time. I can explain everything later."

"Then what was all that in the notebook?"

"It was just ideas for a novel. Ideas for a murder." I shrugged. "I told you, I'm writing a thriller. Maybe I used David's name in the notebook, but only because I was stressed out about him at the time. Really, sweetheart. I had nothing to do with it. Honestly."

She was about to say something but at that moment Valentina walked back in the room.

"How are we doing?" she asked.

"Fine," Maria said, looking away from me. I stood up looking at her, wondering what she was thinking.

"Harry, why don't you go out and get some coffee for Mama," was all she said. "I think you could use some air." Her face then screwed up. "Owaaa," she screamed out. "That was a big one!"

I could only stand there, not wanting to leave.

"Harry, go," she begged. "You're making me nervous."

"Fine," I said. "I'll go."

I went outside for a smoke, hating myself. How could I have been so careless? I should have burned the damn thing in France. What if she told her mother? And where the hell was the doctor? It was getting light now. I took another cigarette, inhaling it deeply into my lungs.

There was a café across the street with its lights on. I walked over and stood at the long zinc bar while the waiter finished putting the tables out on the terrace. He came in and served me a double espresso. The waiter looked at me with his cold French eyes and a look of worry. I'm sure he's wondering what the hell's wrong with me. I'm getting awfully slow, I thought. Somebody will take me down any day now. Maybe even Maria.

"Goodbye," I said and left coins on the bar.

"Au revoir, monsieur."

I took two black coffees in plastic cups and went back up the stairs, and onto the floor where Maria's room was. I opened the door and the room was empty. I went down to the end of the hall where there were lights and noise. I opened the door slightly and could see Maria lying there. She was covered in bloody sheets, and two nurses and one doctor, our doctor, were rushing around either side of her.

"Harry!"

I turned around. It was Valentina. "Harry, I was looking for you." She seemed frantic.

"What's happened? Is she okay?"

"I don't know. She had pain and started bleeding and then she passed out and was rushed away."

"Oh my God." I could see through the door that she had a mask over her face and was breathing rapidly. There was so much blood, and the doctor's hands were covered in the stuff. I opened the door and shouted for the nurse. Taking her eyes away from Maria for a second, she came over.

"Monsieur, we are doing all we can," she said calmly. "But you must wait outside."

"But what's wrong?" I cried. "Is she okay?"

"Please," she insisted. "You must wait outside."

The door swung closed. Valentina was crying now so I went over and put my arm around her, but when I did she backed away. I stood looking at her. Of course Maria had told her, I thought.

I went down the hall and into the room she was last in and sat down on the chair. Poor Maria. I felt sick. I stood up and went to the window, hoping to open it for some fresh air, but it was bolted shut.

Why was there so much blood? Was the baby okay? Had our conversation put stress on her?

I wanted a drink of water and found the bell on a cord by the bed and rang it but nobody came. I don't know what I would do if we lose the baby. Could we lose our baby? Was that even a possibility? I couldn't lose another.

I slammed my body against the window until it opened slightly and lit a cigarette. What if Maria should die, I thought weakly. Could God really be that cruel?

No, she won't die, I told myself. People don't die in childbirth anymore. Maybe twenty years ago. But it's 1960 now. That sort of thing does not happen these days.

But what if she does die, asked a terrible voice in my head. She can't die, I protested. We've gone through so much and come too far for her to die like this.

It's just nature giving her hell. And that's all it is. Suddenly the door swung open and Liv came running into the room.

"Harry Bear!" she shouted and jumped onto me. I picked her up and gave her a kiss.

"Hey, snowflake."

"Where is Mama?" she asked.

"She's with the doctors."

"Is she sick?"

"No." I shook my head. "She's fine. She's just working on getting you a baby brother or sister."

"I want a sister." Liv grinned up at me.

"I know you do, snowflake," I said. "But just to make sure, I'll tell the doctors."

She wanted to climb down but I couldn't let her go. I just held her tight.

"Harry!" her mother shouted from the hall. I ran down with Liv in my arms. Valentina was there, accompanied now by Maria's father.

"What is it?" I asked, unable to keep panic from my voice.

"They just came out of the room and rushed her to the elevator."

"Well, did they say anything?" I asked. "Where did she go?"

"I don't know, they wouldn't say." She shook her head. "They just told us to stay here."

"Do something, Harry," her husband urged me in his bad English. I nodded, handed Liv over, and dashed toward the elevator. I could see that the elevator had stopped on the fifth floor. I kicked open the stairwell door and ran up the two flights of stairs before pelting down the hallway, checking each room with a light on.

Then I saw her, but I was too afraid to go in. There were six people all around her now. I stood frozen, watching through the small window of the door. A nurse saw me and told the doctor. He turned to look at me and then came out.

"Doctor, what the hell's going on?" I demanded. He took off his paper mask.

"We have an obstructed labor and the baby is not getting enough oxygen," he said. "I'm sorry, but we are running the risk of losing the baby."

I breathed. "And Maria?"

"She's holding on, but it's hell for her." The doctor shook his head. "We need to get the baby out now by Caesarean."

"Do whatever you need, doctor," I said, grabbing his arm. "Just save them both. Please."

"I will try," he said, taking my hand. "We are keeping Maria as comfortable as possible, but she's not conscious. I have her hydrated and on antibiotics. But I have to tell you, once we get the baby out, she will be at massive risk of postpartum bleeding. She's already lost a lot of blood."

"What's that?"

"It's when a woman loses the child," the doctor explained gently. "She then loses a lot of blood."

"But that's not going to happen, right?" I asked, looking from the doctor to Maria on the operating table. "You can fix all this, right, doctor?"

"I will try," he sighed. "We have to focus now on the baby. But I need to know, if it comes down to saving Maria or the baby...?"

"You save Maria," I said without a trace of doubt.

"Okay. Understood." He put his hand on my shoulder and gave me a brave smile before rushing back in.

I went downstairs like a walking ghost and gave the news to her parents. We all came up to the fifth-floor waiting room. Liv played cards with Leonardo on the floor.

There was sunlight coming in through the windows, and I looked around the room at the bare walls and two chairs and my legs were jumpy, and after three hours of not hearing anything Valentina started to cry. I asked Leonardo to take Liv to the café across the street for some breakfast, and we all felt utterly useless and I kept going down the hallway and looking into the window, but the scene never changed. They were working hard and I paced the hallway again and again.

I stood at the door window and saw the doctor turn a dial and then look at his watch. He then turned toward me and came out the door.

"I'm sorry," were the first words spoken. "She had one hemorrhage after another and we lost the baby. She lost too much blood. I'm so sorry."

"Is she dead?" I asked, looking into his face. He looked away.

"I need you to say it! Is she dead?"

"Yes, she's dead," he said. "I'm so sorry, Mr. Hoffman."

I put my hands up to my mouth and could feel my legs starting to give way, and the doctor grabbed me and pulled me toward the chair and I bent down and put my head in my hands and sobbed. The doctor sat down next to me, and we stayed like that for some minutes.

"Can I see her?"

"Of course you can. Come with me." He helped me up and I entered the empty room. My legs were jelly. It was quiet now and the doctor walked out slowly.

Maria was lying there. She didn't look dead, only pale. Her eyes were closed. I walked over and took her hand; it still felt slightly warm.

I sat down on the chair in front of the bed. Reports hung on clips at the side and I looked out of the window. I could see nothing but the rain falling across the light from the window. So that was it.

What would I tell Liv? Maria was so strong and healthy and beautiful, even in death. How could this happen? Did the doctors do something wrong, or was it me? Had our conversation given her stress and made this happen? Beautiful, kind-hearted Maria, who I loved so much. She didn't deserve this.

I had no religion in that moment. I wished to hell it was me lying there instead of her.

"Oh, darling, what will I do without you?" I asked her, willing her to wake up and answer me with a sleepy smile.

The nurse came to the door but did not come in. After a while I went to the door and opened it very softly and looked out. I could not see at first because there was such a bright light in the hall. Then I saw the nurse sitting by a desk.

I turned around and sobbed uncontrollably and stayed like that until the sobbing eased away. Slowly I gathered the courage to walk out.

I went down the hallway and the nurse looked up, and then into the waiting room, and from my pale face and red eyes, they already knew. Valentina fell down onto the chair and started to scream out Maria's name. Leonardo came over and put his arm around her and cried. I looked over at Liv. She was looking up from the floor, trying to understand what was going on. I walked over and picked her up and tried my best to explain without crying.

I carried her to the room so she could say goodbye. I was shaking now and she could feel it. I placed her on the bed, and Maria's parents came in and stood by the door.

"Give her a kiss goodbye, snowflake," I whispered. Behind me I heard Valentina let out a cry and walk away.

"Mama, wake up." She shook her arm. "Why won't she wake up?" she asked, looking up at me.

"Because she can't, sweetheart," I said, my voice breaking. "She's not here anymore."

"Why?" Liv asked, a small, confused frown gathered on her forehead. She started to cry.

"Because she was sick," I said with a lump in my throat.

"And my sister?" she asked.

"She's gone too," I said. I was trying to hold it together but the tears were now streaming down my face.

"Please, snowflake, give her a kiss and say goodbye," I said. She leaned over and kissed her cheek and held her mother tight. She understood what was happening now and let out a scream, frantic. Her legs were now kicking, and she threw her arms around on the bed. I began to cry. I picked her up but she didn't want to leave Maria's side. She grabbed onto the covers and pulled them onto the floor as I lifted her off the bed. I held her for a moment until she calmed down.

"What happened, Harry Bear?" she said as she rubbed her eyes.

"She was sick, and now she's left us and has gone to heaven."

"But I want my Mummy," she screamed out. "Please wake up Mummy." I sat down with her on my lap on the chair next to the bed and held her tight.

"Will you also leave me now?" she turned and asked.

"Oh, sweetheart," I said, shaking my head. "I'm not going anywhere if you don't want me to."

We went to the door of the room and turned off the light and shut the door, and I tried to say goodbye, but it wasn't any good. It was like saying goodbye to a statue.

I carried her out down the hall and felt like I wasn't really there, like this wasn't really happening. We all drove home in silence, and when we arrived home I put Liv in our bed, shut the door, and turned off the light.

CHAPTER XXXI

THE BEGINNING WAS FRIGHTENING and overwhelming. Is there anything more painful, I asked myself? Do I even have the energy to get through something like this? I was unsure of who I was now. I felt confused. Feeling disoriented is natural, I thought. I know it's important to mourn and I know there is a need to mourn. Mourning is an open expression of your thoughts and feelings. It's an essential part of healing. Then there's grief. Grief is different, I thought. Grief is unique because no one had the same relationship as I had with Maria. Grieve in your own way, I thought, and don't try to compare it with others'.

Perhaps I should consider the one-day-at-a-time approach. It's all starting to affect my head. Maybe it's too hard work, grief. It's called work for a reason. Am I losing my mind? I hope I don't lose my mind. I need my mind. I should really get out of bed. It's been two days now. I pulled myself out of bed and sat on the edge. I turned to look at Liv. She was still sleeping. She had been having nightmares the last nights and would let out screams that would startle me awake. She would then wake up but not be really awake. She would become lost. "Poor snowflake," I said out loud. What time is it? It was still dark. I went to the bathroom and I could hear Valentia crying and see the light on in her room. I got back into bed and pulled Liv close.

The days that followed felt like I was on autopilot because trying to absorb such an enormous shock was not an option. Nothing seemed real. Of course, I knew the truth deep down, but I now had a daughter to care for. I started to play the "what if" game. But once you let it in, it just consumes you. I was not so much exhausted with the process of grief, but now it was more about how busy my mind had become with everything but grief. I would lie awake at night going over and over how, why, or what if. I became obsessed, convinced that if I worked out how, I could change that day or blame someone else. I could somehow bring her back. I would withdraw from talking about Maria's death. I wanted to talk about her every day. On the fourth day, I searched for the notebook, but it was gone. Maria had put it somewhere and I couldn't find it.

At nights I could still feel her hand inside mine. Hers was so small and beautiful that it disappeared into mine every time I took hold of it. I loved her hands. They were soft and delicate, and they were also a place where compassion could be felt. A touch from Maria could soothe me in a way few other things could. Her eyes were where love could be seen and would always be a place to shelter me. I wondered if I gave her the same looks and the same comfort. I suspected I did, but I couldn't know for sure. Loving her was as natural as breathing for me.

"God, I miss her," I said under the blanket, and began to sob. Was there a path to forgiveness for me? I guessed whatever happened from here on out would not change my love for her.

CHAPTER XXXII

VALENTINA ARRANGED THE CREMATION in Paris for Maria and our baby girl and then the funeral, which was to be held back in Bologna the following week.

On that morning over that breakfast, Valentina changed her tone and talked to me in an almost businesslike manner.

"Harry, we need to talk about Liv," she said.

"Please not now, Valentina," I said with a plea in my voice.

"Harry, we have to talk," she said firmly. "Please don't make this harder than it has to be. We are all hurting."

"What's the point?" I asked, shaking my head. "The conversation will end by you telling me that you're taking Liv away. I already know how this ends."

I stood up and put the dishes in the sink.

"Well, I'm sorry to say it, but you didn't get married," she said. "And you don't have legal custody over Liv."

"Valentina, you can't take Liv away from me," I protested, staring into the sink. "She's all I have now. I've been like a father to her. Go ask her who she wants to live with! It should be her choice."

"Harry, she's six years old!" Valentina cried. "She can't make these types of decisions."

"Yes, she can."

"No, she can't," she sighed. "I know you love her and I know you would do anything for her. But you have to understand, as the divorce papers were never signed, Roberto has full legal right over Liv. And he wants Liv back."

"She can't go back to Roberto!" I cried. "He doesn't care about her. He's just doing this to spite me."

"Harry, I know this and I know she would rather be with you," she said. "But it's out of our hands. I would much prefer you to raise her, but Roberto is her biological father and technically still married to our Maria. We have to take her back. I'm sorry, Harry."

"You lay this on me now," I seethed. "Five days after Maria died! I can't take this. Is this because of what Maria said to you?"

"About what?" she asked.

"About what," I laughed, shaking my head. "About the notebook she found?"

"I don't know what you're talking about, Harry." She frowned up at me. "And please don't shout."

"You know exactly what I'm talking about," I spat out. "And I'll tell you this: that's just the tip of the iceberg."

I stormed off and went into the bedroom, slammed the door, and sank down on the bed. I just can't let them take Liv. We need a plan and we need to leave, just the two of us. I had enough money to start a new life together. We didn't need much.

I jumped up off the bed and took out a bag, starting to pack only what I could carry. Things I couldn't take we would buy later. We just needed to be together. But where to go? I searched for a map in my box of books, found one, and spread it across the bed.

We could go to one of the Greek islands, or the ones just off the coast of Sicily—Lapari for example. They would never think I was dumb enough to take her back to Italy. It would be the last place they would look.

A knock at the door came and the handle turned, but the door was locked.

"Just a minute," I shouted and threw the map under the bed covers.

"Harry, we are going out for a walk to clear our heads," Valentina shouted from behind the door. I went over and opened it. She stood there looking at me, sympathy etched across her face.

"Do you feel like joining us?" she asked gently.

"No. I just want to spend some time with Liv."

"Oh, we just dressed her and planned to take her with us."

"I'd rather she stayed and we play together," I said, though I could already see in Valentina's eyes that she did not trust me anymore. Her look was different now.

"Well, we can stay then," she said.

"No, I'd really prefer to have some alone time with her if you don't mind," I said, trying to sound persuasive not insistent. "And I'm sorry for what I said earlier, Valentina. I'm just upset and emotional."

I gave her a reassuring smile.

"Okay. Well, we won't be too long."

I gave a false smile and closed the door.

I heard them talking loudly in Italian in the hallway and then saying goodbye to Liv before the door closed. I walked into Liv's room.

"Hey, snowflake." She was playing on the floor.

"Hi, Harry Bear," she said, smiling back, looking up from her drawing.

"Listen, we are going to play a game," I said. "If you only had one bag, let's say this one, and you were going away on a long holiday, what would you put in it? You can choose anything."

"Are we going on holiday?" she asked me.

"Yes, we are," I said. "So I need you to focus and only take the things you really love and care about. Like that picture of Mummy. Okay?"

"Okay."

"Start now and I'll be back in a few minutes."

I went over to her wardrobe and grabbed a handful of clothes, some shoes and a jacket, and stuffed them into my bag and went back to the bedroom and finished my packing.

She came in some minutes later, pulling her small red suitcase that we had bought her for Christmas.

"So are you ready?" I asked.

"Si," she nodded.

"Well, then let's go!" I said brightly.

"What about Grandma and Papa?" she asked. "Are they coming too?"

"Yes, they will meet us there," I said, putting on her jacket. I zipped it to the top and took one last look around the apartment before we left.

We walked down the stairs and onto the street and then made the short walk to the garage. I'd figured flying would be useless. They would almost certainly stop us before we got on the plane. I gave us at least three hours before Valentina notified the police and another hour before it got to the right people. It would be at least six hours before the French border patrol was alerted. I believed that gave us enough time to get out of the country.

We drove to the Gare du Lyon and left the car in the parking station and booked us onto the first direct train to Marseille, which left in forty-five minutes. This gave me enough time to call a few ferry-liners to get some information. There was one ferry leaving at nine o'clock tonight direct to Palermo. From there we could make our way to Lipari. It was a twelve-hour trip, but they had private cabins with beds. I didn't reserve the tickets, as I didn't want to give our names, but I was assured that there was plenty space left to buy tickets at the port of Marseille.

We stood waiting alone under the fouled glass dome, relic of the seventies, era of the Crystal Palace; my hands, a vague gray color that only twenty-four hours can produce, were placed in my coat pockets to conceal the trembling fingers. I put on my hat. I was scarcely recognizable.

The well-to-do Parisians poured through the station onto the platforms with frank new faces, intelligent, considerate, thoughtless, and the occasional English or American face among them seemed sharp and emergent. Suddenly I was involved in a human contact and I felt scared. Only after a hundred years did the train finally arrive and we boarded and settled in.

Unlike English trains that were absorbed with scornful people, this train was part of the country through which it passed. Its breath stirred peacefully and quietly from the dust of the station, out toward our future, and the cinders mingled with the lushness of the land. Liv was sure she could lean from the window and pull the flowers with her hand.

By the time we got off the train and boarded the ferry, we were both exhausted. I was living on espressos and my twitching nerves. Liv was fast asleep now as I carried her to the cabin. There was only one bed, so I opened the tight sheets and took off her jacket. Her hands were freezing. I wrapped her up and she stayed asleep.

I sat down next to her on the edge of the bed and sobbed. My hands were shaking and my body was tense. Had I done the right thing? Had I even thought this through? I hadn't thought, I just acted. I really didn't know anymore. All I knew was that I had lost Maria and I'd be damned if I was going to lose Liv as well. I then collapsed in a heap on the floor next to our luggage and fell fast asleep.

I awoke to the sound of the engines starting up and the movement of the ferry. I slowly raised myself up and felt better. It was nine-thirty and it looked like we were on our way. I figured we had been lucky enough to get out of the country as fast as we did. I'm sure they had alerted the police by now. I was sad for Maria's parents and what I was putting them through.

As we set off, there was a feeling of uneasiness that I couldn't shake; something about Italy gnawed at me. Perhaps it was a bad idea to stay in Europe. I had a strange feeling that something was going to happen, and it gave me a sudden chill. Murder and now kidnapping: what was next? The scandal of it all was almost too much to comprehend. Famous author kidnaps six-year-old girl of dead mother. I could see it now in the morning papers. I guessed we could travel to South America after Sicily. We could ferry down to North Africa, train it to Johannesburg, and then jump on a boat to Rio. I could probably get work writing for a small-town newspaper. We would figure it out. What's important is that we are together.

My mind went off in such directions for the next hour, and then I decided to go out for a smoke. I locked the cabin door and walked down the corridor. As the ship moved from side to side I had to hold my arms up and steady myself on the walls. Outside it was utterly dark and the stars were out. It was bitterly cold. I walked around sizing up everyone I came across. I smoked one more before I went back and set the alarm and fell fast to sleep. She woke five times during the night screaming with nightmares. Every time I would go over and sing to her and then crawl back down to the floor.

I awakened to the sound of Liv talking in her bed. I raised myself off the floor and felt shaky and lightheaded and looked at the clock. We had thirty minutes until we reached the port of Palermo. I opened the curtains and the glare of the sun hurt my eyes. Liv jumped up on the bed and looked out the small cabin window.

We got washed from the basin and dressed and closed the cabin door, and I carried our luggage out on to the deck and Liv walked alongside. The ferry was approaching the port now. I picked her up and held onto the white rusted railings, and she gave me a warm and slightly moist kiss on the cheek and I felt good again. The town was getting closer and the surrounding land looked dry and primitive and the air was warm and there was no wind, and I opened my bag and took out my blue baseball cap. The port and city rose up above us and felt like a mirage ahead. Solid ground that we could walk on, and where our future was to begin.

As we came slowly to dock, I could see a police car and then in front of it a dark-haired man in a long black trench coat. He looked out of place in the crowd of cars and people. Next to him stood a younger policeman in full Italian uniform, his arms folded across his chest. I could see the dark-haired man was holding binoculars and looking straight at us. I rubbed my eyes to try and focus, but I couldn't catch his face. We were still too far away. I took my glasses out and placed them carefully on my face and looked again. Then, with a jolt of panic, I realized it was the inspector. I put Liv down and unzipped my bag and took out my knife and placed it into my jacket pocket, and they stared back at us and I felt the adrenaline rush hit me like a punch to the gut and could see in the distance a newsstand and the headline:

BRITISH SERIAL KILLER HARRY HOFFMAN AT LARGE IN ITALY. MANHUNT INITIATED.

In that moment I knew what I had to do. I would not let them take Liv. They would have to kill me first.

"Are you okay, Harry Bear?" Liv looked up at me, and I looked down at her sweet innocent face.

"Everything is just fine, snowflake. Everything is just fine."

— THE END —

ABOUT THE AUTHOR

Maxwell P. Jacobs was born in the north of England in 1981. Raised by his postwar grandparents, Jacobs spent his early years in much poverty. At sixteen, after dropping out of school, he began an apprenticeship with a local newspaper, trying to realize his ambition as a journalist. At twenty, this dream took him to New York where he found work at a well-known publishing house. Two years later he moved to Paris and fell between the expatriate artists and writers of the time and quickly found love with a local girl, and not long after married. During these early Paris years, Jacobs took on a variety of jobs to pay the rent. Unsure of his true calling he continued to write in his spare time. His marriage soon failed, and he left Paris and secluded himself to a small fishing village close to Marseille. This period was highly creative for Jacobs and he began to write down his experiences and completed his first manuscript. This small volume included three vignettes and sixteen short stories and with a hope of getting published, he went back to Paris. Unable to find a publisher, Jacobs self-published the book but it did not sell well and never got the attention it deserved.

Looking for a change, and with very little money, Jacobs decided to move to Mexico because the exchange rate made it an inexpensive place to live. He arrived in Monterrey early spring with a plan of starting his first novel. Not knowing anyone and unable to speak the language, he slipped into isolation. He rented a small house and converted the second floor into a writing studio. After only eleven months, and a failed attempt at a novel, Jacobs ended up fleeing the country after a tip off that he was targeted for a kidnapping operation with the local cartel. He quickly fled to Mexico City before returning to Paris. There he renewed his earlier friendships with the young writers and artists and their encouragement and criticism began to play a valuable part in the formation of his fiction and established his name more widely. The following year, he began writing a collection of sketches and stories based on his grandparent's wartime activity. This publication, "Of Time & War" attracted a great deal of attention and began a fine future for him as a creative fiction writer.

A few years later, Jacobs left Paris to spend the winter in Switzerland and to begin work on his next collection of short stories. There he met a Swiss girl with whom he became infatuated with and they started off a thrilling romance. This set off a creative surge and a hunger for expression and he began writing a sprawling semi autobiographical novel called Confessions of an Expat and later changed to the title In Another Country, and Besides. This story, set in post war Europe, is a pilgrimage of youth and especially of an English expatriate. It begins in Venice, where our protagonist meets Cleo, who offers him a chance to start over. It takes them through a variety of profoundly moving experiences— To Zurich, and the Swiss Alps, thence to the Cote d'Azur and finally to Paris, irresistibly drawn back to the great, sprawling city he had once fled in bitterness and disgust. This story is a moving tragedy. From its violence, ignorance and cruelty, joy and mystery, it shows vividly Jacobs own expatriate experiences and by doing so, has created a confessional story with the mass and movement of an epic novel.

Morgan James
Speakers Group

www.TheMorganJamesSpeakersGroup.com

We connect Morgan James published authors with live and online events and audiences whom will benefit from their expertise.

obtained

1B/922/P

CPSIA information can
at www.ICGtesting.com
Printed in the USA
BVOW09s1235210218
508743BV000